WEATHERHEAD BOOKS ON ASIA   WEATHERHEAD EAST ASIAN INSTITUTE, COLUMBIA UNIVERSITY

river *of* fire
and other stories

LITERATURE
David Der-wei Wang, Editor

Ye Zhaoyan, *Nanjing 1937: A Love Story*,
    translated by Michael Berry (2003)
Oda Makato, *The Breaking Jewel*, translated by
    Donald Keene (2003)
Han Shaogong, *A Dictionary of Maqiao*,
    translated by Julia Lovell (2003)
Takahashi Takako, *Lonely Woman*, translated
    by Maryellen Toman Mori (2004)
Chen Ran, *A Private Life*, translated by John
    Howard-Gibbon (2004)
Eileen Chang, *Written on Water*, translated by
    Andrew F. Jones (2004)
*Writing Women in Modern China: The
    Revolutionary Years, 1936–1976*, edited by
    Amy D. Dooling (2005)
Han Bangqing, *The Sing-song Girls of
    Shanghai*, first translated by Eileen Chang,
    revised and edited by Eva Hung (2005)
*Loud Sparrows: Contemporary Chinese Short-
    Shorts*, translated and edited by Aili Mu,
    Julie Chiu, and Howard Goldblatt (2006)
Hiratsuka Raichō, *In the Beginning, Woman
    Was the Sun*, translated by Teruko Craig
    (2006)
Zhu Wen, *I Love Dollars and Other Stories of
    China*, translated by Julia Lovell (2007)
Kim Sowŏl, *Azaleas: A Book of Poems*,
    translated by David McCann (2007)
Wang Anyi, *The Song of Everlasting Sorrow: A
    Novel of Shanghai*, translated by Michael
    Berry with Susan Chan Egan (2008)
Ch'oe Yun, *There a Petal Silently Falls: Three
    Stories by Ch'oe Yun*, translated by Bruce
    and Ju-Chan Fulton (2008)
Inoue Yasushi, *The Blue Wolf: A Novel of the
    Life of Chinggis Khan*, translated by Joshua
    A. Fogel (2009)
Anonymous, *Courtesans and Opium:
    Romantic Illusions of the Fool of Yangzhou*,
    translated by Patrick Hanan (2009)

Cao Naiqian, *There's Nothing I Can Do When
    I Think of You Late at Night*, translated by
    John Balcom (2009)
Park Wan-suh, *Who Ate Up All the Shinga? An
    Autobiographical Novel*, translated by Yu
    Young-nan and Stephen J. Epstein (2009)
Yi T'aejun, *Eastern Sentiments*, translated by
    Janet Poole (2009)
Hwang Sunwŏn, *Lost Souls: Stories*, translated
    by Bruce and Ju-Chan Fulton (2009)
Kim Sŏk-pŏm, *The Curious Tale of Mandogi's
    Ghost*, translated by Cindy Textor (2010)
Xiaomei Chen, editor, *The Columbia
    Anthology of Modern Chinese Drama* (2011)
Qian Zhongshu, *Humans, Beasts, and Ghosts:
    Stories and Essays*, edited by Christopher
    G. Rea, translated by Dennis T. Hu,
    Nathan K. Mao, Yiran Mao, Christopher
    G. Rea, and Philip F. Williams (2011)
Dung Kai-cheung, *Atlas: The Archaeology of
    an Imaginary City*, translated by Dung Kai-
    cheung, Anders Hansson, and Bonnie S.
    McDougall (2012)

HISTORY, SOCIETY, AND CULTURE
Carol Gluck, Editor

Takeuchi Yoshimi, *What Is Modernity?
    Writings of Takeuchi Yoshimi*, edited and
    translated, with an introduction, by
    Richard F. Calichman (2005)
Contemporary Japanese Thought, edited and
    translated by Richard F. Calichman (2005)
Overcoming Modernity, edited and translated
    by Richard F. Calichman (2008)
Natsume Sōseki, *Theory of Literature
    and Other Critical Writings*, edited and
    translated by Michael Bourdaghs, Atsuko
    Ueda, and Joseph A. Murphy (2009)
Kojin Karatani, *History and Repetition*, edited
    by Seiji M. Lippit (2012)

river *of fire*
and other stories

O CHŎNG HŬI

TRANSLATED BY
BRUCE AND JU-CHAN FULTON

COLUMBIA UNIVERSITY PRESS ☖ NEW YORK

This publication has been supported by the Richard W. Weatherhead Publication Fund of the Weatherhead East Asian Institute, Columbia University.

The translation of these stories was supported by a National Endowment for the Arts Translation Fellowship.

Support for the editing and publication of this work was provided by the Sunshik Min Endowment for the Advancement of Korean Literature at the Korea Institute, Harvard University.

Columbia University Press
Publishers Since 1893
New York   Chichester, West Sussex
cup.columbia.edu

"Morning Star" reprinted from *Seeing the Invisible*, ed. Frank Stewart and Bruce Fulton, *Manoa: A Pacific Journal of International Writing* 8, no. 2 (1996).

Library of Congress Cataloging-in-Publication Data

O, Chŏng-hŭi.
[Short stories. English. Selections]
River of fire and other stories / O Chŏng-hŭi ; translated by Bruce and Ju-Chan Fulton.
    p.   cm. — (Weatherhead books on Asia)
ISBN 978-0-231-16066-7 (cloth : acid-free paper) — ISBN 978-0-231-50411-9 (electronic)
1. O, Chŏng-hŏi—Translations into English. I. Fulton, Bruce. II. Fulton, Ju-Chan. III. Title.
PL992.58.C63A2   2012
895.7'35—dc23   211038624

Columbia University Press books are printed on permanent and durable acid-free paper.
This book was printed on paper with recycled content.
Printed in the United States of America
c 10 9 8 7 6 5 4 3 2 1

CONTENTS

THE TOY SHOP WOMAN

It was time. The sun gathered its last rays and darkness stole in, claiming the windowsills, enveloping the light, blanketing the classroom like a dense fog. I felt like I was in a tomb. As the darkness settled, the breaths and conversations lingering in the light that had managed to penetrate the worn-out curtains died away. I was left with emptiness, as if I were yelling yet hearing only the echo of my voice. The thirty-two double desks, eight rows deep by four rows wide, came to life as everything else in the classroom vanished into nothingness. Their gridlike layout frightened me. The two black maws of each pair of desks sucked in the gloom;

I stared at those openings with the familiar mix of apprehension and dread, as if looking into a cave filled with precious treasure. My heart quickened at the knowledge that the classroom was empty, that its sixty-four desks were all mine.

I broke the silence: "Shall we begin?" But who would answer? There was only the darkness to swallow my blubbered syllables.

First the desks beside the windows. My groping hand found a seat cushion in one, a pencil case in another. I opened the pencil case and emptied the contents into my schoolbag. Still another desk yielded a pair of canvas slip-ons. I removed my own, tossed them across the room, stepped into the ones I had found. A bit tight. I rocked back on the heels, enjoying their stiff sensation— brand new! Then a desk stuffed with used Kleenex. Next a lunchbox, which I opened to reveal a ragged-looking clump of mashed-down rice that the owner had only picked at. Its fishy smell and sweetish taste nearly made me retch. "No wonder you don't eat that stuff!" I strained to listen. My scolding voice sounded so hollow—as if it had made its way back to me through a series of tunnels and become another person's voice in the process.

I wanted to talk with someone. I wanted to talk about the world I awakened to in this dark, empty classroom, about the self-righting dolls I collected with the proceeds of my gainful employment here, about the woman with the missing legs in the toy shop. The windows were rattling in the wind. Not much of value in the next few desks. I grew impatient—bored, even. But I couldn't just leave the remaining half-dozen rows untouched.

I was about to stick my hand into the next desk when I heard the scuffing of slippers in the hall. I crouched low on the wooden floor. It sounded like several of them. They'd passed by yesterday and the day before, scuffing along, not entering the classroom. Even so, my heart pounded—I kept thinking they were going to fling open the door and call out my name, or that they knew exactly what I was up to but chose to ignore me for the time being while making sure I'd heard them. I imagined two piercing eyes examining me in the darkness. "Is someone there?" I ventured, so fearful I actually hoped for an answer. But of course there was none.

Back to the desks. I tensed. That flat, sleek thing—was it a coin purse? My hand hesitated inside the desk. *I'm sure it's a coin purse,* I had told myself more than once, only to find a glasses case or a plastic folder holding a couple of streetcar passes. I felt the object again, and when I was sure of what I'd found I took it out and un-zipped it. The coins poured onto the floor. That clinking—*please* stop. On to the next desk. I passed a hand across my forehead; it was sticky with sweat.

My hand played around inside the desk. But I was only go-ing through the motions, giddy with delight at finding the coin purse. By now the classroom was dark. My schoolbag was much heavier with its ink bottle and other booty. I approached the mir-ror at the back of the classroom. My form appeared on the dark, shiny surface, and close behind it the entire room. The desks I'd rifled sat in disarray. I continued to gaze at the reflection of the classroom. The windows rattled louder than ever. Out to the hall I went.

The fake marble floor glittered in the faint flickers of light es-caping from the small night-duty room at the end of the hall. The sky outside was pitch black. The spotless appearance of the hall oppressed me. I felt like dumping my heavy schoolbag and rolling around on the marble. I felt like hoisting my stiff skirt and urinat-ing where I stood. Instead I spat. Spit was constantly gathering in my mouth. Again I spat, and then again. Strange how the gummy stuff always went *splat* on the fake marble. Now my mouth felt dry. I recognized the smell coming from it—the smell I'd noticed in the summer when I woke from a nap after several days of not brushing my teeth. Something was buzzing in my ear. I'd felt it climb through my throat, and now my right ear was buzzing and growing, growing and buzzing. My enlarged ear transformed the rattling of the windows into the shaking of the concrete school building. The buzz escalated to a roar. I pressed my ear shut, opening my mouth wide, exhaling till I was short of breath. But I couldn't close my mouth or I'd breathe in the smell coming from it, and that would make me throw up.

Water streamed down the rain-soaked street. There in the toy shop's brightly lit display window stood the red plastic self-righting dolls. And behind them the woman in her wheelchair, gazing out at the street. Her face looked freshly scrubbed. On sunny days she looked gloomy but now, through the rain, cleanliness seemed to radiate from her. In her gray crewneck sweater, a pendant with a carving of a Muslim woman's face lying like a still life upon her meager bosom, she resembled a huge toy doll.

If I pushed open the glass door with my schoolbag and walked in, she would ask if she could help me—knowing full well I never left without buying one of the dolls. Then again, she might not have remembered. A man and woman wearing raincoats went in. The toy shop woman made a shadow exit to greet them. I was terribly jealous of the couple. Disappearing behind some toys, the toy shop woman reappeared with a grin on her face. Smiling made her look twenty years older, from late teens to fortyish. I'd grown familiar with each of her facial expressions, each gesture, and yes, I missed them. People brushed past, glancing at me as I pressed myself against the window and peered inside. I forced myself to leave, fighting to control the jealousy that coursed through me like an electric current, trying to contain my hatred for the itchy sensuality reawakening inside me. I noticed a small boy hawking umbrellas and realized my neck was wet from the rain. I bought a yellow umbrella. But now my calves were itching, chafed by my skirt, which had drunk in the rain and was thick and close. Would someone *please* take care of this chafing? There, across the street, a drugstore. I bought some sticking plaster and found a sheltered place beneath a tall building where I could hoist my skirt and apply one of the broad cloth bandages to each calf. Relief at last. If only I could bandage myself all over, weighed down as I was by my wet clothing. Maybe then I could begin to unburden myself of the hatred that had settled, mucus-thick, in every joint of me. I missed the toy shop woman's room, its curtains with the tiny flower pattern, its pale light. Above all I missed that thin woman herself. But I couldn't bear to visit her again. My behavior that first night was still as fresh in my mind as an obscene picture, and even now I could almost feel the woman's body heat and the stumps of her amputated legs, which I had touched in the darkness of her room.

By sheer coincidence, I'd seen my mother that same evening. She was walking down the street with a grocery basket, looking at the displays of the salons that sold Western-style clothing. She didn't seem to be in a hurry, and I decided to follow her. I kept right behind her, but she didn't seem to notice. I stopped just long enough to put some distance between us, then caught up with her again. Still she seemed unaware. This was fun, following Mother from a distance and then up close. I crossed the street and followed her from the other side. Mother was looking like she'd soon have a baby. I couldn't believe how swollen her stomach was. Her eyes were circled by rings of discoloration that looked almost like a pair of glasses.

I was used to seeing her distended form. Since my childhood, this housekeeper who'd become my mother always looked pregnant. She dawdled along, sometimes stopping to rest. How long had it been since she'd gone away with her six-year-old girl? Three years? Four? I couldn't remember exactly, but it didn't matter. There was Mother, pregnant, just like before. Again she stopped. Above her was a large sign—LESSONS. After some hesitation, she gathered up her skirt and walked down the alley indicated by the arrow on the sign. I hastened across the street, but Mother had already disappeared. The LESSONS building appeared a couple of turns down the alley. At the entrance was a boy dressed like Fist Boss. He intercepted me: no students allowed. "I have to find someone—it's an emergency." I really did feel I should find

Mother and say something to her. "Okay," the boy said, shrugging, as if I'd put him on the spot. Not the kind of gesture Fist Boss would make.

I found myself inside a large, dimly lit space. Aha—a dance hall. It must have been early—all I could hear was the noisy, incessant whir of a fan and occasional whispers. My eyes gradually adjusted and I found her. She'd put on sunglasses. Then I saw the fan, hanging from the ceiling. The air moved by it felt humid and it ruffled Mother's hair, making it stand on end. With upswept hair and dark glasses, she looked like a circus clown. Eventually the hall filled up, the men sitting in one area, the women in another. The band started up, and at center stage a heavyset woman began singing in a low-pitched voice. The dance hall lurched into motion as the men straggled toward the women to find a partner. Mother seemed as anxious as the other women not yet approached. She turned to look at the couples dancing, her shoulders rising as if she was having difficulty breathing. Once more her bulging stomach caught my eye. Poor Mother, a woman cut from different cloth than I, a woman who used to spend an hour in the bathroom in her red nightie every morning, who was callous toward me but pretended otherwise. By now the singer was practically sobbing into the microphone she clutched. The couples swayed on the dance floor beneath lights that changed from crimson to blue and back again.

I used to dream about setting fire to the house, about sharpening a knife to kill Mother and her children. Those knowing looks from her had made me feel so guilty, so scared.

Finally the singer finished her song and left the stage. The dancers bowed to their partners and most of them returned to their seats. Those who remained extended sweaty palms toward the fan. The music started up again. Darn it—would I have to go home without seeing Mother dance? But the next moment she was out on the floor. Her partner put his arm around her waist. Mother's stiff nylon skirt fluttered in the breeze from the fan. The band played "The Blue Danube." Mother was breathing hard. The man looked uncomfortable holding her. He must have had second thoughts. Could he feel the baby kicking in her stomach? Would he jerk back in surprise? I imagined him waiting desperately for the song to end so he could free himself of this big-bellied woman in the dark glasses.

I wanted to cry. Every time the man turned Mother in a circle, the quilted socks that showed beneath the fluttering folds of her skirt looked like boots. I wanted to jump between Mother, as she turned with abandon, and the man, who held her uncomfortably. I wanted to drag her outside and scream and cry. And then, slowly, my hatred for her, coursing through me like blood, sustaining me, began to dissolve. I felt wrung out. As soon as the band finished for the evening, Mother hoisted herself to her feet and disappeared.

That was the night I went to the toy shop. The woman greeted me in silence. The lights were still on and she was looking out at the street. She didn't seem surprised at having a late-night visitor. What was I supposed to say? "You remember me, don't you?" I squeaked. An equivocal smile appeared on her face. It was too late to go home, I told her—could I spend the night there? To my relief she grinned. "Would you like something to eat?" I shook my head. All I wanted was to rest, and the sooner the better. She called the errand girl and told her to close up, then wheeled herself into the room at the back of the shop in which she lived. As I followed her, I wondered if perhaps she had kept the lights glaring out onto the empty street just for me. "Give me a hand, would you?" she asked, reaching toward me. I helped her out of the wheelchair and settled her into her bedding on the floor. Then she had me lie down beside her. After a time she turned to me. She cupped my neck in her hand. Before I knew it we were locked in a tight embrace.

Without a word being spoken, our lips met. Hers were lukewarm.

"Once I had a baby," she murmured breathlessly, her arm still tight around my neck. "I dreamed of making a lot of money and building myself a house without any stairs. But here I am living with a bunch of things that don't move. Nothing moves by itself." Closer and closer she held me.

I listened in the dark to the rustling of the quilt that covered us, to my senses coming alive with the force of a swift current.

We pressed ourselves against each other and I felt the throbbing of her heart. She looked much more like a grownup now as she filled my arms.

I woke to the tolling of a church bell. It was still dark. I counted the chimes. *I'll get up at the tenth one*, I told myself, but at the count of ten, instead of getting up I covered my face with my hands. The woman lay with her back toward me. She was probably awake, but didn't budge. I couldn't hear her breathe. I shut my eyes tight beneath my palms. The bell chimed on. I opened my eyes and winced at the sight of my underwear, flung aside like sloughed-off skin.

When it was bright outside I could wait no longer. I got up, overcome with shame, and put on my clothes. I passed my fingers through my mussed-up hair. As I was about to leave, the woman looked up at me. Her face shone with the traces of tears.

I never visited her again. I couldn't—everything we had done that night cast me in a sinister light, condemning me. But I was jealous of everything she came in contact with. All I could do was gaze at her through the window of the shop. Sometimes I dreamed about her—dreamed her naked body was filling my embrace. And when I woke I found it difficult to deal with the sensuality and the hatred that reared up yet again inside me.

A hundred self-righting dolls, all with the same face, each with the same expression, neatly arranged on my desk. When I pushed one of them over, it pitched and rolled, then stood up straight again.

I counted them, pointing to each in turn—exactly one hundred. There had been no additions to my collection after that night with the woman. Now too she'd be gazing out the window at the street from her wheelchair. One at a time, I set my dolls rolling on the floor. Soon they were a sea of red dots. A hundred dolls—a hundred lovely alter egos. Just me and them in a world all our own.

It was on a day when the sky seemed to swell to bursting and the sun gleamed flash-point white that I first saw the toy shop. I'd been hit with a terrible dizzy spell and was tottering along when I noticed the shop crammed with self-righting dolls. Sitting behind their close array was a woman in a wheelchair. I was bewildered— the woman looked like a doll herself. It wasn't the dizziness that gave me this impression, but rather a series of thoughts flashing through my mind like a moving picture—a balcony showered in sunlight, a gloomy Japanese-style eight-mat room, a boy pushing himself about in a wheelchair, drawings all over the walls.

I rubbed my eyes and opened the door, and there she was, along with a pair of crutches resting in the corner. My gaze came to rest on the colorful toys that filled the shop, looking quietly alive as if the woman's breath had invigorated them. The woman looked not quite forty, but her face had a sprinkling of dark spots characteristic of someone much older. I hesitated at the entrance. Could she help me? the woman asked. I pointed to the self-righting dolls—not because I'd decided to buy one of them but because my gaze had stopped where they filled one of the counters. The woman called into the room at the back of the shop; a girl came out and presented me with one of the red plastic dolls.

That night I dreamed of my little brother who had died, and from then on I dropped by the toy shop every night and bought a doll. It was as if this routine, rather like lighting a succession of lamps, gave meaning to my cold, dreary inner world. Sometimes I felt as if one stout cocoon after another were being woven inside me. These growths weighed heavily upon my heart, and when I held one of the round dolls I could almost feel its red exterior knocking against the shell of the cocoons. I was daunted by the handicapped woman and the imagined silent movements of her various toys, but the dolls I was collecting comforted me.

Seeing the toy shop woman triggered all the old memories— the second floor our family had rented in an old Japanese-style house; my little brother in his wheelchair; our housekeeper, later my mother, with her ponderous bosom and cheerful voice. And I recalled the rooms with the tatami mats—large but tasteless, dark and gloomy. Only the balcony was sunny. I recalled our furniture, which I'd made my private playground—the smelly wardrobes and the huge piano that rested against the wall. None of us knew how long we had owned this old instrument. It had lost its black lacquer; its ivory keys had yellowed, and some of them produced a muffled tone. My little brother had polio and spent most of his day in the wheelchair, making pictures on the white walls as high as he could reach. The steeple of the chapel, the housekeeper's frizzy hair—everything his eye caught was transformed by his hand into a mural. And when there was nothing else to draw, he undressed and made an elaborate drawing of his body. He insisted on drawing me naked too. And so the murals were joined by men and women of various shapes in the most unaffected poses. It didn't take long for Brother to fill the walls with his drawings, which ended at a certain height as if confined by a border. One day the housekeeper giggled while passing her unshapely hands over them. Brother began to pester her: "Take off your clothes, Auntie, and I'll do you too!" The housekeeper gave him a know-ing smile and rapped him gently on the head. He cried the rest of the day, asking her over and over to undress.

One day I returned from school to find him waiting for me at the top of the stairs with a piece of drawing paper filled with his work. He gave me a joyful shout, and I started up the stairs. Sud-denly he was careening toward me in the wheelchair, his hands clutching the wheels. His shrieks seemed to come from every direction, and then he came smashing down on the cement floor. His head was a bloody mess, his face swollen like that of a corpse.

Pieces of the wheelchair lay every which way. I removed the drawing paper from Brother's hand. The paper ripped, a corner of it remaining between his fingers. With a lump in my throat I stared at the paper, embracing what was left of the wheelchair, until they came and carried Brother away. Some flowers—cockscombs, perhaps—had been drawn in red crayon. It was the first time he'd drawn flowers—you couldn't see them from the second floor. Behind the flowers was a nude woman. In my mind it was the housekeeper. The face bore no resemblance to hers, but no one else where we lived had the frizzy hair and the absurdly huge breasts of the woman in the picture.

After Brother's death it was just me and the housekeeper. The days dragged by. I always held to the illusion that Brother's face, pale like a full moon before sunset, flickered among his artwork on the walls. The sight of his drawings tore at my heart.

Father, who had lived apart from us all along, returned after Brother's death. He stayed for a while and was always affectionate with me. Every evening he took me to the docks, where the boats were moored all in a row. He let me tag along with him when he went saltwater fishing, and when we returned we'd have goby fish cooked in soy sauce and spices to go along with our evening rice and soup.

One morning I woke to find that everything had changed. The housekeeper emerged from Father's room, patting down her bushy hair, and when it came time for me to leave for school she didn't comb my hair or prepare my breakfast as she usually did. I left for school in tears, my hair tangled like a magpie's nest. All the memories of my little brother came back to me. And that night Father left.

The situation at home changed, but no one ever told me why. Father visited frequently and the housekeeper always spent the night in his room. Gradually she assumed the role of my mother and her cheerful voice could be heard everywhere in the house. She constantly produced babies—or so it seemed to me at the time. Their crying never stopped, but at least it spiced up life at home. They would survive until their first birthday, but around the time the next sibling was due to arrive they would develop diarrhea and die. At first the housekeeper looked after me in every way. She even attended the PTA meetings, though she dressed like a refugee from the countryside. But her kindness eventually turned to heartlessness. If I told her I needed money for pencils or notebooks, she would look at me accusingly as if to say that what I really wanted was to buy snacks. I began sneaking pencils and crayons from my classmates. Pretty soon no one wanted to sit next to me, and my homeroom teacher got in the habit of turning my schoolbag upside down and emptying it out. My response was to hide a piece of chalk in my pocket and take my sweet time scrawling on the walls of the toilet, "Teacher's a bitch, Mom's a bitch."

I went into a hard shell, and the further I withdrew, the more fiercely I hated Mother. The memories of my little brother grew ever more vivid. And then Mother proceeded to clean the walls of all his drawings—those drawings in which he still lived, drawings that had captured my affection. One by one she scrubbed at them with a wet rag. I clung to her, trying to stop her, but she pushed me away. "It's your fault he died," she said, her tone distant. "If you'd come home a little earlier or a little later it never would have happened. He played so well by himself—why did he have to die?" Our relationship grew frigid. The hatred that clung to my soul, my readiness to confront others, to feel victimized, wound my nerves tight. My hatred for Mother began to feel like the driving force of my life.

Finally I wrote a letter to the toy shop woman: "I dreamed about you again last night. Every night I dream of you, naked. I suffer from the unbearable shame of it all. Do you remember the night I came to you? If only you could forget. Please, put it out of your mind and let me into your world once more." I read it aloud. It sounded kind of theatrical, but there was some genuine feeling to it.

For days a sign had been posted on the toy shop window: CLOSED FOR REMODELING. I was frantic. Now I couldn't even look through the window at her in the evening, much less visit her. The letter I'd written her got smudged from my handling; its creases grew frayed.

A tearoom appeared where the toy shop had been. The locked door was now open. The celebratory bouquets lining the entrance gave the place a carnival atmosphere. I went inside, half expecting the toy shop to appear and the woman, bathed in its bright lights and surrounded by all the toys, to welcome me. "I love you," the speakers blared, "I love you." The new owner greeted me from the counter with a sumptuous smile. Her fingernails were neatly trimmed. I looked around. I never would have guessed the toy shop had been there. But even with the red and blue lights, the lovers who filled the chairs, and the huge aquarium where tropical fish made bubbles and more bubbles, I could visualize where the toy shop woman had always sat, where her crutches had rested, where all those lifelike toys had been placed. I walked outside. The same tremulous voice still cried "I love you" over the speakers.

I imagined the woman rolling in her wheelchair in search of a new life, followed by the charming toy cars and behind them the self-righting dolls wobbling along, the other dolls walking stiffly. But they might as well have been in a foreign country, so far out of my reach were they now. For a moment I felt liberated. But I also felt a loneliness that would never end. Soon I would shrink back inside my hard shell like a snail, there to embrace visions of my little brother and my hatred for Mother, together with the obscene images of my liaison with the toy shop woman. I would have to get rid of the dolls waiting for me on my desk. I could live without them—I had to. But this thought failed to console me. My legs wouldn't stop trembling. No stars in the sky. My heart was drying up—how much longer before it crumbled?

ONE SPRING DAY

Better water the flowers before the sun hits them. Telling myself this, I hopped down from the veranda to the yard, and the first thing I noticed was that one of the stems of the rosebush was broken. I swore under my breath.

"Say what?" said Sŭngu from the edge of the veranda, where he stood swilling a bottle of Coke and stifling a yawn. He craned his neck in my direction.

"This stem is broken."

His only reaction was to bring the bottle to his lips again, a faraway look in his eyes.

He always acted like this, planting his ponderous torso behind me as I went about my work. Even so, I was irritated by his lackadaisical attitude. I started with the annuals, which had already grown a couple of inches, swinging the watering can roughly from side to side. In no time I'd scoured the earth around the base of the stalks and drenched the tiny stems and leaves. But I kept it up, even after I'd practically washed the roots bare.

It didn't seem to have rained, and I hadn't noticed the broken stem the previous evening, so the wind or the rats must have done the damage overnight. The stem was a thin young sucker, so it wouldn't have blossomed that well anyway. No harm removing one shoot to produce a healthier rosebush.

I liked the way the suckers were taking water and branching out, and I'd decided to prune the bush before the summer rains. Still, it was so vexing to see the sap oozing from the broken stem.

Sŭngu finished his Coke and added the bottle to the pile of empties in the apple box. I frowned. Three boxes of empties and we were about to fill a fourth. Awful the way we guzzled that stuff. Indigestion, insomnia, loneliness—whatever the excuse, we consumed a steady supply of Coke. Anytime, anywhere, we always found a good reason. Sometimes we had nothing else to do, sometimes we drank it because it was raining. Suddenly I had a hollow feeling—something about that pile of bottles unsettled me.

"Hello, ladies—sleep well?"

While I was lost in thought, Sŭngu had come down to the yard and was peering into the chicken coop, a tangle of slats and wire supported by wooden posts.

"What are we keeping those things for, anyway?" I snapped at him. "We'll never get any eggs out of them. Plus, they're attracting a swarm of rats."

He looked at me with such a serious expression that I thought he might actually reply. But instead he took the rice pot, which

I'd brought from the kitchen, and deposited the dregs inside the coop.

Our dog, lying dead still all this time, got up and went to Sŭngu and wormed its way between his legs, whimpering. Sŭngu lifted the dog high and sat it on his shoulders. Shreds of fur started fluttering down. I resumed my angry sprinkling. In no time my throat was tickling. Dog fur had long since infiltrated the house. Sŭngu's hair was full of the shiny silver stuff—it made him look prematurely gray—and every movement of his head dislodged some of it. The drifting shreds of fur followed us everywhere, getting between our toes, into the basin when we washed our faces, into the soap when we lathered. There was no escaping them.

The greater part of our lives was taken up with Coke bottles and the fur that penetrated every available space like little silver stingers. *Dog hair floating in space—our only constant possession.* There was something strangely oppressive about those desiccated hairs, identical in length and shape. Whenever I saw or felt the dry, coarse stuff, I thought of tiny hidden crevices left by termites at work and sensed a destructive power capable of bringing down a house. But I felt helpless to lift a finger in response. All I could do was shudder.

I set down the watering can and gently pounded the small of my back to get the kinks out.

"I want to eat," I heard Sŭngu say.

We had our usual early breakfast, even though it was Sunday and Sŭngu didn't have to go to work. After rinsing his mouth with rice water, he prepared to leave.

He told me he'd be home after supper, and then he was gone. I sat down again, but after a few token spoonfuls of rice water I pushed the meal table aside. My stomach was churning over that broken sucker, which had somehow transferred itself to my shoulder and made it feel out of joint.

I poured stew over the leftover rice in my bowl and called the dog, who was rooting around in the garbage can. It jumped onto the veranda and curled up in the folds of my skirt.

I patted the dog with one hand and poured the stew and rice into a separate bowl with the other, making sure I didn't spill any. The dog slurped it up, stopping only to whimper at me.

I buried my hand in the pretty fur of its neck. The dog's warmth spread up from my fingertips, gentle as affection. "Shalom." At the sound of its name the dog lifted its head and nuzzled me, its snout flecked with white grains of rice. *Shalom*—the Yiddish word for peace. What exactly did peace signify? In history class we had learned it was something obtained only through blood sacrifice.

Peace filled our home, imbued my relationship with Sŭngu, a peace absolute and invulnerable in which no leaf on a tree could be disturbed. But what had I sacrificed for it? Our relationship was like stagnant water—stale, peaceful.

I caressed the dog more firmly. Its silver fur collected on my skirt and the back of my hand with a frightening persistence.

I washed and dried the dishes and stacked them one by one in the cupboard. The sun was still low. Time to clean the house. I flung open the windows and cleared the cobwebs from the ceiling with my duster. Changed the curtains. Swept the floors and wiped them with a wet rag until my knees gave out. The morning began to feel endless.

I spread Sŭngu's bedding over the wall outside where it would catch the sun, then returned to his room to fetch his balled-up socks and handkerchiefs, which I tossed into the laundry basin in the yard. I searched his room once more, but that seemed to be it for the laundry. I trotted back outside and ripped away the linings of the bedding, which still had a bright shine as if freshly bleached. *Pop-pop-pop-pop* went the seams. After washing the linings, I would resew them to the bedding. Then it was back inside to peel off his spotless pillowcase. I opened his wardrobe, took the dress shirts that had been pressed at the cleaner's, rolled them up in a bundle, and added them to the basin to soak. I put in the detergent, then rolled up my sleeves, squatted, and watched the water in the basin bubble and foam. Anxiety rose from my chest, eating at my nerves like a corrosive fog. . Was I coming down with something? Was something supposed to happen today? No, nothing I could think of.

I imagined Sŭngu staggering home drunk again, crumpled up like a rag, leaving it to me to remove his shoes and undress him, acting like a little boy who's been forgiven for something or who's cried himself into a manageable state. Maybe his shirt pocket would yield a rubber doll that produced a mewling cry if you poked its belly button. You never knew. More than once I'd plopped down in shock while hanging his clothes—there in his pocket a squirrel, or a wind-up robot with flashing eyes, or worse, a pair of guinea pigs or an owl, wings folded, with big round eyes that looked like glass and didn't move. Whether he was being eccentric or just trying to please me, I couldn't tell. But nobody was going to make a mess in my house, and fortunately the animals died off after a few days, even if I fed them and changed their water. Sŭngu didn't seem distressed when he had to consign them to a deep grave in the corner of the yard.

I removed my kerchief, used it to dust myself off, then rolled down my sleeves. It was twelve noon. I went into Sŭngu's room and searched his clothes hanging on the wall. I pulled each pants pocket inside out and shook it. Coins clinked onto the floor. I tried his suit jacket—nothing. Never say die. I reached into his windbreaker. Aha—hello, cuties! Inside the sleek pack were five cigarettes in a nice cozy line. After heaving a sigh of relief, I found matches and lit up.

I watched the smoke trailing from my fingertips. "What next," I muttered. I began to count the number of tiles on the angular eaves of the house next door. But before I could reach twenty my eyes were playing tricks on me. I had to start over. The over-

lapping tiles were a series of uniform ripples—it was only natural you'd lose count and have to give up halfway through. So
from this side, at any rate, I'd never been able to figure out how
many tiles there were. This time, as usual, I only made it to two
dozen or so.

On to the house sites outside our front gate. Winding along
the hillside beyond them was a road pounded out of the ocher
soil. A small dark object bobbed like a kite above that road, the
only movement in the noontide stillness. I followed it along the
slope. My eyes were feeling the strain of squinting when the object enlarged to where I could identify it—a woman balancing a
wide-mouthed basin on her head.

"Flowers for sale, get your flowers, flowers for love love love!"

The woman was still in the distance, but her bawling voice carried over the wall to our house. She must have been picking wildflowers on the hillside.

I waited for the woman to approach and called out to her, but
she didn't seem to hear me—she must have been caught up in the
merriment of the old ballad. I kept calling, and finally I realized
she was ignoring me. She could probably command a much better price downtown for her wildflower bouquets than she could
traipsing around here on the outskirts. From my vantage point on
the veranda I had a clear view of yellow cornel blossoms mixed
with sprigs of azalea that hadn't yet flowered.

Long after the woman had made her impassioned transit past
our house, I kept listening to her singing, which was punctu-
ated by a hacking cough. Sunlight seethed above the road, which
would take her to the bus stop. Finally my eyes had had enough of
the dazzling light—I rubbed them furiously.

A spring day so exhilarating that it stifled me. A day when
plant seed floating on ripples of air could blossom as soon as it
touched down, whether on my hair caressed by the wind, on my
dry, colorless face, or on the laundry hanging loose like an array
of flags. A day on which the peddler woman's coughing drifted

like pollen blending with air. I had a vague feeling something was going to happen.

I yawned, stretched, and lay down on the veranda, my feet hanging over the threshold of the sliding door. I felt bright sunlight wash over my insteps. The sloping roof next door gently screened off the sky.

Helplessly I watched that roof: no emotion, oblivious to all thoughts and feelings, a sheet of white unfolding like a curtain inside my head. And all because of the sunlight, which was everywhere, too much of it, bringing everything to a stop. Back I went in time, years back, to exactly when I couldn't say. Devoid of sentiment, the memory rose like sunlight, tickling the back of my hand and settling around my eyes, like a thick layer of dust dispersed with a single breath.

It was the day I'd left home more than five months pregnant, determined to kill myself. A drought had persisted into the torrid part of the summer, and the sweat trickled from my armpits, behind my knees, from every fold in my body.

I came to the glen. The stream was dry, and I saw carp lying belly up on the fiery surface of the bleached rocks.

I found a small stagnant pool and let my hair fall into it. Despite the mosquito larvae, the rotten vegetation, and the water moss, I could only think how refreshing it felt. And that was all I was hoping for.

I tilted closer to the dark blue pool. The clouds dotting the sky appeared on the surface and began to rotate. Faster and faster they whirled, until I felt it was I who was spinning in circles. My hair trailed away like an amphibious creature.

And then I was upside down, head in the water. My legs scuffed against the rocks, and after a struggle I righted myself.

I flopped back against the rocks, feeling like a piece of laundry drying in the sun. There I lay, looking up at the sky. It was hot.

Maybe it was that feverish heat, but the sunlight seemed to have solidified, as if you were seeing it in a mirror. Time too had congealed, and together with the sunlight it weighed me down. And then time changing into sunlight licked upward from my toes. I felt like my blood was evaporating.

Nothing moved. Everything had swollen in the heat, losing its shape, melting into time, leaving no trace. I myself felt only a tautness. But then, the strangest thing—this body I wanted to dispose of began to dissolve into utter solitude and peace. My consciousness ebbed and I slipped into a languid state of exhaustion and well-being. Birdcalls from somewhere in the hills penetrated my blanket of fever. In my mind those calls transformed into beaks pecking away at a thick glass screen. I wondered how long the birds had been calling. I imagined their tender beaks, bloodied by their diligent efforts, finally breaking through the glass screen of sunlight, fever, and time. It sounded like the birds in the stream valley were calling all at once. I sprang up, opening the white curtain that draped my consciousness, and a sharp pain attacked me—I thought my head would crack open.

I looked around—nothing had changed. I felt not a breath of wind. Everything was still except for the piercing birdcalls and the trembling leaves, the only indication of air movement. A band of dark clouds had formed, deepening the bluish-green foliage in the glen. Sensation began to return, starting with the tips of my fingers and toes, as if I were awakening from anesthesia. What I was doing here? While the baby of that unfaithful man who had abandoned me was growing in my belly, my lifeblood was drying up—I felt empty and decrepit. One drink and I couldn't even keep my skirt hitched up properly. What an idiot I was, coming here on a sweltering day to kill myself. *I'll get rid of the baby*, I thought, figuring it would be as simple as erasing the writing that fills a blackboard. *I'll clean my hands, of this mess, pretend it never happened, erase the memory.*

Back home I had screwed up my courage and had an abortion, feeling as if I were excising a malignant cyst. But even now, years later, I knew with certainty that I had failed to free myself of the bogey of that six-month-old fetus. Never breaking the surface of my life, it had, if anything, lodged more deeply within me, stirring at odd moments like rheumatic joints when they sense imminent rain. My memories of my desire to become pregnant, to nurture a fetus, to reproduce, together with my remorse at my inability, bubbled up in a sticky lather, removing the façade of my daily life as if peeling off a membrane. And when that swamp of memory drew me in I could feel my belly waxing, my womb filling with fluid, my breathing growing labored. Unless I emptied myself of that fluid, I would drown. In my mind I struggled desperately to avoid that fate. But when the fluid rose to my neck I would gasp with thirst and search for water—a glass of pure water.

Lying on the veranda, I covered my eyes, the radiant sun gathering inside the closed lids just like it had that day in the past.

The dog was barking. Which was unusual—it couldn't have been Sŭngu, whose footsteps the dog was sure to recognize, and we never had visitors.

It was suppertime, and I was in the kitchen looking for leftovers. While the dog barked, I listened for any movement outside. The dog scratched at the ground and barked more fiercely. Maybe we actually did have a visitor.

I looked out the window. Who could it be? A shadow projected from the base of the front gate.

I went out to the yard. "Who is it?" I asked sharply, my voice quavering as I tried to make myself heard above the barking.

The face of a young man shot up above the gate.

"Is Sŭngu in? I'm a friend of his from over the hill there."

I unlatched the gate. The young man was resting a hand on the handlebars of a bicycle. He bowed in greeting.

He must have wondered why I was silent, but instead of giving me a chance to answer, he chattered on.

"You must be Sŭngu's wife," he said deferentially. "We've never met, but I could tell right away. Sŭngu asked me over for a game of *paduk*."

It finally occurred to me that this was the young man Sŭngu went to play *paduk* with every Sunday. They were friends from back home.

"By the way, do I have the right place? He is here, isn't he?"

Instead of answering, I moved aside to let him in. With no hesitation, he brought his bicycle inside.

"Is he in the middle of something?" he asked with a doubtful look.

I waited until he had propped up his bicycle, then answered slowly, trying to buy time. "He's not in at the moment."

"Hmm, we had a bet riding on the game. . . . He asked me to come over—where the hell could he be?"

With a bemused expression the young man scratched his head and placed a hand on the carrying rack of his bicycle, as if to leave.

I quickly reassured him: "He'll be right back—he just went out for a haircut." Then blurted, "Why don't you come in for a minute?" I'd had no intention of lying, and it did occur to me that perhaps Sŭngu was at the barber's just then, getting a shampoo or leafing through a newspaper.

But the visitor seemed determined not to enter if Sŭngu wasn't there.

"Then he's at the barbershop? It can't be that far. I'll go find him."

He began to turn his bicycle around.

"That won't be necessary."

He flinched at the firmness in my voice. We were caught in an awkward moment of tension. I examined his face. In contrast with the knobby knuckles of his hand on the bicycle, his eyes were boyish and lively beneath the mussed-up shock of hair that testified to his journey here.

"He told me to expect a visitor and ask him in. If you go back now and don't cross paths, it's all in vain," I said gently, taking the big-sister approach.

Finally he bent over to unlace his sneakers. The dog, momentarily silent, started barking again. The young man looked as if he'd done something wrong.

"Say, that's one vicious animal."

He winked and produced a mischievous smile, but I could tell he was still trying to ease the awkwardness between us.

"Shhh. Shalom—bad dog! No barking—I'm going to muzzle you if you don't stop."

I waited patiently while he undid his laces. Then I led him past Sŭngu's room to mine, slid the door wide open, and went in.

He came right in behind me and with no preliminaries perched himself on my bed.

"Could I trouble you for a drink of water, ma'am? I'm really hot."

I practically ran to the kitchen. My legs were shaky, like when I smoked too many cigarettes, and my hands kept trembling as I tried to pour a bowl of water from the tap. I had to keep emptying and filling the bowl to get the right level. But when I placed it on the serving tray I noticed the water was milky because of all the tiny bubbles from our chlorinated water supply. So I served him a Coke instead.

"This is what we always drink. Can't get by without it."

I examined his reaction as I poured him a glass.

"Better if we didn't drink so much of it, but it's addictive, you know."

He waited for the fizzing to stop, then took a gulp. But he was only being polite—the glass remained three quarters full.

"I guess you don't much care for it."

"No, it's not that. It's just that I can do without it." He smiled gently.

The evening sunlight, still hot, gave a red tinge to the projections of the plaster figures I used as models for sketching; the recesses remained deep in shadow.

"It's really hot," said the young man, and he proved it with a gush of breath, panting so forcefully I could see his ribs moving through his thin cotton pullover. My cramped room felt like it was all the warmer for our body heat and the awkward silence that filled the space like electricity charging a battery.

I opened the window.

"Doesn't that feel good?" he said.

"It sure does."

Again there was silence. The young man looked vacantly out the window, as if searching for a thread to keep the conversation going.

"You know, he may not have told you this, but I'm in medical school."

"So you're going to be a doctor."

"I've got a ways to go—just started interning at the university hospital."

But I noticed an air of superiority that he wasn't quite able to conceal behind his all-forgiving smile as he stuck out his chest.

"Well, guess who majored in painting?"

"He did? Well, he must have done a U-turn after he graduated. I guess I got it all wrong—never heard him say he was taking fine arts. I guess a person's major and his career aren't necessarily related."

No longer was he trying to hide the pride he felt in the knowledge that his major would guarantee him a career.

"*He* didn't major in fine arts—*I* did," I said desperately. "All four years I was crazy about painting."

"Really?" he said without the slightest interest, nodding halfheartedly. He took a sip of Coke. His expression read something like this: *You know, a major is something women have only when they're in college. It's like a uniform they wear for four years, and by the time they graduate it's all worn out.*

"Ma'am, mind if I have one of Sŭngu's cigarettes? I was in such a rush to get here I forgot to buy my own," he said, without a trace of humility.

I passed him one of the two remaining cigarettes in the pack I'd found earlier.

"And a light?"

I pushed the matches toward him and put the last cigarette in my mouth. His expression hardened, but he was quick to strike a match and offer it to me.

While he sipped at his Coke, eyes lowered, I stared at the tufts of hair sticking out from the back of his head, which made him look like an elementary school boy, and the neck protruding innocently from the collar of his pullover. I felt a stinging pain—was this what heartbreak felt like?

"Do you always stay home alone like this?"

"Yes, just like this."

"What do you do with yourself?"

"I read my palms."

"That's interesting. Were you born under a lucky star?"

"I'm not sure. To me a lucky star means that one day a brave, handsome prince on a white horse comes to rescue a sweet, beautiful princess confined in a tower, and the two of them live happily ever after. Maybe I was born to be bored all my life. Shall I read your palm? I can tell if *you* were born under a lucky star. If you've got a circle beneath this long line across the top of your palm, it's a lucky sign." I moved closer to him.

"That's all right. I don't believe in lucky stars and such, and besides, it's too dark to see." He subtly drew in his hand and moved away. Slowly I reached for his hand, making no attempt to hide the wicked smile on my face. I felt like an unlucky old woman. Sitting across from him on the bed, I couldn't make out the contours of his face or see his expression. It was indeed quite dark. Just as my hand was about to touch his, he eased himself farther away.

"We'd better turn on the light. Where's the switch?" he asked casually, his voice muted, trying his best to pretend it was too dark for him to realize what I was doing.

I got up and turned on the light.

"How about a game of *paduk*? Do you play?"

"No, I'm afraid I don't."

"Too bad. Well, could you bring me the newspaper or something?"

"No paper on Sunday—sorry. How about a cup of coffee?"

"No thanks—can't get to sleep if I drink coffee in the evening."

So there we sat like dullards. I did my best to avoid eye contact. Eyes lowered like mine, he fumbled with the sheets. He'd finished his Coke. The fluorescent light gave the transparent glass a bluish tinge. Suddenly I felt a chill. The pale light offered neither warmth nor welcome. Was the phosphorescence on the face of a corpse pale like that? I was pretty sure that if I turned off the light I could still see his white teeth, the tidy cuffs sticking out from his black pullover, and after he had left, the place where his soft, warm lips had touched the empty glass sitting by itself in the middle of the room.

He brought his wristwatch close to his face.

"Where could he be? Well, it's getting too late to play *paduk* anyway."

He stood up, but instead of leaving he spent the longest time smoothing out the wrinkles in his trousers.

I didn't try to detain him. I felt a sense of betrayal, unfounded but nevertheless unpleasant. *You're not much fun, are you? No manners, no charm. If you were going to turn tail, you should have done it a long time ago.*

"It's a bitch of a ride and the light on the bicycle is practically useless."

He went out to the yard, hefted the bicycle, and carried it out the gate. The dog barked its head off, and I made no effort to quiet it.

"I can see why it needs a muzzle."*Ha ha.* I didn't smile.

"Ma'am, you look awful."

"It's this godawful spring—makes me damn tired—I'm always coming down with something."

"Well, you drop on by the hospital anytime you want a checkup."

He pushed off hard, gave me a wave, and flew away into the darkness. In no time he had disappeared, quiet as an alley cat on the prowl. I leaned against the gate and looked down this road that led to the outside world, now buried in dusk—it was where the peddler woman had gone. With a shudder I went back in and latched the gate.

The yard was dark, and with every step I felt the gloom weigh heavy on me like quicksilver. I held my breath so as not to disturb the silence, an emptiness like that of a dry well enveloping the house.

I went into my room, sat on my bed, and found my hand mirror. Confined within it was the haggard face of an aging woman, the color of her pupils badly faded, washed out. What had happened to me just now? Something had wormed its way into my life. But there was nothing to show for it. Nothing except the night. In the mirror I saw myself begin silently to cry.

A shadow—I see a shadow. Light is flickering, ghostlike, inside a long tunnel. The shadow, pursued by its substance, projects from the tunnel wall. On the other side of that darkness, flowing into it, hiding there, is time. Time—the unknown that's hidden in a hard, compact bud. A monk told me that. Time is a bud that hasn't yet bloomed. But to me time felt like the gray robe the monk wore. I remember the desiccated vines of ivy that covered his desolate retreat, how they left countless crevices in the walls.

Yes. Time—through which silkworm larvae spin lovely raw silk out of mulberry leaves. Time—the formlessness that transforms floating dust and other objects the way a blotter soaks up ink. You can't see it—you can only feel it. Time exists in the chill you feel when you grope for a light switch when it starts to get dark. It's there in the whiff from the armpit of the man sitting across from you in the tearoom when he lifts his cup of lukewarm liquid after wearing you out with his chatter. The first disease whose name you can remember, the pleasant sensation you get from a slight fever, the secret pleasure you take from doing something bad, the first time you made love, the times you've kissed someone—they all sink into the swamp of time and dissolve, finally to reappear, skillfully woven back together, each with its own sound, color, tint. Thus rewoven, they look so different from how they first appeared.

Tracking down the ghosts of the past is like searching for something in a well-worn photo album—what do you get from it? It's like trying to unravel a tightly woven carpet by pulling a single strand.

I'm weeding a bean field. Scuffing along on my knees, I weed two rows with my short hoe, my unlined jacket sticking to my back and chafing the flesh. In the heat that spreads over the field, the wilting leaves of the plants droop practically to the ground. *You've got to get rid of those yellow leaves, got to get rid of those weeds that shoot out of the ground even in a drought—they're your enemies,* I tell myself. The ground is hard as a turtle shell, and I feel the blade of the hoe begin to give way—when will I ever be done with all this weeding, and why do I have to relieve myself so frequently? I look around to see if anyone's coming, look up at the sky where cumulus clouds billow like flowers blooming in a time-lapse clip, set down my hoe, and squat, and as I flip my skirt up I hear the shrill crying of a baby from the far end of this eternal field.

It wasn't that hot under the blazing sun of my dream, but I awakened burning with fever. The fever left me with a peculiar clarity of thought that made the crying of the baby sound like the chirping of a slender bird rubbing its beak against a branch outside my window. I felt as if my eyes, ears, and fingertips were luminous, as if I were groping through a tunnel for that sound.

I came to the end of the tunnel and it was morning. Morning visits when you least expect it, always with a feast of presentiments and anticipation. Greedily I breathed in the fresh air. Then I found the bowl of lukewarm water beside my bed, the pure, salt-free fresh water that I prefer, and gulped it down. I flung open the curtain. Whether it was the mist of morning or the previous evening's haze, a collection of tiny particles crawled along the window, clustering on its surface.

The spine of the hill across from our house was the color of an eggplant. Enveloped in the lingering gloom of dawn, the hill looked like a crouching beast approaching me.

The birds hadn't started singing. When the gloom lifted, the hill would come alive with movement like an animal that catches a stray bullet, and all together the startled birds would begin their morning chorus.

I felt a draft, and with a shudder I gathered my rumpled nightie closer. Whenever I had a disturbing dream I sensed things ominous and my heart would start to pound—it never failed. But the shrill crying of the baby was not just something I heard in my dreams. When I sliced tofu, when I was pinching off the fibrous tails of soybean sprouts, when I held a flopping fish by its scarlet gills and scraped away its glittering scales, I heard every now and then the innocent cries that were like a medium between me and the baby. I would stop what I was doing, feel my sight and hearing begin to sharpen, and imagine myself searching for the origin of the sound. My destination was always the ocean. I didn't go so far as to call it a journey, merely told myself I was visiting the sea. But

I never carried out this plan. It was just as well, for the gray, impassive ocean would have offered no relief.

It was not the ocean itself I longed to see. What I wanted was harsher, more wrathful than the biblical flood, a deluge building and swelling like the sea at high tide, overflowing dikes, swallowing houses, washing away hills.

Like a glass being filled, like the moon waxing full, my body, mature enough to bear, began to fill with water, starting from the tips of my toes, my insteps tickling, the level gradually rising. But my lips were blackish, parched, chapped, pinched like a clam, and finally my fever erupted like a dancer whirling to a fast rhythm.

I heard an airplane, its roar somber like the rush of waves on a shore at night. Sweat clung to my forehead. I needed a bath, but first I wanted to to give my hair a good soak, then throw off my clothes and wash myself with water from the pump, cold water pure as dew, flowing unseen from deep within the earth. That water streaming over me at dawn was cold enough to leave me gasping, to make my veins stand out and bring a mottling of red to my feverish body, but I would pour it over me until my hot flash went away. I'd grit my teeth and screw up my resolve, vicious in my determination. But first I ran to the kitchen, uncapped a Coke, and poured the cool, biting liquid deep down my throat.

A PORTRAIT OF MAGNOLIAS

It looked hazy outside, and I wondered if the wind was kicking up dirt. But when I wiped the condensation from the window with my sleeve, it was snowflakes I saw, falling in fits and starts like swirls of dust.

Taking advantage of the remaining light of the fleeting winter afternoon, I continued to work on my still life, warming my hands in my armpits as I needed to.

"No more magnolias? Then how about a mandala?"

I flinched—the voice was so loud in the empty studio—and I felt a draft on my back. I turned and there was Hansu, leaning against the door frame, his face flushed with drink. He must have recalled how obsessed I was with magnolias, how foolish I was in trying to paint them.

To paint a magnolia—I must be dreaming.

Magnolias, purple magnolias, white magnolias—trees that in times past were not to be found in a family's courtyard, the flowers meant instead for invoking spirits of the dead. One of those spirits had burst into bloom from my mother's bones, bobbing in the air, the soul of an undefiled maiden, its blossoms firm like artificial flowers, its color soft and white like an incandescent bulb. It bloomed till daybreak, countless eerie mouths, suction cups drawing in the secretions of the night.

"Try finding a flower to work from at this time of year," I answered. A poor excuse, but the best I could come up with. The real reason was, I just couldn't picture a magnolia in my mind.

White magnolias bloomed at night from Mother's cursed bones—bones that wouldn't bleach out even after the thatch that shrouded them had turned to dust and drifted away. Every night the blossoms that sprang from her bones were spirited away to fill the firmament, but still the bones were dark and mottled.

I had tried to paint those magnolias, scattering dots of white color over a blue background. "A mandala!" Hansu had once exclaimed, looking over my shoulder. *He knew!* Chilled by his remark, I had turned the canvas face down and left the studio without a word.

And now he snatched the vase and the pomegranates I was using for my still life. Squeezing one of the pomegranates, he managed to split it in two, then handed half to me and bit into the kernels of the other half.

"Sour, isn't it? See, that's the essence of pomegranates—they're sour."

"I'm afraid I don't understand."

"What you don't understand, my dear, is the Zen dialectic." Hansu's mouth puckered up and he tapped his lips with his fingers as if to soothe them. "Go, gentle lady, and look after your kid. You're just faking it with those pictures."

I was about to leave anyway, and yes, I really was deluding myself thinking I could paint magnolias. Vases and fruit I could paint day and night, true to life, one cute replica after another, but never would I be able to paint magnolias in bloom, those magnolias that reminded me of a two-headed viper coiled to strike.

I laid my unfinished still life face down on the table and put on my coat. Now what? Should I put up with more of Hansu's venomous remarks, or simply nod and leave, hoping he wouldn't continue to block the door?

"Sorry if I bothered you," he said, placing a hand on my shoulder.

I felt like an overwound spring that had snapped. Would he try me to hug me? I felt dizzy. Then I was hit by the reek of liquor. "Goodness!" Before I knew it I had pushed past him out to the hall. His head followed me out from the studio. He was staring at me as if to say, *What the hell's gotten into you?* But all he said was, "So long."

I tried to collect myself. "Lucky I didn't fall on my face," I mumbled before setting off slowly down the concrete hall. The stairway at the end of this rundown building was steep and unlit, and I practically had to tiptoe down.

Go look after your kid. That's what my husband used to tell me. I remember feeling the color drain from my face, but in time I developed a thick skin and stood up to him, free of my heart-pounding anger and humiliation. "If she needed looking after, I wouldn't be here now, would I?" I'd once told him. Sad to say, there was nobody I could make snappy answers to anymore. My circle of friends had long since realized it was a mistake to mention my husband or daughter in front of me. They were all so very careful—not for my sake, but to deprive me of any opportunity to respond with something embarrassing about them.

Sŏni was old enough to be in kindergarten by now. "Butterfly, butterfly, up to the green hills we go"—she'd been able to mimic me singing that song. Before long she'd be singing a kindergarten song instead: "Butterfly, butterfly, come flutter, come fly to me."

I had learned the first of those songs from Mother:

Butterfly, butterfly, up to the green hills we go,
Swallowtail, swallowtail, you come too.
Autumn leaves, colored autumn leaves,
Bitten by the frost, falling, falling. . . .

To little me, when I asked abou those green hills, Mother would casually reply as she lighted one of her hand-rolled cigarettes, "That's where people go when they die."

The snowflakes were larger now. I reached into my pocket for my scarf and realized I'd left it at the studio. I turned up the collar of my coat instead.

Go look after your kid. I sighed. Did Hansu know my husband and I were separated, that I'd left Sŏni with my in-laws? Either way, he probably hadn't meant anything by it. It was just the way he talked. He didn't see anything special about human history—to him it was like a river, it just kept flowing. He acted like he was above it all.

We'd gone out drinking a couple of times and the result was the same—I got stinko. The first time was a blank—I don't remember how late we stayed out or where we said good-bye. My only recollection of the second time is that I made a fool of myself bawling on his shoulder. It wasn't easy looking at myself in the mirror afterward.

My husband and I never really tried to mend our relationship. After we separated, I got so depressed I slept most of the time, and when I drank I'd sing the butterfly song, call Sŏni's name, and start crying. I was aware of how I carried on and it disturbed me, but I was helpless to change my ways. I used to drink with a certain crowd, and one of the men once reminded me of my mawkish behavior. I could have strangled him. There were fingernail marks in my palms where I'd clenched my fists.

Hansu probably knew about these proclivities too. Did he also know about the butterfly song coiled deep inside me that emerged every night the magnolias bloomed in my dreams? Maybe that was why he'd teased me—*No more magnolias? Then how about a mandala?*

"How far do you plan on going? At that pace you could probably go forever."

I turned just in time to see Hansu come up beside me. He was breathing heavily.

"I was watching the way you walked. You were going so slow I couldn't help catching up with you," he said triumphantly. Catching up with me seemed to have made him more agreeable than he'd been back at the studio. But what he really seemed to be saying was something like, *You figured if you took your sweet time I'd look down from the studio and notice you.* I wished I could have given him a decent answer.

"Look at all this wonderful snow—don't tell me you're going straight home."

I snorted. Hansu swaggered off and I followed, my gaze fixed on his heels. I had to pull my collar up over my head to keep the snow from melting and streaming down my face.

If his flushed face and smart mouth were any indication, Hansu wouldn't be satisfied with the standard one cup of coffee. He kept peeking into drinking places, though it was too early to be drinking—for me, anyway. *Not today,* I said to myself, punctuating the decision by shaking my head—already I was building things out of proportion.... *Darling, I've known for some time that you've been living with your parents. I'm sorry, but I haven't had the courage to write until now. Yesterday I started counting the days—I'll be leaving on the 28th....* I uncovered my face and and tried to wipe it dry with my hand. In front of me Hansu kept digging out his handker-

chief and mopping the back of his neck. I assumed the handkerchief was so grimy you couldn't tell the color—an observation I
probably wouldn't have made if I'd never had to look after a man.
Socks with holes, soiled collars, dirty handkerchiefs—useless
worries, but things I noticed, it never failed. . . . *Let's you, Sŏni, and
I get a place with a big yard outside the city. I've saved up for it. I wish
I knew why so many of us get wrapped up in such trivial matters—
we're wasting our lives. . . . Darling, I love you. We can start all over
again. We'll be happier than we ever were before. My life here is terrible. Some nights I can't sleep because of the rain and the mosquitoes,
and I get so angry—I can't believe what an idiot I was. I want to come
home. . . .*

I made a more forceful attempt to dry my face. So, my husband
wanted to come home from distant Africa, the Dark Continent.
We can start all over again. But there's no such thing as a new beginning. I had told him as much when I left him three years ago:
It's wishful thinking. He didn't try to stop me. And when I finally
convinced him I was leaving for good, he said I was poison.

Like other women with cheating husbands, I felt like invad-
ing his mistress's place, throwing the chamberpot at her mirror,
ripping her quilts to shreds, yanking her by the hair. Instead,
I waited for him in the dark at the alley to our house. When it
rained I'd stand there until dawn with an umbrella, twirling it
like a pinwheel. It was then, in the early hours of the morning,
that I saw the idealized image of my mother, freshly washed face
and all.

Mother had lived alone in a secluded house in an island village. I never really thought about it because I never really knew
her—couldn't remember ever living with her. It was Father, Stepmother, and my stepbrothers and stepsisters that I lived with.
None of them tried to hide the facts—that Mother had developed childbed fever after giving birth to me, that the toxin had
settled in her legs and made her virtually lame, that finally she'd
been possessed.

Whenever a shaman ritual took place, you could see Mother in her sky blue jacket, crimson skirt, long indigo vest, and black shaman's hat, her fan and bells in hand. She was a tall, raw-boned woman, which paradoxically made her look all the more nimble as she balanced herself and performed her jumps on the blue steel of the two straw-cutter blades, with nary a nick on her feet to show for it. But by the time she finished the ceremony she could barely stand, and she had to squat like a crab as she took leave of the gathering.

She wasn't pretty to look at. Her square face with its high, protruding cheekbones always had a bluish cast, and her lips were even darker. I think this blueness resulted from smoking. When she balanced herself on the blades of the straw cutter, drops of sweat raining down her face, her features contorted as if pain were being wrung out of her, she looked like pictures I'd seen of the Spirit General. I couldn't bring myself to believe that this was the woman who had given birth to me, and because of that, nothing about Mother affected me.

I was fond of the rice cakes, chestnuts, dates, and other goodies she always gave me, and I would visit her at all hours. Father and Stepmother didn't try to stop me. If I got back after dark and rattled the locked door, Stepmother would take her time opening it and tell me in a voice barren of emotion that she thought I'd decided to live with the spirit madam and never come home again. I could hear Father roll over in bed and groan. Embarrassed by the silence, I held my breath and hugged the wall as I skirted my stepbrothers and stepsisters, arranged in their sleep like cordwood. No matter how bothersome it must have been for Stepmother to save me a place to sleep or unlock the door for me, it never occurred to me to spend the night at Mother's house, which I believed to be occupied by the spirits of the dead, judging from the portrait of the Spirit General, the shaman knives and spears, and the candles burning day and night that seemed to make the gaudy paper flowers bloom so brightly. And I remembered being told that Mother served a spirit in her home at night, which was why she had arranged another woman for Father and had left him.

Mother always asked about Father when she was feeding me. I was so busy eating I couldn't immediately answer, and so with a sigh Mother would reach for the matchbox, light a cigarette with a grand motion, and sing, her shoulders moving in time with the song:

Butterfly, butterfly, up to the green hills we go.
Swallowtail, swallowtail, you come too.
Autumn leaves, colored autumn leaves,
Bitten by the frost, falling, falling.
Our lives as fleeting as the dew on the grass,
With nothing we come, with nothing we go.

This was the image of my mother that came to mind while I waited for my husband until the wee hours. Eventually I'd find myself singing that song Mother had sung to vent her passion, her sorrow, her spite. And when the clean, cold air of dawn began to feel suffocating, I'd hurry home through the winding alley.

"This place might do," said Hansu, looking to me for approval of the bar with the canvas-draped entrance that he'd just poked his head inside.

"Looks okay to me." And after a moment's hesitation, I followed him in. It was early in the evening and we had the place almost to ourselves.

"What would you like?"

"Do I have a choice?"

Hansu whistled for service and a woman soon appeared with a small bottle of *soju* and two shot glasses upside down on a tray. Hansu uncapped the bottle with his teeth and poured me a drink. I wanted him to give me the bottle so I could return the favor, but he shook his head with a serious expression and proceeded to fill his own glass and gulp the drink thirstily. I looked down at my drink, happy to gaze at the transparent liquor, which seemed to reflect nothingness. I picked up the shot glass and holding it tightly, swirled the liquid gently. It came perilously close to the rim, but didn't spill.

There were times when I had slipped out of bed at dawn on my husband's birthday and gone out to the soulless, freshly cleaned street to buy flowers for him. When Sŏni was a hundred days old we took her to a photographer's studio and sat her between us, a mural of a distant church and a steeple providing the background. The man photographed her while shaking a rattle and babbling to her. And one day we went to the opera. My husband had burst into tears at Madame Butterfly's song, "I'd rather die than live in disgrace. . . ." I had reached for his hand, repeating the sentence silently.

"You're not drinking. What's on your mind?"

"I was wondering if there's anything as clear as *soju*."

Hansu gave a hearty laugh. I noticed that his hand holding the glass was quivering. A touch of palsy, was the first thought that came to mind.

"Once upon a time I devoted a great deal of thought to a very important question—what could possibly be as clear as darkness, as clear as the night?" he said. "Have you ever listened to the sounds of the night?"

You want to talk about the night? I silently asked him. Well, I knew something about that. Nights, memories of nights, memories we all kept hidden deep in our hearts. I tossed down my *soju*.

Deep in the night, Father had left Mother's island village with my stepmother, their children, and me in a rowboat that he worked with a single oar. Frightened and seasick, I listened until dawn to Mother singing the butterfly song. Accompanied by bamboo flutes, single-string fiddle, and drum, it came to me like a dream. It sounded as if the sea were crying out to me. That song has awakened me at night ever since, dream or no dream, forewarning me, terrifying me, threatening to occupy every nook of my existence, muffling my passion for living and tainting life's purity.

"The night? Yes, I know enough about sounds of the night," I said proudly while hoisting my second shot of *soju* to my lips.

"You mean those magnolias you're always dreaming about?"

"Did I tell you that? Well, I could tell you another story too."

"We all have a story about our own night, don't we? Me included," said Hansu. "A story that symbolizes the night for us— does that make sense? My story's about a man who played the bamboo flute."

Hansu's eyes were still bloodshot from whatever he'd been drinking that afternoon. I listened carefully, feeling the liquor burn in my chest and churn in my stomach like a miracle drug I shouldn't have taken, the strong, hot tipsiness kindling every part of me.

This was the story Hansu told:

One day a man came drifting into a mountain village. All the villagers had the same surname; the stranger's name was different. Nothing was known about him. He didn't seem to have a regular calling and his wife never appeared from their dwelling—all of which helped to convince the intolerant, parochial people of this village, which the mountains surrounded so closely that the wind could scarcely penetrate, that he possessed some extraordinary talent. Occasionally he earned a few coppers repairing chimneys, rebuilding collapsed mud walls, or thatching roofs after the harvest. But he performed this labor the way others cultivated hobbies, leading the villagers to believe that he didn't have to work in order to eat.

To these villagers he became known as a master of the bamboo flute. And yet no one had seen him play that instrument; no one had heard the sound of it riding on the wind to his ears. But no one doubted he was a master, or that the sounds he produced on his flute were more abstruse and delicate than the sighing of the wind from high up in the mountains or the whisper of the springtime freshet that deigned to visited the village only after dawdling away the long hard winter.

A rumor began circulating that the flute master communicated with a ghost. How long he had been doing this, no one knew. A supernatural power supposedly infused him on moonless nights, and then again on nights when the moon waxed round and full. This belief may have arisen from his calm demeanor, which suggested to the villagers that he had long ago divested himself of mundane affairs. He really did give the impression that he saw the world and even his own life from a distance, as if he were watching a house on fire from a safe vantage point.

His wife was young and pretty, and it was known throughout the village that the relationship between this man who was entering middle age and his delicate, youthful wife who rarely ventured out was unusually harmonious. But nothing more was known about them. The master and his wife lived like hermits, maintaining their distance from the tenacious stares of the villagers, who made it their business to know details such as the exact number of spoons possessed by so-and-so, whose lives were as tedious and unchanging as stagnant water.

The man was neither too close to nor too distant with anyone. He lived in the village, but he didn't really belong there.

When people inquired about his pretty wife or his flute, he answered with a mere chuckle. Never would he play the flute, whatever the occasion. Those who politely made a second request ended up chuckling along with him. His attitude led even the doubters to conclude for a certainty that he was a master of the flute, for no master could play when the spirit didn't move him, just as a cloudless sky couldn't bring rain.

On moonless nights and on nights when the full moon shone and he didn't need a lantern, he liked to drink by himself at the village tavern till the wee hours.

It was around the time of the winter solstice, and a group of young fellows displaced by the elders from their cozy den at home were gambling for tobacco in the tavern's inner room. Already the game had grown stale.

At this time of year it could be unbearably lonely late at night. So when sporadic barking in the distance caught the attention of the young gamblers, they began to murmur about whose dog it was and whether a stranger might have arrived, their curiosity overcoming any lingering enthusiasm for card playing. And when the solitude of the world outside the tavern touched them and coursed through their bodies, they suddenly sensed the solitude of their own lives, along with memories of the dead returning from oblivion. Such moments were sure to be followed by another round of drinks, and if a glib fellow came up with a dirty joke, the rest would pound dutifully on their knees in laughter, trying to fill the emptiness they had momentarily confronted.

On this particular night you could hear wild animals howling in the distance, and outside it was so bone-chillingly cold that the mere sound of the wind raking the mountain valleys could drain the warmth from you. One of the young men happened to point out the flute master, who was about to leave the tavern. It didn't escape the young man and his friends that the master had a curiously listless look as he unobtrusively paid his bill and walked out.

Because the master had no children, the villagers liked to say that he treated his wife's body with undue respect, that an overly harmonious marriage would anger the three gods who governed childbirth. What was it, they wondered, that made for such a good marriage between the tottering, scruffy-looking master, that husk of a man, and his wife with eyes so long and lids so thin?

The gambling resumed—it rose to one last fever pitch but quickly died down. No longer was the tavernkeeper busy serving kettles of brew. The midnight hour of this long moonless night had passed, and the young men knew that on such a night the master would communicate with a ghost. The dealer cut the deck of flower cards and declared that the first to draw a plum blossom must learn the secret of the master's mystical talent that very night.

The fellow whose lot it was to follow the master saw him walking like a phantom, swinging his arms in the dark. Where the village came to an end, the master encountered a barking dog. With a sudden sweep of his arm he drove it back, the supple movement of a dancing phantom. The follower's eyes glittered in the darkness and a lump rose in his throat. The dog disappeared and the master continued on his way, swinging his arms and dancing.

The master's house lay apart from the dwellings that fanned out like a skirt at the foot of the nearest mountain. Passing houses lying still as death, the master arrived at the low mud wall of his home. Out from his vest pocket came his flute, and with a deep breath he started to play. Strange were the sounds he produced—like the staccato hissing of snakes slithering through the grass of early summer, looking for mates.

Instead of passing through the brushwood gate, the master walked around the wall of the house, playing all the while. When he had completed a couple of circuits the door opened, its cavity looming large in the light of a lamp whose flickering reached out to the stone step. A shadow emerged from the doorway, only to disappear into a darkness deeper than the gloom surrounding the dwelling. The door closed and the light was extinguished. Pocketing his flute, the master opened the gate.

And that was all the young observer from the tavern could see, for the moonless night would admit no shadow and reveal no footprint.

"It sounds like the Ch'ŏyong story."

"Doesn't it?" Hansu responded with a weak laugh. He was looking toward me but seemed to be gazing far off—listening perhaps for the sound of a flute? It was absolutely dark beyond the canvas. Tears gathered in my eyes; I wondered if it was the liquor. Warmth and weariness spread through me. *If only I could lay my head down on the table and fall into a dreamless sleep.* And that's when the hem of Mother's shaman vest slid into view before my watery eyes. Would I dream about magnolias like I had other nights I'd gone to bed drunk?

Mother was consumed in a blaze. The image that remains with me is a tree radiating flames. She had crawled out of her room onto the veranda. I had stood petrified at the brushwood gate, only a few steps away. The fire had crawled along the main crossbeam, engulfed the thick rafters, and spread unobstructed through the house.

Mother managed to cross the veranda, but just as I thought she was about to roll down onto the stone shoe ledge, she suddenly stood up. I couldn't believe how tall she looked. By then the fire had reached the sleeves of her jacket, the flames fluttering like a curtain in a breeze. Mother was a tree on fire. For a moment it seemed she would give in and rush off to extinguish the flames, but instead she began sweeping her long arms in the air and leaping up and down, dancing in a shaman ritual, a large flaming tree. Hiding among the flustered onlookers who dared not go to her rescue, I watched until the end, thinking Mother wasn't dying but instead was calling forth all the spirits to perform a grand, once-in-a-lifetime ceremony.

My soul, oh my soul,
Green willows, deep mountains, your first visit there,
Place my soul in its vessel, my god-given body in a casket.
Up above I see valley after mountain valley, peak after peak;
Down below, a white, sandy wasteland.
Here, I'm here. Borrowing the body of this spirit madam,
    I speak through her mouth; unfulfilled in my life, I am
    bound for the hereafter.

I realized then that Mother was singing the song from the *chinogwi* ritual—the ceremony for the restless dead that she used to perform. And then she collapsed. But like a green pine bough, she kept burning for the longest time, the flames feeding on the oil from her body. And then, like a great hanging serpent, the main crossbeam fell onto her.

Mother's body was left covered with grass on a hill behind the village. The villagers believed that only after the grass died, her flesh rotted, and her bones turned white would her spirit travel to the hereafter. All summer and autumn her body swarmed with blowflies, was violated by every bird and beast imaginable. The snows of winter enveloped her bones, but still they didn't turn white. The following spring the thick covering of grass dried up and scattered, but even then her bones with their bits of charred flesh were black.

It was at night that her bones shone white and flowered, flaring open with bluish-white sparks. A white flower bloomed from every joint, and finally the flowers merged into one huge blossom. But the next morning the bones looked even darker and more decomposed, like a tree that had bloomed for myriad years and was now mere bark hanging from a rotten stump.

How imposing Mother had looked, how tall she had stood—a woman who normally moved only in a squatting position. Nor could I forget the spectacle of her collapsing like a flaming tree. And it had always bothered me that her bones never turned white.

Her death was the cause of endless whispering among the villagers. Some said she had caught fire because she violated cleanliness taboos during a period of purification, and her bones hadn't turned white because no one had performed a *chinogwi* ritual to pave her way to the hereafter. On nights of rain and nights of thick fog you could supposedly hear the spirit madam's sad song of grief over her untimely death. On those nights I got used to seeing the faces of my father and stepmother turn pale in the light of the kerosene lamp.

We had left Mother—left in a rowboat one foggy night. As an adult I continued to dream of Mother, to see magnolias blossom from her bones. I sublimated my deep-seated hatred for my husband in a burning desire to paint the magnolias that I saw in my dreams whenever he didn't come home.

As soon as we finished our second bottle of *soju*, Hansu summoned the woman, this time clapping his hands, and she brought us another. His hand trembled as he poured himself a drink. I took the bottle from him and filled my own glass carefully so nothing would spill. It seemed to be snowing harder. Newcomers coated with snow stamped their feet as they came inside.

As Hansu was about to order bottle number four, I took him by the arm and led him outside. He began to lurch along as if he'd forgotten how to walk, whereas I was feeling clear-headed. I put my arm around him for support, and we walked down an alley lined with drinking houses. We'd just emerged onto the street when Hansu wrenched himself free, squatted, and began vomiting. *Good heavens.* I could feel myself scowl. I began patting his back.

"It's okay—don't bother."

He tried to push me away while he retched, and I continued to pat him on the back. I could feel his ribs beneath the single layer of his jacket. The gentle tattoo of my hand produced muffled thumps. I stopped for a moment and rested my palm against his back—how warm it felt. *During these awful nights of rain and mosquitoes, I think only of returning to you. I love you. We can start all over again. . . .*

"I'd rather die than live in disgrace"—we'd cried listening to that song.

Instinctively I shook my head. The snowflakes on my face couldn't cool the fever I felt.

"We can go now," said Hansu.

With a hand in each armpit, I helped him up. His stomach must have felt better, because he wasn't trying to resist me anymore, and I left my hands where they were.

"I'll walk you to the bus stop. Which way are you going?"

He didn't answer. The traffic was flying by as people raced home ahead of the curfew. The slush covering the asphalt glittered in the glare of the streetlights, and still it snowed. The two of us stood there on the sidewalk until finally I asked again where he was going. Barely opening his mouth, he grumbled, "You know better than I do." My head snapped up. He was looking at me without a trace of a smile. I let go of him and covered my face, feeling the same torrents of darkness rush over me as I had the night we abandoned Mother. Deeper inside I heard white magnolias exploding, saw blossoms that would ultimately submerge me in a darkness even more profound. *So this is what I've been living on,* I'd realized when I woke in the early morning from the chaotic field of dreams induced by my husband's nightlong absence. *I've been living on blind sensation, like an insect through its feelers.* And I'd shuddered from the chill as I dipped my hands in the washbasin. Every time this lucid realization pierced me, a tiny chisel poised at the joints of my skull, every time I felt a nagging urge to make a mess of myself—a torrid, overwhelming desire for all manner of degradation, a burning desire to sin—I sensed within me, gently reminding me of their presence, the magnolias that had blossomed from Mother's bones.

"All right." I linked arms with Hansu and it felt very comfortable.

All about us the snow swept pell-mell into sight, a gray cloud, a vague fathomless blur, except when stray flakes were caught like fluttering butterflies in the headlights of passing cars.

We looked at each other as perfect strangers might, not trying to hide our hostility toward the signs of weakness we each saw, then set off on our lonely journey down the street like wayfarers seeking the witch of legend who left in her trail an endless scattering of white rice flour.

Butterfly, butterfly, up in the hills we go.
Where, you say? Here, right here.

Across the sea of darkness we rushed. And all that night the butterfly song was a constant refrain, tying me in knots of tension.

My soul, oh my soul,
Green willows, deep mountains, your first visit there,
Place my soul in its vessel. . . .

It would take an infinity of such nights—nights of hopelessness, ecstasy, and despair yielding finally to deep sleep—to root out the magnolias that bloomed inside me. Blossoming on the nights I'd waited for my husband, blooming everywhere he'd left his brand on me, those magnolias had turned into thousands, tens of thousands of scattered mandalas, and I would never, ever be able to paint them.

RIVER OF FIRE

To someone else he might have looked like a little boy, or maybe an old hunchback, the way he sat on the sill of the open window with his knees drawn up and his back bent way over. But to me he was a drop of mercury compressed by surface tension, and I felt a shiver thinking the weight of that drop might pull it over the edge. Fortunately the window was protected by a grate, so I could observe him dispassionately, adjusting the focus of my camera-like gaze.

This tension ran in his blood, so that his constant habit of curling up as if to minimize the aspect he presented to others made him seem to be living ever so cautious a life. And I always felt as if he had a little smile stored away inside his mouth, something he could produce whenever he had to tell someone he was sorry, so terribly sorry.

The grate sectioned the mackerel sky into precise hexagons in which the clouds spreading placidly across it were tinged with the red of sunset. When a bright moon shone through the grate, I sometimes awakened in the grip of an infantile terror, feeling I was being watched by the compound eye of a dragonfly or fruit fly.

Hunched up on the windowsill, he began whistling. But the sound was muffled by the wind and I couldn't make out the tune.

Feeling a chill on my back, I took his jacket from the wall and put it around my shoulders, then sat back down and picked up my embroidery hoop. Soon my hands were turning red; I imagined them shriveling from the cold. I almost asked him to close the window, but thought better of it and instead sat on my hands to warm them. Then I took up my needle and looked at the pattern—a crane standing on one leg, its wings spreading above a pine bough. I just couldn't get the position of that leg to look natural. I'd probably have to pull out the thread and start all over again.

He looked up under the eaves, frowning.

"What is it?" I asked, wondering if he'd found a hole in the rusty gutter.

With a serious expression, he craned his neck and moved his head this way and that, inspecting whatever it was he had noticed.

"Did you find something?" This time I tried to sound nonchalant.

"No, nothing." But then, a short time later, "There's a spider web."

"Really?" I was praying that tonight, for once, he'd stay home. I turned back to my embroidery.

"The spider's carrying all its young on its back."

As I'd expected, he sounded irritated at my casual response.

"It's probably their nature," I said.

"Not a pretty sight," he said with a look of disgust.

"Well, like I said, that's the way they are."

Finally I got up and went to him, leaving the needle stuck in the cloth. I'd finished half of the right wing. From the window it looked as if the other half had broken off.

"How come it's making a web way up here on top of the building?" he mumbled to himself.

The edge of the roof was directly above the window. A water tank had been installed up there and it was always leaking, though nobody seemed to know where from. There were moisture stains on the side of the building, but the spider web was positioned so as to avoid the leaks. There in the web was a charcoal-colored spider the size of your thumbnail crawling laboriously yet acrobatically, its young on its back. I'd heard older people say that young spiders will nibble away at their mother's back until only a husk is left, something you can blow away with one big puff—so a person should kill the unfilial creatures whenever he sees them. Whether the spider sensed our tenacious gaze or the rare sensation of human breath, at intervals it came to a stop and curled up its legs as if playing dead. He whistled once, a piercing sound; it seemed so nasty to me. The web rocked and the spider, its stratagem discovered, began scuttling precariously. The abrupt motion sent some of the young from the mother's back into the web and others to the ground six floors below. But the loss of her young didn't concern the mother, who never paused.

I looked into his small, childlike face with all its wrinkles. He had stayed out again the previous night, returning around dawn, his face haggard and looking utterly aged. He had work that needed finishing by morning, he had said.

Deep beneath his languid expression was a gloomy tension—a sign that he would leave again tonight. I no longer felt that I could stop him.

His nighttime sojourns were much more frequent, almost a routine. He would return at dawn, wait until the sun went down, then fish for an excuse to sneak out, either cracking his knuckles or passing his hand through his hair and saying how long it had grown—"Looks awful, doesn't it?"—or mentioning that he felt sticky all over and ought to visit the public baths. I could only put on a sad face. His doubtful manner made me reluctant to complain or question him—why was he leaving, where was he going, who was he seeing? And that, combined with the glimpses I'd caught of his unyielding side, prevented me from pestering him to take me along. Weak-spirited, perhaps he would have stayed home had I forced the issue. But I wasn't confident enough to try to assuage his anxiety and fretfulness when he was cooped up (and he couldn't have felt other than cooped up here). I didn't know of any games we could play that would serve that purpose. I could fill my tambour with embroidery and I could fill the bobbin on my sewing machine, but I couldn't fill our time together by myself. Time isn't something you consume like a cup of tea. It would be a whole lot easier learning to write poetry, I grumbled to myself.

He lost interest in the spider, and before long his gaze was playing along the Han River below.

Beyond his curled-up back was a bare stretch of riverbed, the wind kicking up sand, and the sun-bleached riverbank where we used to go strolling after we got married. At a broad, U-shaped bend in the river stood the power plant. Its dreary-looking smokestack began to sparkle in the setting sun as if it had sprouted fish scales, then took on a fiery glow. The top of the smokestack seemed almost within reach of our window. But whether it was because of my astigmatism, which was especially bad when I had to look into the sun, or because the power plant was diagonal to our apartment, I could never figure out the shape of that gloomy gray structure. I knew only that its three stories had once housed a small steam-powered plant that for some reason had closed down not long after it was built. And then, when the river trade still thrived, it was used to unload seafood shipped upstream from the West Sea. And for a long time afterward ice was made there, but then the ice-making industry slumped, and once again the building was vacant, used only occasionally as a setting for a gangster movie.

On the far side of the river was Yŏŭi Island, which invariably flooded during the rainy season, only the crowns of its tall poplars left to wave in the breeze like river grass. The summer-long dynamiting had removed every trace of the island's volcanic origins and the alluvial deposits left by the floods. Army trucks bringing soldiers on work detail came and went along the shattered rock and the sandy soil, throwing up dust and avoiding the bulldozers that were busy leveling the island in preparation for the runway deemed necessary by the military strategists. The village on the island had disappeared, the ferry docks had closed down.

Ever since we'd moved into our top-floor apartment, the vista below had been undergoing changes, some drastic and others so gradual we hadn't noticed them at first. Rumor had it that the power plant too, which had stood for almost half a century, would soon be demolished. I'll never forget the first time I saw it, a gray concrete building that gave me such a vivid impression of inscrutable hostility, its only distinguishing characteristic the low-voltage high-tension lines that ran above the lofty smokestack and the roof.

We'd had no hobbies or favorite entertainments back then, and when he wasn't working nights we liked to take an evening stroll along the riverbank. On one of those strolls he pointed out the power plant and related the following story in an unassuming yet proud manner, the way a student might explain his ancestral home's prize attraction to an outsider:

"This is where we lived after the war, here on the riverbank, in a tent. We were the lucky ones—most of the homeless people who landed here had nothing but a straw mat. First thing in the morning, we'd go piss in the river. We were always hungry, but what could we do? Well, one thing we did was go swimming in the river, and we stayed in as long as possible. We liked to swim over to the island and grub around in the peanut fields—even though the peanuts were only half ripe. By the time we reached the island we were pretty wrung out. We'd flop down on one of the sandbars and gawk at the power station on the other side. That power plant looked awesome, but I think it was because we were so weak from hunger. You'd think someone would have occupied that big old building, but everyone kept to their huts—I don't know that anyone ever considered living in it. There was a massacre there during the war. People were herded inside and slaughtered like animals. I remember people telling me you could see bloodstains and bits of flesh stuck to the walls. I heard other stories too. The bloody fetuses we used to find in the river came from there, and the place was haunted at night by the ghosts of people who got electrocuted when the plant was operating, and unwed mothers went there to deliver their babies in secret and then killed them, and then they went crazy and came back looking for them. You hear rumors like that and your imagination tends to run wild. Well, it wasn't long before we were telling each other that mysterious beings lived there, and we started spinning ghost stories. The door to the plant was always locked. We liked to think of it as a haunted castle with lots of rooms and mazes, a place you could get into but not out of. And it just seemed to get bigger and bigger. Sometimes a bunch of kids would tear the planks off one of the windows and sneak inside. Later they'd brag about the rooms and the mazes and the wind whistling through the power lines— they made it sound like an adventure in a bat cave. But I was too chicken to go inside, so it just kept getting bigger in my imagination. It was always there in my mind, a symbol of everything that was hostile. Of course I realized when I was older that a building has to have a way out as well as a way in, but we moved away before I had a chance to look in.

His words buzzed inside my ears as I watched the dark pro-
jection of the smokestack lose its sparkle in the waning twilight.
And then I felt it come alive with a sinister hostility that left me
in despair.

"Didn't I hear they're going to tear it down?" I asked, looking
toward the power plant, where his eyes had come to rest.

"Mmm, that's what they say."

"It's about time. I can't believe they let a building sit useless for
the last fifty years. But it's so solid, how are they going to bring it
down? The shelling during the war didn't seem to faze it."

"So I've heard."

"They'll probably have to dynamite it. More noise to put
up with."

I thought about the explosions, the heavy booms that we'd
heard night and day, all summer long, from across the river. The
sudden earthshaking rumble, the lingering roar as if from a bomb
going off in the distance, always prompted me to shut the window. But in spite of my instinctive fear, I knew the explosions
weren't capable of leaving even a gossamer crack in our walls.

I heard a glass break in one of the other units. The shattering
sound sent a refreshing chill through the air, cutting through the
tension that bound us like tightly woven fabric. The next thing I
knew, I was hearing all sorts of sounds floating up from ground
level, as if the gap in our tension had given them passage.

He got down from the windowsill, found the socks he had left
on the unheated part of the floor, and reclaimed his jacket from me.

"You're going out?"

Though I kept my eyes on the bare expanse of riverbed, I could
imagine his every movement.

"I've got some work to finish. But I'll be back before morning.
You can go ahead with dinner and you don't need to wait up." The
usual answer, but still it flustered him because he wasn't a skillful
liar. I could hear him changing his pants.

"What about *your* dinner?" I asked, still looking outside.

He mumbled something I didn't catch, probably telling me not to worry.

Out he went, and when I could no longer hear his hasty foot-steps on the stairs I rushed to the kitchen, retrieved the half-smoked cigarette I'd hidden behind the dishes in the cupboard that morning, and lit up. Back in the living room, I watched his small figure walk down the slope leading from our building. The gently angled roof of the dye factory next to the power plant caught my eye, followed by the fabrics awash with color hanging like curtains in the factory yard.

And there, the black cat, creeping along the tar surface of that roof, which looked almost flat from here. Early on foggy morn-ings, or in the scattered shafts of afternoon sunlight, the cat never quite seemed real to me as it moved shadowlike over the roof. And yet the sight of it always drew a sigh from me as I felt the familiar frustration, the tightness in my chest, return like a forgot-ten scene, my frustration with the monotony of the time he and I were consuming—the way we ourselves crept about, the flow-ers in the vase withering to a deep purple, the inertia of our life together, our breath tinged with stale conversation. Morning and evening, the smell of his workplace, clinging to him like the bits of thread on his clothes, was sucked into the air in our eleven-*p'yŏng* apartment with an osmotic power that was frightening.

Until a few years ago, or, more specifically, for some time after the death of our baby, I used to call him at the factory at dinner-time. The whir of the sewing machines sounded like static in the receiver. I could hear someone calling him, and then his cautious voice came on the line. He always answered with a soft exclama-tion, as if he were surprised at getting a call.

"It's going to be another long night—we're getting behind. . . . And everything has to go through me."

Whenever he paused for breath, the noise from the sewing machines sneaked back into our conversation, the whir sounding like the grinding of teeth as it traveled the line toward me.

"I guess it's not much fun being home alone—why don't you go out and catch a movie or something?"

I pictured him at his machine as he whispered to me, his wristlet-covered arms turning the handwheel, his feet in constant motion as they trod the pedals, his clothing adorned with threads.

"Be sure to lock up before you go to bed. Yeah, I know, a burglar would have pretty slim pickings at our place. He'd probably give us a donation instead."

I could hear him stifle a chuckle.

"No need to worry. Okay, so long."

I sighed as I hung up, and the sigh turned into a shudder as I thought once again of the factory and of his bloodshot eyes as he sat at his sewing machine, turning the handwheel. The mood that trailed him home from work, the endless rhythm of the whirring machines—was this the only impetus that kept our lives in motion?

"Sometimes when I've been working the pedals for a while," he liked to say, "I nod off and dream I'm on a bicycle trip. I don't stop unless I want to find out where I am, and then I wake up and I'm back in the cutting room."

I could never respond to his smile with one of my own. I just wished his jokes would improve.

"What do you do there anyway?" I once asked.

"Lay out measurements on the fabric, cut it, stitch it, hem it, and add the interfacing—all day long."

"The same thing every day?"

"Sure—the same thing. Pants, jackets, vests—every day."

Even though he took an artisan's pride in his work, I was surprised at the loathing I detected in his voice.

"All I ever hear is the machine, whether I'm home or on the bus. I feel like the pedals are attached to my ears. Sometimes I think I'm going crazy. Your breathing at night—that gets me thinking of the machine too. It really bothers me—I don't want to be stuck in a cage like a squirrel turning a wheel for the rest of my life."

"That's life."

Cheerless words for sure, something a crotchety old woman would say. Though I'd never seen his workplace, I could imagine what it was like. But I refused to sympathize with him. In his absence I was left with the hum of the sewing machines, which I imagined with more certainty when he was gone—along with his stained clothing, the withered flowers, the wasted moments buried in the old wallpaper, and my hatred of the power plant that loomed so close anytime I opened the window. But I felt no immediate desire to change the flow of our life. A dying goldfish might end its life with its snout to the surface of the fishbowl, pursing its mouth in a futile attempt to take in more oxygen. Not me.

The sun had vanished. The darkening surface of the river was calmer, the outline of the power plant more distinct.

Finally, time to go out. I applied fresh lipstick in front of the mirror, added a couple of extra coatings for good measure, then drew my scarf snug about my neck and put on my coat and raised the collar. I locked the window and put the embroidery hoop in my sewing basket. Outside, just before locking the door, I remembered something and went back in to scribble a message: "I'm going out for a little while—I'll leave the key with the custodian." I folded the note four times, stuck it in the crack of the doorway, and rushed down the stairs. Nowhere in particular I wanted to go, but as soon as I'd stepped out the door I'd felt an irresistible sense of urgency.

The breeze from the river cut a stinging swath across my ears. I pulled my coat collar close.

From where it sat on a prominence on this side of the dark river, the power plant looked more like a fortress, huge and sturdy, than in daytime. Its skeletal interior was visible where light leaked out around the boards nailed in an X over the windows, and through the occasional window where the boards had fallen off. I saw men running up and down the steep spiral staircase and a group of people in outline. It looked like they were filming again. I recalled scenes I had watched beneath the red lights: corpses with throats slit being tossed into the river; the playing out of a deadly love affair; the lynching of a traitor.

I took a cigarette from my coat pocket and tried to light it, but the breeze blew out the match. I tried again, this time cupping my hands around the match, and watched it flare up, coloring my palms red.

Not so long ago we had been here at the riverside. Lying prone at the foot of the bank, he rubbed dry grass between his palms, then asked me out of the blue, "Ever wonder how people used to make fire?"

"Didn't they save the coals from fires caused by lightning? That's what I learned in school."

"But to *start* a fire, you had to rub two sticks together like this until they began to burn. It took tens of thousands of years for people to make matches out of sticks."

He handed me the grass he'd been rubbing. It was warm. *I don't like this,* I remembered thinking. There must have been a change going on inside him, or at least a growing desire to be different, to escape the orbit of his life, the whir of the sewing machine. In any event, his sudden interest in fire bothered me even more than the fact that he secretly wrote poetry. But I didn't start wondering until the day I found matches in his pocket—and he didn't smoke. Almost every day after that I found a box of matches in his pocket.

As we were lying there, he lit a match and set the grass on fire. The flames illuminated his face. He looked serious, absorbed with the fire.

"I didn't know you liked to collect matchboxes," I said, noticing how skillfully he had struck the matches.

He jerked his hands back.

"Why not—they give them away at restaurants."

He realized I'd caught on to something.

"Well, what's wrong with matchboxes? People carry around fancy pocket knives and good-luck charms, right?"

By now there were no flames to be seen, only white smoke rising faintly in the dark. But in no time an area the size of my palm had been charred.

The breeze felt dry. He rolled up his sleeves and stuck out his forearms. Then he began sniffing, a human weathervane seeking the wind.

"First of all, you have to know which direction the wind's coming from. A dry wind's best, the kind that makes the tiny hairs on your arms stand up. Then you don't need fire to light something—the contact itself does the trick. Friction—*that's* how primitive people made fire."

The fire was spreading. I stamped it out.

Until then I'd had no idea why he was carrying matches. I had consigned them to the same category occupied by the occasional ardent lyric I found written on the back of an order for a suit or an invoice—"Where did the dreams of the river boy go?" Even though he had no dreams of being a poet, he must have believed that by writing these verses of lamentation he was chiding and insulting himself, agonizing over a life spent chained to a noisy sewing machine, that he was compensating for his failed attempts to break free and escape. But he was no longer writing poetry. Manifest in his intensity as he struck matches, a seriousness of purpose that made me imagine a fire worshiper, was a desire for arson that must have been budding inside him. I was quite certain of this realization, vague though it was, and it alarmed me.

I began asking where he'd come from when he sneaked in at night.

"I was watching a fire—damn, it was something to see." His voice was rough, husky, excited, And he reeked of smoke.

And sometimes I saw blood o his shirt collar.

"A couple of guys got into a fight. I wasn't part of it—I just helped break it up."

I touched the tip of my cigarette to the grass where I was sitting. A dry wind was blowing. Spring was just around the corner.

The winter had been cold and dry, and the farmers were probably concerned about the spring plowing.

I spat on the charred, smoking grass, spread dirt over it with my foot, and rose. The movie lights inside the power plant seemed to be floating, disconnected. I could hear the buzz from the crew as they thronged about.

Our sixth-floor apartment was dark, the custodian's booth padlocked. Should I wait longer at the booth, or go up? Maybe he was back by now. I went up. "It takes a while to get up to our bird cage," I muttered, thinking of the grate over our window.

My note was still in the door frame. I made sure no one had opened it, then crumpled it and pressed the bell. I listened carefully as the clear tremor carried deep into the apartment and then back out, then pressed the bell again and again and again. The door was locked, just as I'd left it, and I heard no one inside. Not that I'd expected to. I pushed and yanked at the doorknob, then stuck a hairpin in the keyhole and jiggled it—useless efforts to ward off the anxiety gathering in my chest.

I imagined utter chaos inside—the rooms babbling, the broom and dustpan bouncing around, the cooking bowls, spoons, and frying pans giggling, jumping, slipping and sliding, rattling.

Somewhere below, a baby screamed.

I sat down at the top of the staircase, which accessed just our apartment and the one opposite, pulled up my knees, and had a cigarette. He still didn't know I smoked, and for no particular reason I kept it a secret. I always brushed my teeth and opened the window to get rid of the smoke before he came home. But like most men who don't smoke, he was sensitive to the smell. So maybe he was just pretending not to know, the way I pretended not to know that there were always matches in his pocket and that he wrote poetry.

It had come as a surprise when he first told me he didn't smoke.

"You *don't*?" I had said. He'd given me a look.

"What's so strange about that? Smoking would raise hell with my work. You make one mistake, just one, and the clothing is no good. So the boss doesn't like it."

"Wow, you're something else!"

I sighed. The baby's crying had changed to whimpering.

I heard mismatched footsteps on the stairs. It was the young couple in the other apartment. They were walking side by side, the man practically carrying the woman as she sagged against him. I scrunched up close to the wall to give them room.

They went inside, and I heard the chain being drawn. I lit a fresh cigarette from the butt of the old one, thinking that couple ought to be having a baby before long. Which reminded me of our baby who had died two years ago, the thought reviving my heartache. He'd died from severe dehydration not long after his first birthday. It couldn't have been helped. I drew my upraised knees closer to my chest and thought back to when my husband had worked at a "tailor shop"—actually a corner room in someone's house—sewing all night and coming back home looking pale and aged. As for me, I was so absorbed in embroidering the wings of cranes that couldn't fly that I was oblivious to the weather outside. That was pretty much our life. Whenever I tried to imagine bringing a baby into that life, I thought about the story of the sickly boy who lived in an attic working a sewing machine and watching a beanstalk grow outside as he himself slowly died. Children who grew up not seeing the sun would probably turn into hunchbacks or, worse, develop a degenerative spinal disorder and end up looking like mollusks.

The sky was black. Before I had smoked half my cigarette I tossed it out the window of the landing and stood up. The cigarette, its filter daubed with lipstick, drew a long arc, a spark hanging in the sky like a firefly, then dropped into the gloom.

The custodian's booth was still dark, but I started downstairs anyway to check.

The door to one of the third-floor apartments was open. A woman, her back to me, was frying something on the stove, and just beyond her at the verge of the living room was a boy with a large head. W The boy was sobbing. As I gaped at him, I could smell cheap cooking oil and coal briquettes burning.

The boy wailed at the sight of me, a stranger. The woman whirled around, glared at me, then slapped the boy just as he was about to stop. Which set him to crying breathlessly.

"Well, it looks like we have an audience. Seems our neighbors like to poke their noses—"

And then the door slammed shut.

My face burned as if were I who had been slapped by the woman's wet, stinging hand. I covered my face in shame and hurried the rest of the way down.

As before, the custodian's booth was locked.

I knew it was useless, but I went into the telephone booth in the plaza of our apartment complex and dialed the factory.

The receiver filled with the whir of sewing machines. I heard the voice of a middle-aged man: "Kim? He didn't show up tonight. Try again tomorrow morning." Just as I had expected. I looked up at the window of our apartment, made one last check of the custodian's booth, then set out for the bus stop.

It was always an impulse, never a plan, that got me out and walking. While he was fettered to his nighttime duties or out prowling dark, unfamiliar alleys like a nocturnal beast, his shining eyes calculating the direction of the wind, the seeds of fire in his matchbox, I would disappear for a stroll and savor the bright lights of city streets the same way I smoked up my hoarded cigarettes or nursed an occasional glass of *soju*. Back home I would brush my teeth, rinsing the strong taste of the *soju*, briskly roll up my sleeves and wash my face and feet, and strain to listen for a sound I couldn't possibly hear in our concrete apartment complex—the patter of raindrops on grass—thereby eliminating all traces of the streets I had just walked.

As I drew near the bus stop, I knew I'd be back at the apartment by the time the roosters started crowing. I would have left behind the irresponsible men—the ones who made phone calls, bought coffee, drank, bought women, then hastened home after getting everything out of their system. I would embrace my husband's thin waist, and then I would go to bed.

He's in a desert. There are flowers in his hand, dark purple flowers. His face beneath the turban is the leaden color of death. "What are you doing?" I shout. He doesn't budge, just stands erect. One by one the flowers drop to the ground. My voice is absorbed in a rolling landscape of sandy hillocks—there's no echo. The sun isn't visible, but heaven and earth, sky and sand are all red. It's like everything's covered with red cellophane.

Was this a scene from an old movie, a scene that had settled in the swamp of my memory, dark and forgotten? Awakening from this dream, I felt a vast despair even though the scene was fragmented, incomplete, perhaps part of the movie I hadn't paid attention to.

The window brightened and turned red—daybreak was on the way. I slipped back into my dream.

Alcohol was taboo back then, but we somehow found a drinking house and the owner presented us with a bottle of spirits to keep us company on the long journey ahead of us. Thus equipped, we set off across the desert. As before, the landscape was a uniform red. I could sense him walking beside me, a silhouette murky and vague, lacking a physical presence. We came to the end of the desert, thirsty, but the contents of the bottle had evaporated. Up shot the vapor, but it could only whirl and churn; it couldn't find release through the magic bottle's narrow neck. That's when he spoke: "Perfect—the wind's coming out of the southeast."

I heard the distant clamor of a siren. For a moment the hot redness framed by the window made me think of the fire alarm on the stairway. Then the doorbell rang.

I opened the door. There he stood in the dim light of the bulb above the landing, reeking of smoke and ash.

I pulled him inside and shut the door. Then I opened the window and looked out. There, right before my eyes, the power plant, enveloped in flames. Sparks flew like fireworks and the river blazed red. Except for the dauntless smokestack, the building was cloaked in fire.

"Where have you been?" I tried desperately to sound nonchalant.

"Over there—watching. What a fire! Had a hell of a time— getting away from the crowd." He was stuttering and panting.

Fireballs catapulted up and plummeted down to the river. It was bright as day. The blaze continued to feed and flare. The firefighters looked like little toy figures.

"Go to bed now, please—everything's all right."

I helped him off with his clothes, put him to bed, and tucked the quilt under his chin. Soon he was fast asleep. And yet every time the siren blared he jerked and trembled with a muffled sob. I lay down and held him close, as if soothing a baby.

We lay together in a blaze without warmth, the redness in the window filling our room, slow to fade. I cradled his head in my bosom, as though putting a little boy to sleep, but what I held was a charred corpse and what I heard was a wildcat howling in the gloom on the far side of the river of fire, a gloom thicker than that of flowers in shade. All I could do was whimper.

MORNING STAR

Chŏngae didn't know which way was which. The tunnel-shaped hall made several sharp bends, and as she shuffled along, the red carpet muffling her steps, she envisioned the subterranean burial chambers where the early Christians had gathered like ghosts to perform their forbidden rites. *Plaster tombs!* She repeated to herself the standard curse employed by those who had persecuted the worshipers. But in spite of her tipsiness, the sensation that her limbs were weightless and disjoined, Chŏngae knew she was not in the Catacombs, not among plastered vaults. She was in a maze of twists and turns.

A journey through a maze—a rite of passage everyone underwent. White mice trying to find their way out of a laboratory maze run in circles. Daedalus escaped from the endless Labyrinth on wings of feathers and beeswax. Playgrounds have a magic tunnel with a spiderweb of passages. And the home-delivered student study sheets always include a maze. Chŏngae had difficulty solving these mazes, but her children found them a snap—not that they were better at spatial perception, it was just that their lives were still uncomplicated. The problem wasn't finding a way out on the drawing but rather finding an exit from life's abstractions.

And stupid me . . . I can't even find the toilet! Chŏngae lamented, pressing down low on her belly. The ear-splitting music from the band grew indistinct—all she could hear were the intermittent thump of drums and the muted clash of cymbals, mysterious signals coming from who knew where. The others were probably dancing to those signals, dancing in abandon, models of ardent courtship. On to the next bend in this snail shell of a hall—the rest of the way would be the same as before. Chŏngae waddled toward the unseen end of the corridor.

The tables in the murky disco were virtually abandoned while the dance floor seethed with people. Hŭisŏ, sitting across from Chŏngae, motioned with his chin toward the floor.

She couldn't decide whether he was gesturing toward the others or suggesting she join them.

"Go ahead," Chŏngae shouted over the blaring music. "I'll watch your seat."

Hŭisŏ's reply was absorbed by the noise; to Chŏngae he looked like a fish opening and closing its mouth. Instead of asking him to repeat himself, she forced a smile. Hŭisŏ too gave up attempting to shout. Puffing on a cigarette, he gazed at the dance floor.

The candle on the table flared up, sending sooty smoke through the opening in the candle shade. Almost imperceptibly the candle was burning out. The flame brightened one last time, and for a brief moment Hŭisŏ's face flickered red. Whose face was that? The instant Chŏngae saw it, a mystifying chill raked her heart. Was this what people felt when they reached a dead end, or when they asked the existential question of who they were or why they were alive? And then the candle went out and the silhouette of Hŭisŏ's face, turned toward the dance floor, returned to normal. In that sudden last flaring of the candle his masked face—no, a face underneath a mask—had looked quintessentially alien. To Hŭisŏ, her own face probably gave the same impression. Ten or fifteen years ago she couldn't possibly have imagined these faces. But then, who in the future would be able to recognize hers? In the deafening noise and the gloom that revealed nothing but the outlines of her face and his, Chŏngae secretly felt relieved. Without the dim, flickering candlelight, the table appeared more calm and settled.

"Mind if I bum a cigarette?"

Chŏngae saw a woman standing next to her. She offered the pack on the table and the woman deftly extracted a cigarette. Despite the woman's thick makeup, Chŏngae could tell she was no older than twenty.

"Kind of dark, isn't it? I'll have someone bring another candle."

Scowling at the young woman, Hŭisŏ crushed out his cigarette.

As the woman walked off, Chŏngae noticed her outfit: a white blouse and black shorts with broad pleats gathered above the knees. The sight made Chŏngae nostalgic. On sports day at school she and the other girls wore black bloomers purchased from the supply store nearby. Woven from dyed cotton, the bloomers bled when wet, and since it never failed to rain on sports day, the girls were a sorry sight by the time they left for home, black rivulets streaming down their legs. Long ago, or so the story went, the school's elderly custodian had killed a large snake that was about to transform into a dragon and rise to heaven. Its metamorphosis thwarted, the snake vented its bitterness by plaguing every outdoor school event with rain. And so it became a ritual for the girls on the evening before sports day or the school picnic to search the sky through open windows till late at night, at the risk of a scolding from their parents, wondering if the stars were out. Their concern reappeared in their dreams, and as the new day dawned they opened their eyes, anxious, and went out to the drain in the yard and relieved themselves. Squatting, they gazed up, and not until they saw the morning stars, faint and fading, did their anxiety ease.

A waiter brought a fresh candle and placed it beneath the shade. The table turned bright orange. Strobe lights flashed across the semicircular dance floor, making it appear to revolve. Sometimes the flashes seemed to shatter the floor into myriad fragments. One of those flashes revealed Kyŏnghae's pale, grinning face angled toward Chŏngae. As she beckoned Chŏngae and the others, another flash appeared to slice off part of her outstretched hand. The dancers' bodies came alive, lonely bursts of silver leaf, only to disappear into deathlike darkness. Chŏngae drew her hand beneath the table and sneaked a look at her watch: nine o'clock. Time passed so quickly at night! She wasn't feeling anxious, she reassured herself. She just wasn't used to going out in the evening.

A chill wind pounced on the group as they exited the hotel's revolving door. The men hastily turned up their coat collars.

As they fell into line at a taxi stand, Chŏngae checked her watch again. Ten-fifteen. Would the kids be asleep by now? The line seemed impossibly long, and rarely did a taxi bother to stop.

"Let's have a cup of coffee or something," said Hŭisŏ to those behind him while keeping his gaze fixed on the head of the line.

Insu's face brightened at the suggestion. "Yeah, how about Kyŏnghae's?" Hunched up against the cold, he asked Kyŏnghae, "Do you still live there?"

"Live where?"

"The place with the blue door, just below campus—you know."

The place with the blue door was where Kyŏnghae had rented a small room with a kitchen. Her friends had liked to drop by for coffee, and when the weather turned frigid they enjoyed lingering there, warming their bottoms on the heated floor. Three or four people in a close circle pretty much filled the space. More than once Kyŏnghae had displayed her culinary skill for them. She was like a big sister, candid and generous, to these friends who had worked with her on the school newspaper. But wasn't it actually for Hŭisŏ's sake that Kyŏnghae had taken such pains? Chŏngae had often wondered about this—not because Hŭisŏ was the neediest of the group but because, unknown to the others, she herself was interested in him.

"Well, I'd really rather not," said Kyŏnghae, but then she gave in. "I guess I'm a softie—whenever we talk about the good old days, I turn into a jellyfish. But you'll have to promise me—*one* cup of coffee, okay?"

It was time to go home, thought Chŏngae. And the kids ... But she kept these thoughts to herself, anxious though she was about finally breaking out of the familiar pattern of her life. This was the first time in over ten years that she had seen the old gang. And as the saying went, mountain high, river deep, not for a decade do they keep.

They split up into two taxis. Munil, Chŏngae, and Hŭisŏ climbed into the first one. Kyŏnghae now lived in Chŏngnŭng, and she had to repeat her new address to them before they left.

"Maybe we ought to just go home," Munil blurted as the taxi exited an elevated expressway. "This could get complicated. We park ourselves at Kyŏnghae's and it's going to be a long night."

Chŏngae silently agreed. *One* cup of coffee? No way. But instead of voicing her concerns she looked out the window and watched the faint dots of starlight being smothered by the bright lights that floated past overhead.

"Oh, hell," drawled Hŭisŏ from the front seat. "We're not staying long." There was no excitement in his voice, and Chŏngae wondered if maybe he didn't care what they did as long as he was with them and didn't have to hurry home.

Chŏngae realized yet again that her only link with her fellow passengers was her memories of their times together a decade ago. Since then, all three had passed into their thirties, the men had completed their military service and found jobs, and each had married and produced a child or two. Surely during those ten years they had all been trying to toe a line drawn for them by an invisible hand. Yet she couldn't have envisioned the lives her friends now led, so vivid were the memories she'd been treasuring.

Tonight she had abandoned her routine of putting the kids to bed, locking the doors, and waiting for a call from her husband, away on a business trip, and here she was delivering herself up to a taxi rushing to god knows where. Was she longing to re-create a space in her life that she once had shared with these friends? Or maybe she was just being foolish: the plain truth was that life does not demand its own review.

"All done for the semester?" Munil asked Hŭisŏ.

"Two down and one to go—only a week left at the last place."

"How many hours do you teach, anyway?"

"Twenty-four," Hŭisŏ snorted, as if he himself couldn't believe it. The last Chŏngae had seen of Hŭisŏ was thirteen years ago, when he had gone into the army after his junior year. He couldn't postpone his military service indefinitely, but she also suspected he was fed up with his penurious life in the school newspaper office, a gloomy fourth-floor hole in the wall in the humanities department annex, where he slept on a row of chairs. The yellow dust that blew in from China, the spring fever Chŏngae had felt when the flowers blossomed: these were her memories of college. To her eyes, red and moist from tear gas, how innocent and beautiful were the peach trees blooming up behind the school, a sight that brought pure tears to her eyes.

Kyŏnghae lived at one end of the twelfth floor in an apartment building. No one answered the doorbell, and the door was locked.

"Hard to believe this is Chŏngnŭng," said Hŭisŏ as he leaned against the railing of the open corridor and looked out at the apartment complex bristling with high-rises. "We must be half-way up the valley—remember when we used to come here on school picnics?"

The wind blew steadily from the nearby hills, cold and desolate, ruffling the hems of their coats.

Kyŏnghae had said she and Insu would follow in the next taxi, but there was no sign of them.

"Did you get the address right?" Munil asked Chŏngae.

"I think so—I kept repeating it to myself on the way here." Chŏngae displayed her palm, on which she had written the building and apartment numbers.

The window of the neighboring apartment opened briefly, then clicked shut. What was the meaning of all these footsteps, this hum of voices outside the door at such a late hour?

"Think they ran off somewhere?"

"Shouldn't rule out anything with those two."

They all knew that Kyŏnghae and Insu were single and un-attached.

Just then, as if in response, Kyŏnghae emerged from the elevator. Behind her was Insu, his arms wrapped around a grocery bag.

Kyŏnghae led the way inside and turned on the light. The small living room was modestly furnished but clean and well arranged. Recalling the appearance of the room Kyŏnghae had rented in college, Chŏngae had half expected to find clothes, books, coffee cups, and whatnot strewn about. Once again she realized that her memories had frozen in time while everyone was changing. Time seemed to have carried all the others on its wings but left her be-hind. She felt all alone, betrayed somehow.

Kyŏnghae lit her kerosene stove.

"It gets too cold in here. I keep telling myself to get the heating system checked, but I'm too lazy."

"I think the problem's a lack of body heat," joked Insu.

Kyŏnghae went into the bedroom. "Chŏngae, the phone's in here—help yourself," she said through the half-open door.

Chŏngae found Kyŏnghae changing clothes. She was about to dial, then changed her mind and replaced the receiver.

"Don't you want to call home and take the load off your mind?" Kyŏnghae asked.

A nice gesture, Kyŏnghae being mindful of her husband and children, but Chŏngae felt no need to explain that her husband was away on business or that her mother, who was watching the children, was hard of hearing. Lately the old woman's deafness had worsened. She couldn't hear the doorbell and she couldn't hear the phone, even when the ringer was turned up loud enough to blast the receiver off the hook. And despite Chŏngae's warnings, the children would rant, "Grandmother's deaf!" right to the old woman's face. But her mother didn't understand and responded only with quizzical smiles.

"You've turned into such a homebody," Kyŏnghae said, more serious now. "We've been getting together pretty regularly.... You *were* told, weren't you?"

"Yes, but what with having babies, taking care of the house—you know.... I've read your articles, though."

When Chŏngae took stock of the person she herself had become—a woman who locked herself inside a fortress—she had to smile. Kyŏnghae had graduated a year ahead of her and gone to work as a reporter for a women's magazine. She was still so tall that Chŏngae had to look up when they talked, and she still had the broad shoulders and the imposing, ready manner that used to make Chŏngae feel rejected. Chŏngae had read her investigative reports and her features on the unusual lifestyle of people living on remote islands or in other isolated areas.

"Strange the way an empty room picks up dust." Kyŏnghae sighed as she wiped the top of her vanity with an accustomed sweep of her hand.

"That's how it is with furniture that's black," said Chŏngae. "You wipe it clean, and as soon as you turn your back the dust starts settling again."

"Yes, sometimes at work I think about it settling so quietly here—it gives me the shivers," Kyŏnghae murmured as she looked into the mirror. "I guess when something gets old and worn out, dust is all that's left."

Instead of the agreed-upon *one* cup of coffee, Kyŏnghae brought in a table loaded with snacks and all gathered around, sitting on the floor. Four bottles of *soju* appeared from the grocery bag, and in no time two were empty. Added to the drinks at the hotel disco, the liquor took effect quickly, everyone's face turning the color of a ripe tomato except Insu's, which grew ever more pale.

"There's been sightings all over town, you and your James Bond attaché case," Hŭisŏ joked to Munil. "People are beginning to wonder if you're a spy."

"You might as well confirm their suspicions," Munil said, chuckling. His ultramarine-blue, almost purple dress shirt, his cuff links, his designer belt, and other accouterments made him look like a chic middle-aged playboy.

In the school newspaper office Munil had once made a bashful confession to Kyŏnghae over *soju* and dried squid she had provided: it was Rilke who had decided his course in life. Munil's father, a surgeon, had tried to force him to study medicine, but Munil resisted, finding moral support in Rilke's *Letters to a Young Poet*. As a result, his obstinate father had virtually disowned him and Munil had lived a hand-to-mouth existence in college. His despotic father forever insisted it was never too late for Munil to begin his medical studies. He was like Muhammad with the Koran in one hand and a sword in the other. Munil, for his part, remained unyielding as a martyr.

Chŏngae used to wonder what Munil was fighting for. Once she had asked him what he was doing for work. "Drinking," he had replied, handing her a business card bearing the name of a textile company; Munil worked in the export department.

The doorbell rang. The visitors looked wide-eyed toward the door.

"Well, now, who could be knocking on a young lady's door after midnight?"

"Kyŏnghae, there's something you're not telling us."

Unfazed, Kyŏnghae took her time getting up. She seemed to know who her visitor was. And when she opened the door, there appeared a wicker basket and the face of a young woman with large eyes and short, permed hair. The face scanned the visitors.

"You have company and I have a lot of fruit—so I brought some over."

And with that, the face disappeared and the door closed.

"Pretty sexy—there's something about the sight of a woman at night."

"Maybe the fruit is a hint that we're making too much noise."

The basket was filled with apples and tangerines, freshly rinsed.

Kyŏnghae produced a knife and platter and began peeling the apples.

"She lives next door. Divorced, with two daughters. Her ex was quite the lover boy—except with her—so now she's got a thing about men. We got to know each other, and she's been asking if I want to live with her—says we'd be good for each other. She got a chunk of money from the divorce settlement, so we wouldn't have to worry about finances. She'll take care of the housework and I can keep working as long as I enjoy it—so I'd still have my own spending money."

"Not bad," Insu said, chuckling. "Going to take her up on it?"

"Somehow I think we'd be a burden on each other. And what do you do when it's time to break off the relationship? I can see the end of this one before it even begins. . . . I'll admit it, it's a hang-up of mine."

"That's what you get for acting like a smarty-pants grownup," said Insu.

"What about you?" Kyŏngae shot back. "How come you're still living all by your lonesome?"

"As for me, give me liberty or give me death!"

In college Insu was always seen with a poetry notebook under his arm, which earned him the sobriquet "Kim the Bard." He was still an unknown writer but hoped someday to upgrade his nickname to "The Everlasting Poet" or "The Everlasting Vagabond." His face, once pale and attractive, looked shrunken and sallow, and his hair had thinned. His ambition now, he declared, was to drive around with a truckload of wooden beehives and leave them wherever flowers were coming into season. He would live as he wanted and write poetry as freely as a songbird sings.

"Now where did I hear that?" Hŭisŏ asked, pretending to ponder the question.

"In an American movie—where else?" Munil said, guffawing and slapping his knee.

Chŏngae had never drunk so much and was feeling woozy. Still, she didn't object when the others kept refilling her glass. Perhaps the *soju* would calm her nerves. It was after two o'clock by the time she realized the alcohol wasn't settling. Nauseous and terribly dizzy, , she made her way to the bathroom on unsteady legs, stuck a finger down her throat, and vomited. Some of the queasiness went away. She rinsed her mouth and washed her hands, then gazed for a time at a lighted window in a top-floor apartment across the way. Otherwise pitch black, even the stairway lights off, the sleeping building looked like a huge monster. That single light suspended in the void made Chŏngae think of a star. And then of a candle floating down a stream on a dark night. Through the wall she heard running water and a faint voice singing. What worrisome thoughts were keeping someone awake at this hour? She recalled the young woman, the face with the large, nervous eyes that had popped into sight in Kyŏnghae's doorway, then vanished.

No more *soju*, no more cigarettes, and it was three in the morning—a time when no amount of alcohol, tobacco, or fodder for conversation can keep night owls from regretting that they didn't leave for home much earlier.

Hŭisŏ fumbled beneath the table and realized the *soju* was gone. He glanced at his watch.

"Already? Well, folks, let's make our move."

"No way," said Munil, waving off Hŭisŏ. "I'll catch hell from the old lady: 'I was sound asleep and you woke me up!' She can get real bitchy: 'If you can't come straight home from work then don't come home at all!' Poor woman has insomnia—takes her till the wee hours to get to sleep."

Hŭisŏ produced a hollow smile. His wife had had a hysterectomy a week earlier and was recuperating in a hospital ward with four other women who had undergone the same operation. Cancer of the uterus: in spite of the diagnosis, she had kept her spirits up. But when the operation was over and the crisis had passed, she'd begun acting like a child. If Hŭisŏ was momentarily out of sight she called out to him anxiously. A few days earlier she'd pointed out one of the other women. "Her husband's an only son," she whispered. "Their first baby was a girl, and now she can't have any more children. She's only twenty-seven—isn't it a shame? Her mother-in-law was here today—said something nasty about the family line being cut off. She's been crying like that ever since. Not me, though. They say that after a woman has a hysterectomy her husband starts playing around. I'm not concerned—I'm just happy I'm alive." All of this was said matter-of-factly. And then his wife, thirty-one years old and childless, her hopes for motherhood shattered, turned on her side and broke into sobs. It had been her idea not to have children until Hŭisŏ finished his studies. After their marriage, when she was still a nurse at the hospital, she had gotten pregnant three times and had three abortions—not learning until later from her doctor that the scar tissue from an abortion can turn cancerous.

"Hŭisŏ, remember the time I went to the *Korea Daily*?" Chŏngae asked. "To pick up an article from that editor, Kim?"

Hŭisŏ was leaning back against the wall, drowsy, eyes closed. *Oh yeah?* He forced his eyelids open and nodded dubiously. *Could be.* Who was she anyway, this woman who kept gesturing with her chin and pestering him with questions? *Oh yeah, Chŏngae— literature major.* Finally, from the distant past, he recalled her round, freckled face. *What a change! She looks awful.*

Meanwhile, Insu was crooning a song. "The bird knows not what it sings" was all that was coherent. Suddenly he slumped sideways, crashing against the table and sending empty bottles and glasses spilling onto the floor.

"He's hammered."

While Kyŏnghae pushed the table out of the way and cleared the dishes and the upturned ashtrays, Chŏngae folded a seat cushion and placed it under Insu's head. Insu clutched at the air, trying to grab Chŏngae's hand as she propped up his head.

Munil looked down at Insu with concern. "See what booze has done to him?"

Hŭisŏ, eyes closed, continued to lean against the wall.

"Four o'clock," Munil muttered. We need to get going. And Kyŏnghae needs some sleep—she has to go to work soon."

Hŭisŏ finally opened his eyes and spoke up. "Let's wait till four-thirty—then we can go downtown and have some hangover soup. That way everybody's up by the time we get home."

"Good thinking," said Kyŏnghae. "Besides, if you go now you'll never find a cab."

Insu, breathing in fits and starts, looked cold all curled up. Kyŏnghae fetched a blanket and covered him.

A gust of wind rattled the windows.

"We're so high up. The rain sounds a lot louder too. When it's windy like this I feel like I'm out on the ocean and the sea is up—I get such a lonely, miserable feeling sometimes. Funny how the phone never rings when I'm home on Sunday or a holiday. And I'm still not used to walking into a dark apartment at night."

Kyŏnghae's murmured words reminded Chŏngae of a familiar saying: living is like rowing a boat through high seas. She'd long since decided she lacked the energy. Wasn't that why she'd married early? It was an escape. She'd gotten a job after graduation, and it turned out her future husband worked on the floor below. Then came the day the elevator stopped. She'd just finished work and was on her way down to the lobby. It had happened at the eleventh floor—the lights went out and the car stopped. A power outage? A breakdown? She never did find out. In that square black cell she'd lost all sense of time, had thought only of having to die there, suspended in space. Just when she was starting to panic, someone managed to force the doors apart. That was her first encounter with the man she would marry. During the ten years they'd been together, he'd never displayed the heroic energy it takes to deviate from the beaten track—or maybe he'd never had the opportunity. In any case, it was his frightening strength— the ability to force open the obstinate doors of an elevator with his bare hands—that had captured her attention. Had she married him so she could rely on that strength?

Four-thirty came and they prepared to leave. Munil shook Insu awake, but all Insu could do was ask where he was and look around, bleary-eyed, before nodding off. Again Munil roused him and this time got him to stand up. Insu fussed like a little boy, letting his head flop to the side while Kyŏnghae got his arms into his coat sleeves and tucked his scarf snugly around his neck.

At another time and place, four-thirty meant dawn. But they all realized that long hours remained until daybreak on this endless winter night.

As the visitors disappeared down toward the elevator, Kyŏnghae's neighbor stole out of her apartment in her nightgown, opened the door the group had just shut, and went inside.

"Who were *they*?"

"Some old friends."

Kyŏnghae had removed the table and seat cushions to the side of the living room. She yawned loudly.

"What awful people! They all left, right? God, this smoke!"

Kyŏnghae opened the window and a cloud of cigarette smoke drifted out.

"Get in here, will you? Come on. I was so worked up I couldn't sleep—I took a bath, washed my hair, everything."

The woman had tossed her gown aside and climbed into Kyŏnghae's bed, and there she sat, nude from the waist up.

"Can't I get some sleep? I have a story to cover first thing in the morning."

"Will you get in here right now?"

The woman was hissing like an offended cat. As Kyŏnghae listened to her importunate demands, she made a circuit of the entryway, the living room, and the bathroom, turning out the lights.

What's the problem with the elevator? As Chŏngae pressed the unlit call buttons in vain, she stared at the lighted window she had seen, as if through a veil of tears, from Kyŏnghae's bathroom. The light still floated brightly in the gloom.

Hŭisŏ struck a match. "Sign says, 'Not in service, midnight to 5 a.m.'"

"Oh great—we have to walk. What floor are we on, anyway?"

"Twelve," answered Chŏngae.

The security lights were off and the stairway yawned pitch black before them. There wasn't a hint of daylight.

Insu, still drunk, still drowsy, ventured a footstep. Chŏngae took his arm and guided him down the stairs. "Watch your step!"

"Can't see a damned thing," Hŭisŏ grumbled from time to time, striking a match and inspecting what lay below. Each flame flared up, then quickly died out.

Chŏngae kept stopping at the landings to look at the familiar light. As they descended floor by floor, the solitary light floated higher and higher. And when they reached the bottom of the last flight of stairs it suddenly disappeared.

"Dark as hell," Hŭisŏ mumbled.

"It'll be light pretty soon," Munil responded.

No taxis in sight. The air, bitterly cold, sliced through them. Munil had a sneezing fit. Insu shivered violently as if performing a pantomime.

As they set off down a broad avenue in search of a taxi, Chŏngae tried to make out the surroundings. If this was Chŏngnŭng, then her grandmother had brought her here for the mineral water when she was a child. The old woman liked to come here during the May Festival, brass pot in hand, to cook rice with the pure spring water and offer it to the local guardian spirit. And then the two of them would bathe in the mineral water even though it was early in the season. On one of these excursions Chŏngae's shoe had come off and fallen into a stream flowing from the nearby hills. Her grandmother had followed the stream all the way down, looking for the shoe, only to return empty-handed and fuming. Explaining that a person who lost a shoe would die unless the remaining one was thrown away, she ordered Chŏngae to take off her other shoe, then sent it floating down the stream. In the deepening twilight Chŏngae had walked downstream barefoot and in tears. She wondered now where that path could be that had caused her such mortification, that endless path with the old tree where the guardian spirit supposedly lived, the tree with the spooky-looking strips of colored cloth hanging from its branches.

Hŭisŏ watched the taxi bearing Chŏngae turn sharply left at a rotary. "What do you think of her?"

From the front seat of their taxi Munil turned to answer him. "Think of who?"

"Chŏngae. Maybe we kept her out too late? We're used to it, but she's not. And she put away a lot of booze."

"I have to wonder if she's going through a change. When that happens, anything goes. Who knows, maybe she broke up with her husband. I didn't even recognize her. Can't remember the last time I saw her—must have been at school. It's amazing how a woman can change!"

Insu slouched next to Hŭisŏ, his head buried in the seat back. "The bird knows not what it sings. . . ." The motion of the taxi seemed to be making him more drunk.

"Still that ballad of the bird!" Hŭisŏ shook Insu and spoke into his ear. "Where's your place?"

"Yŏngdŭngp'o. Do you know Yŏngdŭngp'o?" Insu asked facetiously, slurring the words. Eyes shut tight, he planted his forehead against the back of the front seat.

"What's our friend here up to these days?" Munil asked Hŭisŏ.

"Editing translations. He says it's lousy work and they hardly give him enough to live on. Ten years now he's been saving up for that truck!"

Munil chuckled in disbelief.

Hŭisŏ got out at Sŏdaemun, and the taxi continued toward Shinch'on. What to do with Insu, now sprawled across the rear seat? Munil could imagine his wife's reaction if he came home at dawn with a drunk in tow. To make sleeping space for an uninvited guest would mean moving the children while his wife scowled at him.

As they passed Yonsei University, Munil made up his mind. People have a nesting instinct. Insu was a vagabond—slept where there was a pillow, ate where there was a meal. He could find his way home; if not, there was always an inn. And soon it would be morning. Munil checked the meter, made a rough guess of the fare, and handed the driver some money.

"Take this gentleman to Yŏngdŭngp'o."

Munil's neighborhood was buried in gloom. He relieved himself in the alley to his house, gazing at the waning moon, a fingernail hanging in the sky. A few stars glittered faintly, looking like tinfoil cutouts made for a children's play. What had happened to the stars of his childhood, their outpouring of light? "The older you get, the harder it is to find time to look at the stars," he muttered. Shivering from the cold, he zipped up his pants.

From where the taxi had left him, Hŭisŏ crossed the street to the hospital. An ambulance pulled away from the main entrance, red warning lights flashing, siren wailing.

The inpatient ward was in a separate building, but Hŭisŏ wanted relief from the harsh wind. He entered the maternity ward, from where a corridor would take him to the other building. A pregnant woman emerged from a taxi and came inside, supported by a bushy-haired man who looked like he'd just been rousted from sleep. The woman toddled like a crab protecting its eggs. Every couple of steps she would make as if to squat in a heap, and the man would urge her a little farther along. But his voice was impotent, lacking conviction. Hŭisŏ could hear the screams of women in labor and the squalling of newborns. Those screams and cries would continue until dawn, longing for each other, inciting each other, until they had cast off the deep, dark curtain of night. Hŭisŏ fled the maternity ward, but the noise kept whirling about his ears. He shook his head, telling himself he was overly sensitive because of his wife's operation.

She was on the third floor, last room down the hall. The nurses' station, brightly lit, appeared at the top of the stairway. A nurse was asleep at the desk. Next to her head sat a bouquet of freesia wrapped in cellophane.

Hŭisŏ bought coffee at a vending machine in the waiting room. As he sipped it, the radiators began clunking as the steam came on. The heating system in this old, run-down building left a lot to be desired. Which reminded him that his wife had asked him to bring her a blanket. The waiting room never really warmed up because of all the windows and the draft that came in whenever the door opened. Hŭisŏ crumpled the paper cup and threw it into the wastebasket, then sat down on the bench near the door to the ward. He wondered if his wife was sound asleep on the other side of that door. Fatigue surged irresistibly into his body. All the previous week he'd slept beside his wife, huddled on a fold-out bed. After the close encounter with her mortality, she wanted him by her side. In his state of exhaustion, the vague cacophony from the maternity ward had been like a saw blade on his taut nerves.

Using his arm for a pillow, he lay down on his side on the hard bench. He had stolen away from his wife's bedside, not to return all night—he could imagine her waiting up for him. He shed his coat, covered himself, and curled up. He knew that it would soon be dawn, that the doctors and nurses would start their rounds, that the hospital would fill with the hubbub of well-wishers bringing flowers, that he wouldn't get enough sleep. But none of this prevented him from drifting off into a restless slumber.

Chŏngae pressed the doorbell beside the gate, but heard no one stirring inside. It was useless, but she kept her finger on the button, hoping a light would come on. The neighborhood dogs had perked up at the click of her high heels, and now they were barking. She paced back and forth to get the blood flowing in her numb toes. The paperboy ran by and college students with satchels walked past on their way to early morning classes. Then came the milkman, the bell on his bicycle jangling. The stars barely twinkled. Soon they would grow faint and die out. "You Are a Treasure Like the Morning Star." The first time she had sung that song—in Sunday school or wherever it was—a star, clear and bright, seemed truly to have touched down in her heart. But before she knew it, that star had been hammered into cold, rusty fragments deep inside her. Life used to be frightening; now it was humiliating.

A light came on in one of the other houses in the alley. A faucet gushed, dishes clattered, a human form flitted past the window. Someone preparing the morning rice?

Chŏngae returned to the gate and tried the doorbell again—and again and again and again. She could hear the bell from inside the house, steady, urgent, and ever so sinister, but her deaf mother couldn't. And the old woman slept so deeply at dawn that thunder couldn't have woken her. But still Chŏngae tried. The dogs responded with a mad chorus of barking. A sliding glass door chattered open.

FIREWORKS

"Pursued by the sons of King Kŭmwa, Chumong arrived at the Ŏm, a stream to the east of the Amnok River. How was he to cross the indigo waters that blocked his progress? 'I am the son of Heaven,' he proclaimed to the stream, 'the grandson of Habaek, the water god. Give me passage.' Whereupon a horde of fish and turtles rose to the surface and formed a bridge for him. . . ."

The magnifying glass funneled the sunlight, forming a tiny spectrum. As Yŏngjo angled the lens for maximum effect, the bright white space framed in yellow became a perfect circle on his notebook page, then an oval. When it shrank to a sharp white point of pure brightness, smoke would rise from the paper.

The magnifying glass belonged to Yŏngjo's father, who used it to read the newspaper. "Can't see a blessed thing without it," he lamented whenever he was looking for it. "How can a man's eyes go bad like this?" The previous night the lens had slipped out of the frame and he had wrapped it in tissue paper and placed it on a shelf on the veranda.

"When Chumong's son was a young man, he went to his mother in tears one day, wanting to know who his father was. 'He is the son of Heaven—a great man, a man of excellence,' his mother replied. 'Beneath the pine tree is an eight-sided rock. Under that rock you will find a token, part of a knife. Your father has the matching part. . . .'"

The teacher didn't sound very interested in the book he was reading from. His drone, combined with the drowsiness of students whose stomachs were full from lunch, blended into the languid summer air that had permeated the classroom and was absorbed by the humid shade outside the range of the magnifying glass.

Last night Yŏngjo had dreamed about a UFO, a sphere of white light resembling a full moon that had come to rest in the poplar grove on Hamyŏn Island, at the far side of the Taebaji River, where it flared like a corona and stretched out to span the river between the island and the wetlands at the near bank. It was so bright that Yŏngjo couldn't make out its source, but the hypermagnetic span and its cold, frosty blue color, as of pure molten steel, terrified him—it was going to blind him, wasn't it?—and told him instinctively that he had encountered something alien. These details, unimaginable though they were to Yŏngjo, were consistent with reports by UFO eyewitnesses. He wasn't sure whether the UFO had disappeared before he awakened, or the other way around. But he had to get up to relieve his swollen bladder, and then he climbed the persimmon tree in the yard. The tree rose higher than the house and offered more distant views. The birds nesting there skittered away at Yŏngjo's approach, leaving only the darkness that precedes daybreak. Hamyŏn Island crouched in the distance, a dark, floating lump. No dot of light to be seen there. It was dangerous to nod off up in the tree, but Yŏngjo nevertheless hunched up against a branch and let himself drift into a dreamy daze as he watched the scattered stars fade and die out, and finally he felt the chill of the dawn air and heard the roosters begin to crow. If only he had binoculars, camera, and flashlight, he could join the UFO Research Club. He'd long ago clipped the notice in the newspaper with the membership details.

The notebook page just wouldn't catch. The small circle seemed to absorb all the light around it, swelling and growing ever more intensely white. Kijung, sitting next to Yŏngjo and sneaking looks, couldn't resist the temptation to reach over and cover the circle with his hand.

"Fuck off—you want to get burned?" Yŏngjo hissed, shoving the hand away. But the circle had vanished and the room suddenly seemed so dark that Yŏngjo felt night-blind. He had to blink slowly, over and over, like you would before starting down the aisle in a movie theater after the film has begun. Only then did he recognize the blurred, wavy outlines of the teacher and the students squeezed between their tiny chairs and desks.

The teacher was at the blackboard, drawing a map of Manchuria and the Korean peninsula. "Koguryŏ, weakened by a series of wars and by the constant menace of Tang China, . . . fell to the united forces of Tang and Shilla 705 years after it was founded. . . ." And with that the teacher erased the red chalk border he'd just drawn across the lower middle of the peninsula. Gone was the kingdom, leaving only the displaced inhabitants and the burned ruins of fortified towns.

In flew a bee through an open window. Blissfully unaware, it flew in calm, lazy circles, stirring the air and the lingering odors of pickled radish, sausage, and other seasoned lunch items as yet undigested. The feeble buzzing awakened those children who were dozing. With fresh enthusiasm, high hopes, and sparkling eyes, they followed the flight of the bee. Imagine their disappointment when it refused to land on the bridge of the teacher's nose or sting one of the other children on the head. Instead it lit for a moment, wings spread, protesting the notion of a long afternoon of incessant motion, before resuming its lazy circling.

The rays of sunlight had retreated to the corner of Yŏngjo's desk. Before long they would disappear across the windowsill. Yŏngjo nudged his chair closer to the light and raised the magnifier. Once again sunlight collected in a circle of intense brightness on the notebook page.

"Write down the following dates and memorize them." The teacher erased the map and began a time line:

37 B.C., founding of Koguryŏ by King Tongmyŏng

No sooner had he turned his back to the class than a squadron of white paper airplanes were launched from all directions, targeting the flitting bee. Up they soared, describing short, wobbly parabolas like doves caught in a battle, before clipping the heads of classmates and nosediving to the floor. When the bee flew too close for comfort, ignoring the stifled laughs of the children, their muffled exclamations, and the ripping of paper from notebooks, the girls flinched and shrieked, sticking their heads under their desks or burying them with their hands. An airplane grazed the bee and suddenly the insect was agitated. Spurred by the children's stifled cries, it bumbled about in search of an exit, missing the large open windows and finally bouncing off a wall. Its frantic flight was reflected in the black zigzag shadows that crossed Yŏngjo's white circle. And then a wisp of smoke rose from the swollen, blistering zenith of the point of light, and ever so slowly the paper caught fire.

313 A.D. (King Mich'ŏn, reign year 14): Nangnang com-
mandery conquered

372 (King Sosurim, reign year 2): importation of Buddhism

410 (King Kwanggaet'o, reign year 20): eastern Puyŏ, near
the Ssunghwa River, conquered

Finally the teacher noticed the clamor. He turned toward the
class, and the next moment the airborne planes plummeted to
the floor while those not yet flightworthy were crumpled in hand.
The children straightened in their seats, looking up at the teacher
with tense expressions as feet inched out from beneath desks to
recover fallen aircraft.

So much for that, thought Yŏngjo as he wiped the magnifying
glass with his shirt and put it in his pocket. He watched the fluttering flame consume the paper. Too bad he couldn't see its scarlet color because of the sunshine.

Kijung poked him in the side, and too late Yŏngjo noticed how
still and tense the classroom was. Before he could look up, the
teacher's hand had snuffed out the flame.

"What the hell are you doing—trying to set the place on fire?"
the teacher shouted, his voice trembling. He slapped Yŏngjo
once, then again and again in quick succession. Black ash scattered over the desk, the scorched remnants of the notebook page
leaving specks of soot on the teacher's puffed-up, reddened palm.

"Go stand in back—you're not fit to be sitting at this desk. Remember what I said about one rotten apple spoiling the barrel?"

Yŏngjo felt like a wormy apple as he scuffed to the back of the
classroom. Whispers followed him down the aisle: "What happened?" "He was playing with fire." "Oh-oh, he'll wet his bed tonight for sure." *Just wait,* Yŏngjo grumbled to himself. *After class
you'll all be kissing my ass—you'll want to set fire to the ants out behind the toilet, or else try to make a big fire with those dry branches.
But not with my magnifying glass—no way!* It was a good thing the

teacher hadn't confiscated it. He stroked his burning, swollen cheeks. No, he wasn't going to return the magnifying glass to his father. It was a war trophy, earned with the slapping he'd endured.

The teacher finished the time line. "You have ten minutes to memorize the board." After clapping his hands to get rid of the chalk dust he sat down, poured himself a glass of water from the kettle on his desk, and had a cigarette.

All together the class began to recite the chronicle: "598 (King Yŏngyang, reign year 9): expulsion of the 300,000-man Sui army; 612 (King Yŏngyang, reign year 23): expulsion of the one-million-man army of Sui emperor Yang. . . ." What was life like back then? Yŏngjo thought about Chumong asking who his father was. How many children during those times had left home to find a papa whose face they didn't remember? The children began drumming on their desks and stamping on the floor in time with the recitation. But Yŏngjo was only half listening to his pubescent class-mates, the husky voices of the boys clashing with the shrill voices of the girls. He was more interested in the children in those old stories. They were all so wise and brave. Surely there must have been a few morons among them? They built character studying by the light of fireflies or the reflection of snow, and they valued keeping their word above all else. If their parents were ill, they cut flesh from their own thighs to nourish them; when the country was in danger, they rushed to the battlefield to offer up their lives. Strong of body and spiritually centered, they grew to be men and women of ardent loyalty.

The bee was still trying to find its way out, still circling above the children. A group of sniveling tykes passed by in the hall, shirt sleeves rolled up to their shoulders. Yŏngjo guessed they had just gotten their encephalitis shots. A sight such as this usually brought catcalls from his classmates: "Babies! Go home and suck your mommy's tit." The teacher would gently rebuke them: "You boys were small fry once—remember?" But today there was a more important issue to occupy the children. "Do any of your parents take sanity pills to keep from going crazy? Tell them I could use some." "You boys ever heard the expression, 'Even dogs won't eat a teacher's crap'? Well, you better believe it." Although their teacher often ranted like this, he rarely resorted to corporal punishment. But now, with no warning, he had pulled Yŏngjo out of his seat and slapped him. He must have meant to make an example of him—an example the other children wouldn't dare forget. Early that spring, on the first day of school, the teacher had kept the windows wide open even though the stove had been removed and his new homeroom students were all huddled together trying to keep warm in the icy classroom. "You'll learn this next year in middle school," he had declared while writing on the board in English, "Boys, be ambitious." The class had to recite the phrase. "Boys, be ambitious!" he repeated in Korean and then English. "And don't you forget it." Shivering from the drafts, goose bumps sprouting on their faces, the children addressed the obscure gateway to their future and called out these words meant to develop in them the bravery that was one of the moral pillars of life.

Yŏngjo heard students in another classroom reciting multiplication tables in unison. The sunlight had retreated beyond the windowsill, but the playground was still a scorching expanse of white that glinted as if grains of sand were popping out of the ground. A dodgeball game was under way. Three girls dressed in skirts stood to the side of the playground, heads lowered, punishment for not reporting to school in gym clothes. "Girls—they're always bleeding," the boys scoffed. And that's the first thing you'd suspect if you saw a girl who wouldn't change into gym clothes, even when the teacher called her to the front of the class and rapped her on the head. The same went for the girls with pasty white faces who volunteered to watch the classroom while everyone else was outside. And when those girls were forced to run, they looked uncomfortable, hunching up their shoulders and hugging themselves. All Yŏngjo noticed was their heaving chests and round bottoms.

Ten minutes had gone by, but the teacher remained at his desk, idly looking outside. *Maybe he's loosening up*, thought Yŏngjo. But then he heard the room seething with muted whispers and busy movements—the regularity of pitch and rhythm that bespoke order in the classroom was coming undone.

Once, before roll call, Yŏngjo had noticed the teacher's hair flecked with chalk dust.

Several days ago, on an errand for his mother, he had visited the teacher's home with a hen, legs bound, and ten eggs padded in straw, all of it inside a mesh bag. "Tell him eggs and a hen are good for beating the heat. And let him know the eggs might look small, but they were fertilized right here at home." The eggs *were* rather small. But Yŏngjo knew they fetched a better price because they were fertilized. Though the sign still hung from their gate— FERTILIZED EGGS, TOP QUALITY, WHOLESALE—people hadn't gone out of their way to visit since last year, when most of the chickens had come down with diarrhea and died. They ought to get rid of the rest of them anyway, only a few were left, his mother said before sending him off. And better to be generous and bestow them on the teacher with her regards than let the weasels get them. "But they won't let me on the bus like this," Yŏngjo complained, feeling disloyal. Embarrassed at having to carry the mesh bag like a girl going to market, he strapped the hen and the padded eggs to the carrying rack of his bicycle and set out. All the way to the teacher's house the hen was on its side, struggling to flap its wings. When people on the street stopped short to take in the spectacle of a cackling hen trying in vain to work its wings, Yŏngjo felt like tossing the bird into the nearest garbage can or unloading it at the market.

The teacher lived in a house with a red slate roof on a hillside accessed by a steep alley. Yŏngjo hesitated at the gate. "Who is it—are you one of the boys from Hyangt'o Middle School?" called the teacher's wife. Yŏngjo found her at the faucet in the yard, washing a naked boy who looked to be around seven. "Your teacher isn't back yet—he might be late." A couple of months ago, on Teachers' Day, Yŏngjo had come here in the evening with Ŭlt'ae, Kijung, and some other boys to offer the teacher a small cake, but the teacher's wife didn't remember him from that visit. The teacher had been out then too, and the boys had turned around and retraced their steps home.

The house was small, but the square yard was large enough to accommodate a vegetable patch in one corner where lettuce, crown daisy, and other lush greens were growing. Two girls were playing house beneath the terrace where the garnish crocks were kept. They wore identical red dresses and had braided hair. They resembled the naked boy. One of the girls picked a couple of leaves of lettuce from the vegetable plot. "Sŏngyŏng!" shouted their mother. "I mean, Hugyŏng! Those greens are precious—why do you keep picking them?" In this brief interval of motherly inattention the boy started to run off, but the next moment he was pulled up short and his mother slapped him on the back. "Oh? You're still here?" she said to Yŏngjo. "Well, what is it?" Blushing in response to the woman's beleaguered expression, Yŏngjo walked his bicycle into the yard and unstrapped the now docile hen. "I brought these—my mom said chicken is good for the heat and these eggs were fertilized at our house," Yŏngjo said in a flurry, wanting to be done with his errand and gone. "So you all raise chickens—roosters too?" The teacher's wife stared in wonder at one of the small eggs. "Yes, but only one rooster's left." "Well, I have to think—now who's going to slaughter it? . . . Say, what's your name? And your class? Wait a minute. I'll get something to write on. I'm not so good at remembering. I used to have a good memory—I wonder what happened to it. . . ." Flustered, she considered Yŏngjo and the hen, then straightened herself with an effort and went inside. In no time the three children had surrounded the hen. From a room with a closed door near the vegetable plot came a muffled shout, but the children ignored it. The boy untied the hen's legs and its wings jerked to life; it staggered a few steps before hopping onto the terrace. A furious chase en-

sued. Yŏngjo joined in, scolding himself for letting the bird loose.
The girls clapped and giggled as the frightened hen flew cackling
to the faucet and then toward the gate. Panting, the naked boy
picked up a rock and chased it back onto the terrace. From there
the bird hopped down to the vegetable plot. Before Yŏngjo could
stop him the boy let fly with the rock. But instead of hitting the
hen, it thunked against the largest of the potbellied crocks, breaking it open and releasing great dribbles of soy sauce. The girls'
mouths, gaping in laughter, remained open in shock and fear.
Their mother appeared with paper and pen. "Good God!" she
shrieked. "We're losing all our soy sauce! Damn stinker of a hen!"
The door to the room near the vegetable plot opened, and out
came an old woman in a sleeveless men's T-shirt, her white hair
cropped like a soldier's. Her hands were tied and she waddled,
squatting, to the edge of the veranda, where she lowered herself
to the yard and said in a plaintive tone, "My dear, did I hear say
someone brought us a chicken? I am simply famished. Would you
boil it up and serve me a bowl?"

The teacher rose and methodically erased the blackboard.

"Yi Yŏngjo, tell us about the founding of Koguryŏ."

Yŏngjo stared at the blank surface, desperately racking his
memory. All he could remember was what he had read in a comic
book—the story of Prince Hodong and Princess Nangnang, a
magic drum that boomed in the absence of any human touch,
and General Yŏn'gaesomun, who wore half a dozen daggers, who
when mounting his horse used a servant's back rather than stir-
rups. But there was no sequence to these images that made any
sense to him. The hand clutching the magnifying glass in his
pocket was slippery with sweat.

"Come on—I didn't make you stand back there just so you
could daydream."

After a further pause, Yŏngjo began: "When Chumong crossed
the river, the turtles and the fish made a bridge for him, and his
son found part of a knife under a rock—"

"I ask the boy to look at the moon and instead he looks at the finger I'm pointing to it with. Let's try again—in what year did Chumong establish Koguryŏ?"

Why was it that the harder the teacher's tone, the less Yŏngjo recalled? Nothing—not one word of what he had heard earlier—was coming to mind. The only thing he was sure of was the feel of the sleek, hard piece of glass in his hand. The playing field still blazed creamy white in the sun. The dodgeball game was still under way. One of the teams was down to its last player, and every time this boy managed to dodge a flying ball with some breathtaking maneuver his teammates cheered him on. The three girls still stood with their heads down, looking in the direction of their squat shadows. Above Yŏngjo saw the national flag, the school flag, the New Village Movement flag—all of them limp in the still air—and the clock tower, which perpetually read 12:10. And in front of the old frame schoolhouse, on a banner with lettering so distinct you could almost smell the paint: CELEBRATING THE ESTABLISHMENT OF THE CITY OF UNYANG. On this particular day, the town in which they lived was to be upgraded to a city, and that evening there would be a grand fireworks display.

"Idiot for life—go back to your seat," the teacher said in a low, weary voice, his lips curled in contempt.

Feeling alone and humiliated, Yŏngjo tightened his grip on the magnifying glass and looked squarely at the teacher. Suddenly he felt a tingle that sent shivers up his spine, but before he could cry out, the edge of the lens had cut into his clenched hand. He felt a hot, sharp pain.

Only a couple of quarts of feed left. She'd have to scrape the bottom of the bag, and that would still give her barely enough for three feedings.

Inja, Yŏngjo's mother, filled a bowl and took it out back. A clucking throng of chickens greeted her at the front of the coop. As soon as she poured the grain into the feed tray, the five hens set to with a purpose while the old rooster, ignoring the feed, pecked at the hens to drive them away. *Animals are just like people,* Inja thought as she grabbed the rooster's wings and flung the bird aside. *It's amazing—the older they are, the more greedy and gluttonous they get.* The rooster's comb used to be full as a cockscomb flower and blood scarlet. Now it was drooping and crooked. Half of its imposing tail feathers had fallen out. It was the shabbiest-looking rooster you'd ever see. *Get rid of the damn thing,* Inja would scold herself whenever she saw it. Fowl weren't pets—you didn't keep them for the duration. Her grandmother had told her a story: "Once upon a time a spirit madam was called to summon the soul of a man who had died. She climbed to the roof of the dead man's house and what do you know? There sat a grand old man in a fine white coat. 'What have we here?' asked the spirit madam. 'Something wicked is afoot. Down below the master lies dead in his house, while up above a demon makes mischief.' In the village there lived a well-known archer. He let fly an arrow toward the roof, and *poof*—the old man vanished and all that was left was bloody feathers." Like many girls, Inja was forever pestering her grandmother to tell her stories from the old days, which the woman recited in a singsong voice. But there were also times, not so infrequent, when Inja had walked a dark, lonely country road and made the unsettling discovery of a live chicken with its feet bound, bedecked with a pair of underwear inscribed in scarlet Chinese characters that read, "Transfer This Calamity."

If a rooster flew up onto the roof, it meant disaster for the family—the master of the house might drop dead. This folk belief aside, there was no reason to keep chickens when they were senile and squawked any time of the day or night and did nothing but peck. It was a job protecting them: the weasels dragged them away by the wings, and the rats took bites out of their backsides. And the birds lost to diarrhea had to be culled. As summer set in, all Inja and her family ate was chicken. Their breath stank of chicken. They could almost feel yellow fat oozing from their pores. It wasn't always that way. The chicks were lovely little balls of fuzz. And when they became hens they filled the shelves of the henhouse, producing faithfully every day on a diet of water and mixed feed. Before sunset Inja would fill her basket with the marvelous eggs, so large and firm. They were like gold to her. Chickens were sensitive creatures, and she studied up on the various taboos. "Ma'am, your red sweater will scare the hens and they won't lay," she might say to a woman who came too close to the henhouse. In addition to raising the hens for unfertilized eggs, Inja let the roosters and brood hens run free and eat together inside the coop. This ensured her a supply of fertilized eggs as well, for which she charged double, those eggs being valued for their supposed restorative effects. "Good for the men," the young wives would say, not bothering to haggle over the price. Along with the pleasant sensation of the money that went through her hands, Inja couldn't get over how well the imposing roosters and the toddling hens got along—could a bouquet of flowers look more harmonious? She liked to think this harmony represented hope. Kwanhŭi, her husband, fed the chickens in the morning before leaving for his shop, and now and then he brought home a book on how to care for them. On Sundays, when the shop stayed closed, he raked up the dried chicken dung and sold it at a farm. Everything seemed to be going right. Their life, shadowed by doubt and held together like a bundle bound with fraying rope, seemed to have settled into a groove.

But with the arrival of the monsoons the chickens began to die off. Inja dumped antibiotic into the feed, but the diarrhea epidemic continued. Each day more of the chickens would nod off, and at night they grew limp as rags and died. By summer's end only 20 of the original 300 remained. Watching three or four die each day, Inja fell out of love with the chickens and lost interest in caring for them.

Sheer cobwebs appeared in the deserted coop. The tin roof, hot as a frying pan in the summer sun, turned rusty red. Sometimes Inja was startled from an anxious sleep by the rush of the wind or the patter of rain. Her hopes had disappeared as suddenly as they had risen—she felt cheated. Though she wished she could get rid of the remaining chickens, she continued to change their water and sprinkle a handful of feed on schedule, telling herself she couldn't allow living things to die. But that was all she did. The neglected hens yielded to the tyranny of the old rooster, once in a while dropping an egg as an afterthought, and when the sun went down they would all roost together to sleep.

The bell sounded; someone was at the front gate. The rooster chimed in with a long, sustained crow, surprising Inja. *Senile old bird.* It wasn't a good sign.

The bell kept ringing as Inja emerged from the backyard and approached the gate. Was it Yŏngjo? But he had ridden away on his bicycle not even thirty minutes ago after returning from school. Whoever was ringing the bell didn't seem to care if someone might actually be responding. The sound was ominous and gave Inja a feeling of urgency.

"Who is it?"

The ringing stopped. In the dead silence, the questions pressing upon her took on absurd proportions.

Inja opened the gate. No one was there. Were the neighborhood children playing tricks? It was so still. Inja shook her head, wondering if she'd been hearing things. She knew that no one was home across the way or next door, or next-next door. All three families had left to watch the fireworks.

As Inja rested her arm against the wooden gatepost, her vacant gaze returned from outside, drawn as if by habit to the persimmon tree in the yard. The foliage, sparse not so long ago, was now lush and dark green. The sun shone through the fork in the limb where Yŏngjo always sat. She watched the hazy sunlight filter through the leaves, as if observing Yŏngjo in his precarious perch.

Crowded into the corner of the front yard, it was an excellent shade tree. But the few persimmons it managed to bear were unshapely, didn't ripen, and were no bigger than acorns. Disease? Bad soil? Inja couldn't tell. Kwanhŭi had suggested cutting it down, but to Inja it was worth saving because of its verdant leaves.

It was a good ten years since that man in his forties had shown up at their house. It was summer, about a month after Kwanhŭi had returned from a trip to the countryside, where he'd gone looking for items to stock the antique shop he was opening. The visitor had stood hesitantly at the gate, looking inside. Was the man of the house in? he asked. When Kwanhŭi emerged, the man said the house was originally his and he couldn't resist stopping by as he passed through the neighborhood. And then he excused himself, entered the yard, and ignoring his host, proceeded to pore over every last crack in the chimney, walls, and front door. He next considered Inja, lingering nearby with Yŏngjo, a suckling at the time, on her back. Cadging a cigarette from Kwanhŭi, he related a story about his days as an army officer. He'd been involved in some incident or other and was sent to prison as a result. By the time he was released he had lost both his youth and his ideals and was middle-aged and gray. He couldn't locate his wife and son, and this, their house, seemed to have changed hands several times. The man's tone of voice was composed until then. But tears came to his eyes as they played over the persimmon, which he said he'd planted after the birth of his son—his only flesh and blood. He was astonished at how it had grown. Inja couldn't recall the incident of which the man spoke, but Kwanhŭi remembered—it was a rebellion that had been the talk of the country, and most of the participants had been executed after a summary trial. Kwanhŭi tried to guess what had remained unspoken in the man's otherwise candid story. Had he been spared in return for betraying a comrade?

The tree always brought to mind images of that visit. As Inja and Kwanhŭi had listened to their visitor and sensed his mysterious unease, she felt as if the three of them had long ago been scripted by events both inevitable and unknowable to bear witness together to the history represented by that persimmon. They were like performers on a dark stage who'd been thrown into the spotlight.

Somewhere in this world a boy was growing older along with this tree; growing into a young man. The persimmon tree was of no use to them, and it left the house more shaded and gloomy. But Inja couldn't bring herself to cut it down.

The dying hens were squawking. The weasels wouldn't be snatching chickens in broad daylight, so it was probably the rooster bedeviling them. .

They'd just had a house built, said the woman, and they'd replaced all their furniture with antiques. Would Kwanhŭi have a suitable ornament for the top of their stationery case? No sooner had he obliged the woman with a brightly painted pair of wooden geese than in came Myŏng, the pharmacist from across the street, with two bottles of tonic. His wife, after arriving late with his lunch, was minding the store, Myŏng explained.

Kwanhŭi's shop was stuffy, ventilated only when the sliding glass door was open.

"First sale of the day?" the pharmacist asked, glancing at the departing customer. "How'd you make out?" He pulled a metal chair toward Kwanhŭi's desk and sat.

"Yeah, a pair of wild geese," Kwanhŭi answered as he gulped the cold beverage. "The kind people use for a wedding gift— they're supposed to be good for marital harmony. But she's no newlywed. Maybe she figures they'll keep her husband from sniffing around."

"I know a better one. It's called a musk pocket or a fox something-or-other. Back in the old days, the wives of the highest-ranking officials would give their last pair of bloomers for it and then stick it you know where. An aphrodisiac, I guess you could call it. I'll bet you've got something like that stashed away."

Kwanhŭi produced a wry smile. "Well, I've handled just about every kind of old junk, or at least I've seen 'most everything, but I haven't run across anything by that description."

"Well, then, how about a game of *paduk*?"

The pharmacist reached under the desk and took out the board. He hated having to tend to the pharmacy all day, and whenever a prospective substitute was momentarily available, the usual cryptic smile would light up his thin yellow face and he would cross the street for a game. Kwanhŭi guessed Myŏng preferred the antique shop because it was quiet and business was slow compared with the hardware store, copy shop, and small supermarket nearby—and also, Kwanhŭi was a good match for Myŏng as a *paduk* player. It was probably the pharmacist's one and only chance to venture out during the day. "Have to keep the old oral cavity in working order"—this was his standard greeting, but in actuality he said little apart from getting the game going.

The two men winced—the gongs were clanging again. The noise must have been coming from a campus festival at the university nearby; the only other possibility—a shaman ritual—was unlikely, because families didn't call in shamans during the day anymore. Whatever the origin, the clanging had continued all morning.

The pharmacist shook his head in annoyance. "Gives me the chills—reminds me of the war."

"The war? Why's that?"

The pharmacist belched and rubbed his stomach. The sleeves of his white pharmacist's smock were rolled up to his elbows, revealing rough, dry forearms. Kwanhŭi also noticed dark rings around his eyes. Myŏng must have come down with something.

The pharmacist liked to exaggerate that for years he had sold virtually nothing but masks and eyedrops for student protection against tear gas. But a rumor was afoot that his wife had bought up land on Hamyŏn Island, expecting it would soon be developed into an amusement park. And there was another rumor, of the "just between you and me" variety, that Myŏng had come down with a terminal illness. *What good's all that money if you're so run-down?* Kwanhŭi silently scolded the man.

"Well, I was only seven when the war broke out. I remember seeing the Chinese soldiers. And hearing stories about gongs and bugles, and Chinese troops crawling like maggots toward Summagi Pass, and snow in every direction. Supposedly they fell back like dominoes when they came under fire, but finally they managed to gain the pass—zigzagged up like they were storming a fortress. I could almost see it before my eyes. We had to quarter some of those soldiers. When it was sunny, they'd strip off their quilted uniforms and crush the lice with their fingernails. At night you could hear them whimpering in their sleep, calling for their mothers. They must have been barely fifteen or sixteen."

"Folks here got pounded during the war, didn't they?" said Kwanhŭi, remembering that the pharmacist, unlike himself, was a native of the area. "Well, this should be a day to remember. All the shamans getting into the act, and we turn into a city and get a new name—whoopee."

For the better part of two months the local media had been building up this day. The town would be christened a city, the idea being to symbolically restore the fortress town that had flourished here two thousand years ago (some would say three thousand), to revive in the people a sense of pride in being cultured citizens of the province. It was back to the roots, something for the entire province and the whole town-turned-city to celebrate. If everything went according to plan, most of the residents would turn out.

"Sure," said Myŏng. "The government needs a rallying point to drive public sentiment. But they need to do more than just upgrade the town to a city. How does our new name grab you, anyway? Unyang—is it supposed to have a familiar ring, make us feel attached to the area? Hardly. You know, the historical records aren't clear on the dates for the fortress town, and there are all sorts of theories about where it was located—some people say around here, some say upper Hamgyŏng Province, others say somewhere in Manchuria. The records only say it existed—not when or where. Well, I guess I better close up early. Something's in the air—I wonder if there's going to be trouble after the festivities." The pharmacist's tone was gloomy as he watched three riot police buses speed past, each filled with dark shapes and bearing a sign, EMERGENCY MOBILIZATION.

"I doubt it. They probably just want to beef up security for the big event. Lots to see this evening—the wife's been after me to go."

Fireworks at the riverside and flower lanterns floating on the water, Inja had said at breakfast that morning. Why not have an early dinner and then go for a walk and watch? Yŏngjo had eaten silently and without responding to his mother's suggestion had left for school, treading on the heels of his sneakers, too lazy to put them on right.

"Lots to see—well, that includes people too," said Myŏng. "My parents always told us to avoid big crowds. I've been wondering about that. You think there's a fear of massacres somewhere in our collective unconscious? Or a large-scale loss of life—maybe that's a better way to put it. Think about all we've experienced—the wars and such, situations nobody should have to go through—just because we were defenseless. And I'm not just talking past tense. One of these days we could all end up dead in a nuclear war. And if you believe in the Bible, all the nonbelievers get cast into hellfire on Judgment Day, like poisonous weeds."

Why's he jabbering so much? Kwanhŭi wondered. Was he afraid that if he didn't keep up the spiel, if he shut his mouth for an instant, the words boiling inside him would be snatched away or else burst out like a flood and overwhelm him?

"You look done in," said Kwanhŭi. "Did you catch a bug?"

"I'm not sleeping very well. I go to bed and just lie there for hours, reading a book or looking through the newspaper. I want to find some of the answers before I die. 'Humans are the only species with the gift of speech. And the only species that knows how to lie.' Remember that one? So, are we fundamentally evil or are we fundamentally good? I suppose the convenient answer is both. Everyone wants to live, but murderers keep murdering. Everyone wants peace, but wars break out everywhere. Paradoxes. . . ."

"Well," said Kwanhŭi, "like the fellow says, every pot needs someone to stir it. And every period in history has its madmen, same as every marketplace has a madwoman." But was that a valid comparison? Kwanhŭi was beginning to feel burdened by the pharmacist's insecurities. It was as if Myŏng, to rid himself of his worries, was responding to a seething urge to blurt anything that came to mind.

And now he fixed Kwanhŭi with a stare.

"All right," he said, almost in a whisper. "I've got leukemia. It's still in an early stage. I haven't told the wife, but she knows something's up. If I can hang on another year or two, maybe they'll find a cure. But my days are numbered, so while I'm still kicking I guess I'd best not look for sympathy or complain about having to go first."

This revelation caught Kwanhŭi off guard. He felt as if he'd been showered with a bucket of cold water."Are you sure about the diagnosis? And why keep it from your wife?"

Other responses had occurred to Kwanhŭi: *Why tell me? Well, we all have to go someday. Yeah, with all the medical advances, maybe they'll come up with a cure.* Each of them meaningless. A person driven to his limits would unburden himself to a passing dog for want of anything better.

Again came the clanging from the direction of the university, and again they winced. The pharmacist shook his head. Kwanhŭi could only imagine the loneliness and the fear of death that must have been mushrooming in Myŏng's mind.

"I don't want her getting into a tizzy," answered the pharmacist. "Actually I need some time to figure out how I want to live the rest of my life—what I have to do before I go. If I tell her now, she'll start treating me like I've got one foot in the grave. She'll find out soon enough, and then she'll want to send me to the hospital, call in a shaman, make me go to church. But before she does that, I want to try being my own doctor, I want some time for myself. You know, whether we like it or not, the life we live is part of a great stream, and it's always moving. Maybe that stream is history. God only knows where it's flowing, but that doesn't stop me from thinking about people, life—the big questions."

Myŏng's wife appeared at the door to the pharmacy, shouted toward them, and beckoned her husband.

The pharmacist stood up. "Looks like we missed out on that game," he said with forced cheer. "Now that it's getting hot, let's go fishing—or else nab a stray mutt and have some dog stew."

After the pharmacist had left, Kwanhŭi realized he was drained. Lowering the bamboo blinds over the door, he pulled two chairs together and lay down. The metal chairs supported his back, yet he felt he was sinking endlessly into the ground. The fan had to work at capacity to circulate the turbid air, which was laden with the odors of camphor, naphthalene, the wild-sesame oil that gave wooden vessels a shine, the patina Kwanhŭi could manufacture by applying sulfur to an object. The cedar clothes chests, the large wooden basins, the mortars, the candlesticks appropriately rusty for their vintage, the incense burners, the dining trays, all these antiques sat weighted down with a thousand years of time. Kwanhŭi closed his eyes and breathed deeply, wishing everything would fade. But there remained his bewilderment, along with an elusive, stifling sensation, as if he'd become a spirit fated to wander underground, and finally words whispered by the pharmacist, his body reduced to a diseased shell—*My days are numbered.* Vibrant, simmering sounds from outside assailed his ears—the whir of tires against pavement, the blaring of horns, the footsteps of passersby.

He rose, closed the door, lay down again. The cramped interior became a coffin and he the corpse of an emperor amid all his burial accessories. Then he was a skeleton, and suddenly he was a child again.

And then the bogeyman came.

"Do you see him? Do you?" his great-grandmother had asked in her breathless tone when young Kwanhŭi put his eye to the hole poked in the paper panel of the door. "I don't see anything," he sullenly replied. But the old woman, known to all as Old Grandmother, was undaunted. She sat down close by, nudged him aside, then said in a hushed voice, "Look—I told you—out there by the road, just this side of the bridge." But Kwanhŭi's eyes detected no bogeyman. Instead, mirror clear in the piercing moonlight, the wraithlike shadow of a bare tree stretched over the pale ground. Enthroned in the tree was a single magpie nest. In the rush of wind the juniper fence swayed, and the chill white frost coating the road and the bare fields glittered and seemed to scatter. The rock pile jutting up from the far side of the road was frost-covered as well. The previous summer Old Grandmother, sweating in the sweltering sun, had for no apparent reason carried the rocks up from the stream, as if this were as routine a task as gathering sheaves of rice stalks.

Old Grandmother sat with her back to the door, her shadow flickering large on the wall. For nights on end she'd been looking through the hole in the door panel. "Those farmers who escaped the flood, they'll be back after the frost," she'd said. But Grandfather had shaken his head. "It wasn't a flood, Mother; there's a war going on." What could Old Grandmother have been seeing? Ghosts supposedly appeared to people in their last years. Those white forms she saw swaying and drifting out beyond the new

marketplace—were they the ghosts of children? Of old people?
Old Grandmother looked so old it was hard for Kwanhŭi to believe she had ever been young enough to give birth to Grandfather. She was so old her hair had turned black again, black as a
crow's, and her dark, barren mouth held only the remnants of
teeth, tiny stubs that resembled silkworm eggs. She liked to sit
where the sun came into the yard and shuck the sunflower seeds
nestled in her skirt, all the while talking: "Once upon a time, in
the broad light of day, the fire dog ate up the sun, and heaven and
earth were plunged into darkness. . . . The gentleman scholars of
the land, dressed in their white topcoats and white hempen hats,
assembled outside the royal palace and wept three days and ten
months for the deceased king. . . . Bands of robbers stormed the
village and set the houses ablaze and carried off the children. . . .
In the *ŭlch'uk* year, in the beautiful days after my marriage, there
came a flood. The mountains crumbled, and under an uprooted
tree were scattered the bones of the old people who long ago were
dressed in new clothes and carried on backracks to Karang Valley
to be abandoned." Old Grandmother remembered everything.
Her head was crammed with a kaleidoscope of vignettes and
anecdotes, random and unconnected. People reckoned she was
more than a hundred by then.

Oblivious to the dying flame in the castor-oil lamp, Old
Grandmother put her eye back to the hole in the door. Young
Kwanhŭi was on the verge of slumber, and the night birds deep in
the mountain valley began calling. The tapping of a woodpecker
on a rotten trunk sounded like distant thunder. The night birds
always sang around dusk. The darkness thickened in time with
their calls, spreading melancholy like a dissolving dye along the
road and through the narrow alleys of the town. It was when
the calls died down that the bogeyman came around and darkness filled the town. It wasn't like that before all the people left,
when the whispers of grandmothers warning the young ones who
were crying—"Sssh, the bogeyman's here!"—and the lamplight

that speckled the tightly shut windows were enough to keep the
bogeyman at bay. With dogs baring their teeth and snarling beneath verandas, the bogeyman would hover beyond the fence
until dawn and its magnificent morning star drove him back
whence he had come. But now he could lurk in any of the abandoned houses, climbing the low mud walls and penetrating the
decomposing roof thatch, no longer intimidated by the dawn. It
was the bogeyman who was responsible for the hollow tolling of
the bronze bell in the pavilion, who scattered the limpid sunshine
lingering after a passing shower, who shook the stalk of a radiant
sunflower that was big as a brass plate. He might be the wind, the
water, the darkness, a sound from an unknown source. He might
be the gigantic shadow of Old Grandmother bobbing on the wall,
and finally the chilling hand that swept over Kwanhŭi, who was
too tense to utter a word.

Already by then Kwanhŭi's grandfather was a fanatic about
water witching. Three years before liberation from Japanese colonial rule, Kwanhŭi's parents had gone into hiding, leaving five-
year-old Kwanhŭi behind. Their disappearance prompted the local constabulary to summon Kwanhŭi's grandfather from time to
time, and after emerging half dead from one such visit, he went to
the township's Catholic church and began learning from a French
missionary how to divine for water. The most learned person in
the village, he often lamented, "What's a man supposed to do in
a world like this?" When this priest reached his sabbatical year
and was preparing to return to his homeland, he impressed upon
his charge the importance of using the newly gained knowledge
while it was still fresh in mind. And that was how Kwanhŭi's grandfather became the one and only water witcher in the area. "At first
glance," he would say, "the ground doesn't look different from any
other. But there's a steady supply of water flowing beneath the surface, and if its course is altered by human hand, that's no good."
Holding a forked willow branch by its two prongs, he would bend
close to the ground and move ever so carefully, as if taking the

earth's pulse, and at the right place the prongs would dip toward
the ground as if to sink roots. He would then drive a stick into the
ground to mark the spot, and if you were to dig a hole there, water would gush from the sodden earth. "It's miraculous!" "What
magic!" people exclaimed. If you wanted to site a grave, locate a
well, find a pure spring for brewing, then Kwanhŭi's grandfather
was your man. One summer six-year-old Kwanhŭi tagged along
behind his grandfather up into the hills, and they came across a
freshly dug hole. "This is rotten ground," the old man said, indicating the turned-up red earth. Many were the stories about people
robbing graves in broad daylight—and the robbers were usually
Japanese colonists and their minions. Like dogs trying to pick up
a scent, they would examine a flat expanse offering no visible evi-
dence of burial mounds and set to with their shovels, after making certain they weren't being observed. Within half a day they'd
be turning up dishes, jars, knives, and whatnot. Was it then that
his grandfather had been captivated by visions of all the objects
that lay undiscovered in graves and other places underground?
Kwanhŭi and his grandfather had filled in the hole, but by now it
was more a rat hole than a grave. Every time they stamped down
the soil their feet left an indentation. Kwanhŭi didn't understand
what his grandfather meant by "dead earth" and "rotten ground"
until much later, when he himself robbed an old burial mound.
When he drove in the stakes, the hard ground seemed to rear up
like a wounded animal, and when with mixed pride and anxiety
he located the undefiled opening, he felt as if he were awakening
from a thousand-year dream in which he had walked down a passage to a tomb and visited the underworld. Closed up until that
moment, the burial mound was like a virgin.

"What does it mean to be human?" Kwanhŭi murmured,
eyes closed, repeating a question the pharmacist had asked. His
grandfather had provided an answer, he now realized. "Look—
mankind," he had said to Kwanhŭi as they stood before the gaping, despoiled grave, indicating the tombstone and a skeleton

with dirt-filled eye sockets. What was the difference between living life and knowing life?

As always in summer, the ferry dock was thronged with people bound for Hamyŏn Island. Their destination seemed so close, but the passengers had to expect a long wait. "Why can't they put in a bridge instead of making us stand in line for the boat?" was the common gripe.

Dust rose from the poplars that bordered the island, and through the haze you could make out figures in yellow hard hats as well as bulldozers leveling the ground. The island was indeed being developed into an amusement park. Yŏngjo propped his bicycle near the bow of the ferry and kept rubbing his eyes at the sight of the approaching land mass—it was as if the island rather than the boat were undulating in the swells of the river. In less than twenty minutes the ferry had arrived. Weaving his away among couples laden with huge rucksacks, ready to spend a night under the stars, Yŏngjo walked his bicycle ashore.

Above the terminal, in a field blocked off by red plastic ribbon, young people in sun visors and white cotton gloves were picking rocks out of the ground. HYANGDO COLLEGE ARCHAEOLOGICAL DIG, read a sign staked at the edge of the field. Yŏngjo walked his bicycle past the sign and turned onto a dirt road that went along the river. He had been here with his class on a picnic and field trip. Hamyŏn Island, their teacher explained, contained artifacts from prehistoric times as well as mud dugouts, dolmens, and a kind of large, flat stone. The dolmens and flat stones marked the graves of those who had lived in the dugouts thousands of years ago, fashioning combware pottery and using hot coals for protection against the cold, the dark, and wild animals. Listening to the teacher, the students had peered into the dugouts, only to retreat with cries of disgust at the dog poop and the odor of urine. And now puppies and children from the nearby village were romping on the dolmens while farmers harvested the ripe golden barley.

Yŏngjo had returned from some of his long bicycle trips so sore he dreamed his legs had turned to stone. But sore legs didn't stop him from planning to set out the next time on a sturdy new bicycle, packing a rucksack with flashlight, camera, and binoculars, and go farther than he ever had before. On these trips he pedaled as hard as he could, the sensation of speed giving him the bittersweet feeling that he was a child of the wind.

At the far end of the island, a woman suddenly appeared, running toward him. Braking to avoid her, he lurched toward a scallion patch beside the road and tumbled to the ground. The woman kept running, her long tresses scattering behind her in the breeze—no apology, no look back. Yŏngjo could see why. A shaggy man was running after her, shouting "Bitch! You bitch!" Furious, Yŏngjo massaged his side where he had landed on the rocky ground. The two figures receding in the distance looked like children playing tag. All he could hear were the man's curses as he stumbled barefoot after the woman. The woman ran for dear life, but would stop to smoothe her hair and straighten her clothing; and when the man came within range, would run off again. It was as if the woman felt obliged to play along with "it" in order to make the game of tag fun for him.

Yŏngjo brushed off his clothes and got to his feet. Dropping down on foot toward the river, he saw an open tent pitched on a marshy sand bar. Behind a crudely lettered tin sign advertising hotpot potato pancakes, and *soju* sat two old women. They looked like something out of a still life as they spooned into *ch'amoe* melons.

"Usually she's as good a girl as you'd want. But when liquor gets into her she's bad to the bone."

"Can't you give her something?" asked the other woman.

"Oh, I've tried. I've fed her shit water, made her eat mashed-up bones—people's bones, mind you. The only thing that's left is poison. You know, it's criminal to make a soul live as long as I have."

"How old are you, anyway?"

"Can you guess? . . . I'm seventy-seven."

"Well, I declare—that makes you my little sister! I'm eighty-one."

The running woman disappeared behind a rise next to a barley field. When again she came into sight, she seemed to stumble on the hem of her skirt and fll in a heap to the ground. The hairy man finally caught up with her and in no time was swinging her around by the hair. "Let me go!" the woman screeched. And then she squirmed loose and fled once more.

"Goodness, if they keep that up someone's going to get hurt. Hadn't you better stop them?" said the older woman.

"Best leave them alone. What could I do, anyway? They'll wear themselves out and sleep it off, and then they'll be all right. . . . We used to be fire-field farmers, but we got flooded out and here we are. Up in the hills we lived like bandits, down here we catch fish from a tiny boat—some life, eh? I'm telling you this because it makes me so mad. We catch enough fish to get by on, thanks to the Buddhists—they buy the fish, then come here to set them free."

"Our blessed ancestors were connected with carp somehow, so each generation's supposed to make the next one promise not to eat it."

"Well, we go to the temple on Buddha's birthday, and here we are selling fish. I don't feel righteous about the fish, but I'll die like everyone else and then I'll be food for the insects."

"So you came down here from the hill country?"

"We surely did. From Ant'ae, yonder side of those mountains there. When it got flooded out, a lot of folks left for the city. But we came here because it's close to home. . . . That one there," she said, indicating the running woman, "she's my youngest—I had nine of 'em, and six died off."

The two women finished their melons and flung the shriveled, paper-thin skins aside, then began to nibble at tomatoes, their murmured conversation continuing even as the hotpot threatened to overflow the shallow pot on the kerosene stove. Spoons and pot lid lay scattered on the sand. An array of boiled eggs caught Yŏngjo's eye, momentarily tempting him before he continued down to the river. The women didn't seem to have noticed him.

Yŏngjo removed socks and shoes, shook the dirt from his shoes, dipped his feet into the water, then stripped down to his underpants and went in the rest of the way. The chill of the water gave him a feverish thrill as his hair stood on end. But soon the water felt gentle and Yŏngjo relaxed. Was the initial coldness from him being in a foreign element, or was it from the water reacting to him? Finally the water felt accommodating enough for him to duck his head under. The slippery weeds growing from the river bottom licked at his feet; passing fish tapped at the fleshy insides of his thighs. If he kept his eyes open and remained still, he could make out the dark backs of carp floating calmly in the murky water like miniature submarines.

"Hey, sonny, watch where you're going! It gets deep over there!" shouted a fisherman in a straw hat sitting on the bank.

Yŏngjo surfaced, grinned, then waved to dismiss the man's concerns. The only way he could describe the sensation of dipping himself in the river was that he felt like a transparent glass tube filling with water. Planting his feet on the smooth, rounded stones of the river bottom, he looked down and saw a short, stubby body surrounded by a milky mass of tiny bubbles along with a pair of underpants, thin and puffed up like a jellyfish, the refraction of the sunlight making them seem to come alive. They looked comical.

Floating like a fish in warm water is what you did in the womb. Swimming is a forgotten memory of your mother's womb, a lost faculty. Ducking under the surface and bringing yourself to rest in the water is an exercise that revives memories. Words Yŏngjo had read. He wondered what memories he had lost when he emerged from his mother's belly, crying in anguish.

Yŏngjo had been taught to swim by his father—it was in first grade, as he recalled. He remembered wailing in terror after his father undressed him and pushed him playfully into the water. "Hey, I thought you were a big boy." His father's hands were merciless. But maybe it wasn't the water that had terrified him as much as those hands that had pushed his head down, hands whose strength was like a magnetic field, blind and ungovernable even by the man himself. *Father's trying to kill me.* Yŏngjo's arms and legs had flailed about, and he kept taking in mouthfuls of water. To this day Yŏngjo had never seen his father naked. When he was too old to go with his mother to the women's section of the public baths, she had urged his father to take him along. But his father hadn't responded, had continued to visit the baths by himself. Was he afraid to remove his clothes in front of his own son? his mother had joked. His father's retort was cryptic: "By the time I was his age, I'd inherited the family line."

"Sonny, you better come out!" the fisherman shouted again. "You're going to get your pecker bitten off." Wondering if there was a drop-off or an eddy nearby, Yŏngjo slowly swam to shore and emerged from the water.

The man was trying to remove a turtle from his hook. He muttered between clenched teeth, gave the approaching Yŏngjo a glance, then cut the hook from his line. "They'll carry it around inside them till they die—tough bastards. If you're not careful, they'll bite off your finger. This is the fourth one I've happened across today."

"Is it a soft-shell or a hard-shell?" Yŏngjo asked. The turtle was so cunning—it continued to play dead even when freed from the line. Its neck and legs were out of sight within the sturdy shell, which was about as big as your two palms side by side.

"Can't you tell from the looks of it? It's a hard-shell. With the soft-shells at least you can drink their blood, but these hard-shells are worthless—all they do is swallow hooks. Last time I was here some Buddhists were out—noisy bunch—and they put this fellow and some others back in the water."

Yŏngjo noticed a small rowboat drifting slowly down the river. The three occupants—a woman in traditional dress and two men—were sprinkling something into the water. Gazing at the surface of the river, they sprinkled slowly, a fistful at a time, as if sowing seed.

"No luck today." The fisherman got up, folded his chair, and gathered an empty basket, a bait can, and the rest of his fishing gear. Yŏngjo watched the turtle trundle clumsily toward the water. "You like pets? Go ahead and take him home. Keep him in a fishbowl and he won't die on you. But be careful, or else he'll bite off your fingers. And don't go in the water again. It's full of those critters, and I'm telling you, they'll chomp your pecker off."

As Yŏngjo reached for the turtle, intending to lift it by its hind leg as the fisherman had suggested, he groaned in spite of himself. The ragged cut in his palm from the sharp edge of the magnifying glass that afternoon had opened, the river water having softened the scab. The blood oozing out was so bright.

Yŏngjo made a fist to stop the bleeding, moved the turtle back away from the water and built a sand bank around it, then flopped down nearby. Wisps of cloud floated low in the sky. Far away was an army base and a grove of poplars. Where could that UFO in his dream have landed? According to witnesses, UFOs left a charred mark where they landed. Yŏngjo heard a gentle rustling near his ear. Thirsty, anxious, drawn by instinct toward water, the sand-covered turtle was trying to break through the sand bank.

The sun was low in the sky. Yŏngjo tried in vain to brush off the sand that had stuck to his skin and dried. The rowboat had returned to the opposite bank, and the two men were helping the woman ashore.

Yŏngjo walked his clattering bicycle up from the riverside, wondering why it felt so damn heavy now. Only one of the two old women was in sight, nodding off inside the tent, flyswatter in hand. The hairy man was asleep on a makeshift wooden bed, breathing heavily. The woman he had chased was cleaning fish. Her face wore an indifferent look.

Six o'clock arrived and Kwanhŭi closed up shop. He usually stayed open till nine, but there wouldn't be much business tonight.

Home was three bus stops away, but he wasn't in a hurry and had to drop by the pharmaceutical supply store, so he decided to walk. Many of the shops along the avenue were shut, with their security doors, some in sections and some pulled down, already in place. The merchants must have arranged among themselves to close early.

The crowds grew the closer he got to downtown. On this sultry summer evening, people from all over the new city were gathering for the festivities. Lanterns covered with sheer fabric in red and indigo blue hung like sleeves from the trees lining the street. A man with a banner draped over his shoulder—ONWARD TO THE THIRD MILLENNIUM—was distributing leaflets. Kwanhŭi glanced at the one he was given: "Our City of Unyang in the Third Millennium and the Major Achievements of the Fifth Republic. . . ."

At the side of the street, in front of a bus serving as a blood bank, a young nurse was parroting an appeal over a loudspeaker: "Share your blood and help save precious life." Kwanhŭi was skeptical. What was the connection between sharing his blood—which he interpreted as his flesh and blood—and saving a life? Then he nodded, laughing at his obtuseness. The young woman wasn't speaking figuratively; she was merely asking people to give blood. Next to the nurse was a desk where staffers at a family-planning organization were asking couples to pledge to have only one child, whether a boy or a girl, and then be sterilized in order to provide a happier, more stable future for their child. The pharmaceutical supply store was only a bus stop away from his shop, but already Kwanhŭi was feeling worn down from the jostling of the crowd. More tedious still was the clamorous shouting issuing from loudspeakers.

Arriving at his destination, Kwanhŭi purchased a couple of pounds of sulfa powder. What next? In spite of the red clusters on the distant horizon heralding the approach of evening, wasn't it too early for the fireworks Inja wanted to see? A girls' marching band paraded down the traffic-cleared avenue. Kwanhŭi recognized "The Ballad of the Han River," "When the Saints Go Marching In," and "Arirang." Then came a procession of black sedans with a police motorcycle escort. Midway up Yangsu Mountain, the occupants of the cars—a group of men in traditional white topcoats—would perform a ceremony marking the site of the ancient fortress town.

A TV van drove by, cameras recording the scene—the large banners reading DILIGENCE, SELF-RELIANCE, COOPERATION, the flock of doves released from City Hall, the lanterns hanging from the trees, the massing throng. A young man with an armband bearing a newspaper logo approached a family standing next to Kwanhŭi.

"Could you give us your thoughts on today's events?"

"I think it's a very meaningful day," the father responded. "It makes me proud to be part of a rich and ancient culture, and I feel more deeply than ever the sublime spirit of our ancestors who lived in this area so long ago. So I brought the wife and children to see it all. Today's a chapter in the book of life."

The man had a smooth delivery and kept the microphone at an appropriate distance as he spoke. Kwanhŭi wondered if he'd practiced for the occasion.

The crowd continued to swell. Faces familiar and unfamiliar approached Kwanhŭi like close-ups on a movie screen, then merged and disappeared. Was this what a 3-D movie was like? Dizzy, almost queasy, he leaned against a tree, but its support offered no relief from his sensation of being sucked into the procession and then regurgitated. Where had this peculiar involution come from? People who believed in life after death said they often dreamed of seeing their souls in limbo, being ushered in an uncertain direction on a crowded thoroughfare.

Kwanhŭi saw children holding their parents' hands and children playing toy trumpets. And where there were children, there also were street vendors shouldering florid displays of balloons and rattles and colorful plastic toys. Other children were riding the shoulders of grownups, giggling in delight, their parents' future incarnate, but to Kwanhŭi the footsteps of the parents amid the pressing throng seemed somehow desperate, like those of a column of refugees, as if the adults were being pursued by some inscrutable entity.

The clock on the City Hall clock tower read 7:10. Inja was probably setting out dinner and waiting for him.

A man with shaggy hair and a long beard, wearing a shirt of coarse fabric, approached Kwanhŭi like an old friend and took his hand. Perplexed, Kwanhŭi started to search his memory, but the man brought him up short.

"Have you been saved?" he boomed, looking Kwanhŭi straight in the eye.

Kwanhŭi produced an awkward smile and tried discreetly to free his hand, but instead found it more firmly grasped. Those occupied with more prosaic matters gave Kwanhŭi a glance both amused and sympathetic before hastening by.

"Have you accepted the Lord as your savior? Have you received the promise of eternal life?"

When Kwanhŭi didn't reply to this second attempt, the man brusquely released his hand and turned to the crowd. "Make this rock speak," he said angrily, and spat.

The blessing of living forever, the curse of never being able to die. There was no date of death to be observed for Kwanhŭi's grandfather because no one knew when he had died. In contrast, when Old Grandmother had died—it was after the villagers who had fled at the outbreak of the war returned to their homes and she no longer had anything to do or anyone to wait for—she came back as a spirit in the palanquin that returned her memorial tablet to the family after her burial. The winter after she died, Kwanhŭi's parents finally returned. "It's a good world we live in now—let's move to the city," they said to Kwanhŭi's grandfather. "We're so busy, and there's much work we have to do." But the old man was consumed as always with water witching. There were no more requests for siting wells and burial mounds, so he'd been wandering the hills and fields with his forked willow stick, feeling for the subterranean veins of water. "You all go first and I'll catch a train next week," he replied with characteristic stubbornness. And so Kwanhŭi left with his parents in a jeep. They arrived in a charred, bombed-out city. A week later, Kwanhŭi was at the train station waiting for his grandfather in the rain. It was a midwinter rain, falling thick as twine. His parents had rented a house untouched by all the bombs. The train station was just across the street, but they sent Kwanhŭi instead of going themselves—as they had said, they were so busy. One room they had set aside for living quarters, and in the remaining two they drafted documents with their "comrades" and questioned different people every day. Kwanhŭi waited all day for his grandfather, and around dinnertime the old man arrived. He had with him his prized possession—the willow stick. "Grandfather, all's that's left here are the ruins of houses—how can you find water?" His grandfather bent toward the ground with the willow stick, then straightened with a smile. "Water flows everywhere under the ground—you can count on it." Kwanhŭi led the way to their house, his grandfather close behind, but in the time it took him to reach inside the gate and unlatch it, the old man disappeared. Kwanhŭi couldn't explain it: there was no other alley his grandfather could have slipped out of, no building where he could have hidden. But there was no trace of him—nothing in the alley except the cold rain and the gathering dusk.

Kwanhŭi's parents had left home before he ever knew their faces, and now, at age twelve, he felt awkward with them and had always to be careful. But then the war situation changed and the bombing intensified, and again Kwanhŭi's parents left. His mother was a strapping woman, rough-and-ready like a man, but as she was led to a jeep with her comrades, she burst into tears. At age twelve Kwanhŭi was all grown up, as the adults would say, and had left the ancestral village. But every night he slept curled up, hands clutched to his groin, and every night the bogeyman came. . . .

Kwanhŭi, using his handkerchief, was trying to get rid of the stickiness from the man's hand when across the street the human wave parted to reveal Yŏngjo, working his way along with difficulty. He had an adult's bicycle with a carrying rack, and it looked too big and heavy for him. Kwanhŭi reached out, intending to call him, but his hand dropped limply to his side. There was something about those eyes lowered in defiance beneath the coarse black hair. The next instant Kwanhŭi saw reflected in Yŏngjo's face both his wife's face and the face of another, vague and unfamiliar. Those arched eyebrows and the firm bones of the chin were not his wife's. But then whose face was it that he saw whenever he encountered his son, an opaque countenance that masked that of Yŏngjo? And why was he ever more fearful of his son growing up?

As Kwanhŭi stared at his son, the boy's form blended into the sea of people, receded, disappeared. Pain shot through Kwanhŭi's temples, and the armpit in which he had wedged the packet of sulfa powder cramped up. Was he that tired?

The twilight deepened and dusk set in. Before Kwanhŭi knew it, blue and red light had begun to seep from the cloth-covered lanterns. He ought to be going home and getting some rest. Or maybe he should go back to the shop. Tomorrow a customer would be coming to pick up some items. Among Kwanhŭi's stock were knives, incense burners, candlesticks, and other metallic objects. By soaking them in a solution containing sulfa powder, he could dull their bright shine and tarnish them, even the new items. And when he removed them from the solution a patina would have formed. Wipe them with a dry towel and scrub them with a wire brush (there were other methods as well), and you could create the corroded appearance of objects entombed for a thousand years.

The people were massing like packs of rats. Where were they going? Toward a void embedded in time, the last strand in a historical chronicle? Toward the missing links of a chain? Toward a dark cave? Listless, Kwanhŭi let himself be eased along.

The last sliver of sun disappeared below the crown of the persimmon tree, clotting the sky crimson.

Dusk arrived, but not Kwanhŭi and Yŏngjo. Waiting for them, Inja tried to gather her wits by sweeping the bare courtyard. That task finished, she sat down just inside the gate.

The dusk deepened and the tree grew darker, its outline more distinct. Yŏngjo was always climbing that tree—he liked to sit on one of the branches and whistle. She could scold him forever, citing the adage that there's no medicine to cure one who falls from a persimmon tree, but it went in one ear and out the other. From his eyes full of dissatisfaction and his polite behavior, she and only she could see the questions he had for her. The longer his outings, the more firmly rooted her anxiety. She could almost see feelers sprouting from his head. Perhaps someday he would leave for the faint but certain home from which his feelers had directed him here—would leave in response to an unseen hand beckoning him, a hand that would retreat one step for every step he took toward it.

The houses on either side showed no ray of light. Their occupants wouldn't return till late that night, after the fireworks were over. Inja released a long sigh, as if by doing so she might gain an appreciative ear, then covered her face.

Was Kwanhŭi on his way home just then? It seemed he had forgotten their plan to watch the fireworks. She had finished preparing dinner some time ago.

Inja crossed the dark yard and went inside. In the kitchen, feeling forlorn, she stood and ate the now cold rice. Lingering there, she poured a gourdful of water onto the concrete floor, she couldn't have explained why. The water choked and gurgled down the drain, and for a moment the odor of filth that always came from there seemed to ease.

The chickens began screeching, the sound all the more strange and disturbing because of the surrounding quiet. A weasel or a rat must have gotten into the coop. Inja found the flashlight and hurried out back.

Sure enough, the section of the coop she'd temporarily secured that morning had come loose and white feathers were scattered all around; of their owner, only the echoes of its screeching remained. A weasel must have made off with it.

Into the henhouse she went. There was almost no light, but Inja knew her way around and usually didn't bother with the flashlight. Now she could hear the frightened chickens skittering about and crowding in a corner, their breathing quick and harsh. She turned on the flashlight and played it about. A hen was missing—there should have been five. Inja squatted and fixed her light on the rooster. The bird was frightened, but the more it tried to escape, the more Inja focused the flashlight on it. The rooster's round eyes with their yellowish border had a vapid glint that startled her.

Inja approached slowly and picked up the rooster. For an instant she felt it claw the dirt and try to stand its ground, but when she put her hands under the bird's wings their warmth seemed to calm it. She could feel the beating of the rooster's heart, racing incredibly fast, as she took it to the kitchen.

She set the rooster on the kitchen floor, filled a pot with water, and lit the kerosene stove. For a moment the rooster seemed confused in this unfamiliar lighted environment, but in no time it began pecking nonchalantly at the rice leavings surrounding the drain. Inja looked intently at the rooster's haughty, showy strut, at its unreserved gluttony. What followed didn't take long. She sharpened her dull kitchen knife against an earthenware jar, stooped down, and carefully took the rooster in her arm. She gathered its wings under her left foot and stroked the bird's throat muscles. The delicate articulation of the neck bones was swollen, as was the craw containing the undigested food the rooster had pecked so greedily. Its claws scratched weakly at the cement floor. Inja separated the down on the bird's neck and drew the knife blade across the tough skin. There was only a dribble of blood. Inja went back to the jar and put a new edge on the knife. The rooster lifted its bleeding neck, took a few unsteady hops, and, yielding to temptation, resumed pecking at the remnants of rice.

The water on the stove began to hiss. Inja washed the shallow pot beside it after emptying the previous day's leftover chicken, which had begun rotting in the heat with a noisome odor.

Again she put the blade to the rooster's neck, and this time the bird's reddish-black comb stood straight up, its eyes changed from gray to colors of alarm and fright—emerald green and salmon—and it began blinking nonstop. The boiling water hissed urgently, and amid the steam Inja, a mass of sweat, gently fondled the rooster. "Come on now, just a little more," she whispered as pressed down on the knife blade. Every spasm of the animal's warm body drew more red speckles like a heat rash on Inja's bare forearms and neck. The sensation of the blade's keen steel felt like an inferno. From this heat came a sharp vibration and then an explosion, and with a shrill cry Inja relaxed the wrist of her knife hand. The rooster's neck and breast were soaked with crimson, but the antiquated bird, the rhythm of its life long since broken down, did not die easily. Breath spewed in bursts from its limp, open beak, and its feeble claws scrabbled uselessly at the floor. Inja was beginning to wonder if she'd have to stay up all night waiting for the rooster to die, but then she realized how foolish was this notion. For now there was only a cruel order to what had separated into flesh, bones, and worthless, sallow-colored fat.

Inja went out to the yard, her alertness and concentration spent. Arms folded across her chest, she looked up at the sky, feeling as if she were recovering from an illness. The neighborhood was dark, but from the direction of the river came the faint popping of firecrackers, along with a small dot of light shooting through the air like an arrow. And then an incomprehensible roar spread through the sky. Who was it? And then she knew. It was the man who had come one spring day when Kwanhŭi was away and she was taking a nap, a man to whom she had been forced to yield—it had been like a dream. Her husband had returned after looking in burial mounds for rusty knives and then her boy had come to term, tearing her uterus and breaking her heart before emerging into the world. Another round of fireworks shot up from the riverside, rending the gloom before scattering to the accompaniment of shouts, laments, sobs, lust, and confusion.

The fireworks blossomed into garish patterns in the dark sky while flower lanterns, blooming like lotus fronds, floated downstream. The children who had been blowing toy horns and flying colored balloons were asleep, food for the swarms of mosquitoes and gnats. The grownups looked out at the dark river—looking with faces darker than the surface of the water at the river flowing from distant antiquity and bearing oil-burning flower lanterns. Those lanterns too would arrive somewhere, before the roosters crowed, before the morning star lit up.

LAKE P'ARO

It was calm as a vessel of water, the lake that lay beyond the steep drop-off. Leaves falling from mountains of crimson plenitude scattered like confetti onto its dark blue surface. As Hyesun watched the lake—Soyang Lake—sink farther in the distance, the bus climbed the mountainside road, the driver downshifting, and she noticed a ringing in her ears. And then the bus lurched around a curve, awakening Kim, who was dozing beside her, head buried in his chest. He heaved a prodigious yawn, then retrieved his porkpie hat from the floor and put it back on. Reaching inside his windbreaker, he fumbled first in his shirt pocket, then in his jacket pockets, and finally, with a downcast look, produced a container of breath mints resembling tiny ball bearings and popped a few into his mouth. His eyes met Hyesun's and he smiled sheepishly—withdrawal symptoms.

Since early that morning, when they had met at the bus station, faces damp from the fog, he had been chewing gum, cracking his knuckles, and fussing with his hands, hands accustomed to holding a cigarette. Hyesun had wanted to offer some advice she'd come across in the newspaper: whenever you feel the urge, drink a glass of cold water—it helps wash out the nicotine that's settled in your bones. Of course, nicotine wasn't the only thing water could flush from the body.

Hyesun was something of an expert about water's cleansing properties, having used it for a time as a sleep aid. The water supply had a high lime content, so she bottled the water and let the lime settle before drinking. If it came back up and made her gag, she'd take a pinch of salt. The briny taste brought relief and her worries faded—no longer in the empty bottle but instead inside her, she could almost hear the limpid sound of flowing water. If she drank too much of it, her face the next morning would be puffy beyond recognition. She wondered about the sense of urgency that had compelled her time and again to empty and cleanse herself with water and to consume it with salt. Was she seeking absolution?

The bus was bound for rural Yanggu, and because of the early hour there were less than half a dozen passengers. Once in a great while there appeared a settlement nestled into the mountainside. And at intervals along the road stood curious-looking structures. To Hyesun they had the shape of a lookout platform in a melon field, only they were coated with tar.

"The army uses them for emergency flares," explained Kim, now wide awake. "We're on a military route."

Used them how? Hyesun wondered. To search out enemy planes? Did that mean the structures themselves were set aflame, to serve as a light source or a kind of signal?

"Takes longer than I thought," Kim muttered. "You must be bored."

Hyesun smiled, shaking her head. "Not at all. I'm enjoying the ride . . . and what a surprise to see the leaves turning."

She had decided to visit Lake P'aro after coming across an article in a local newspaper describing a stratum of prehistoric artifacts turned up when the lake was partly drained during foundation work on the new Peace Dam. Accompanying the article was a black-and-white photograph of the exposed lake bottom with a ridge of distant mountains in the background. What had captured her attention in this bleak expanse was a vague, abstract feeling that she could only describe as an "empty fullness." An impression perhaps strengthened by a visit long before with her husband, Pyŏng'ŏn. VALUABLE RESOURCE FOR STUDYING ANCIENT HISTORY; SHEDDING NEW LIGHT ON THE ORIGINS OF HAN RIVER CULTURE; LARGEST OLD STONE AGE SITE IN NATION. Such headlines reflected the interest generated among academics and journalists. But Hyesun's quest was unrelated to these concerns. She had her own reasons for coming here.

Kim was an old friend of Pyŏng'ŏn and something of a folk historian. He made traditional frames for artwork and also dealt in freshwater-polished stones. Hyesun had dropped by his shop the previous week to order a frame for a painting her children in America had sent her. The painting bore the title "Our Dear Mom" and a message: "Please come back before winter. We wanted to paint your face from memory but ended up having to use a photo." When Kim told her he had been thinking of visiting Lake P'aro to look for stones, Hyesun had asked if she could join him.

The bus completed its mountainside traverse and pulled up at a terminal in a small town. Two passengers boarded. The bus driver poked his head out the window and called out to the girl in the ticket booth: "Go find me some painkiller—I've got a tooth that's killing me. And grab me a cup of coffee while you're at it."

From the bus Hyesun and Kim had an open view of a street lined with traditional tile-roof dwellings, and beyond them a broad expanse of fields.

Kim indicated a three-story granite tower close by.

"Mid-Koryŏ, I'll bet. Provincial cultural asset number, let's see . . . oh, I forget."

"It must have belonged to a good-sized Buddhist temple."

Hyesun's knowledge of towers had come from her grade school readers. Tabo Tower epitomized feminine beauty, and Sŏkka Tower masculine beauty; that's how one of them had expressed it. But as far as she was concerned, this particular tower was undistinguished.

"Last weekend I went to Unju Temple," said Kim. "It has a reclining Buddha carved in an outcrop—what a sight! You know, when people start calling a fist-sized rock a Buddha, then you believe it. I guess seeing is believing. And when they call a little pile of rocks a tower, then you believe that too. It's almost like Koreans express their sentiments or their disposition through habits—piling up rocks, for example. Imagine you're a wayfarer and you've just arrived at a pass. You pick up a rock, and then what? You set it on top of another rock and make a wish. But that wish lasts only a moment, and then it becomes a tower; it becomes Buddha. On my way back from Unju Temple I saw some Buddhas carved in rock walls—quite a few of that type down south. Back in the old days, people believed the Buddha inhabited any number of large rock walls, so the act of carving his likeness in the rock in effect eliminated those parts of the wall that concealed the Buddha. Which means the person hired to do the carving wouldn't have been a stonemason of great talent and skill—he would have been a Buddhist of such perception and purity of belief that he could see the Buddha dwelling in stone."

Were all autodidacts as glib and ready to show off as Kim? Hyesun asked herself. Then again, maybe Kim felt awkward traveling with her. Or maybe his behavior was a side effect of his attempt to quit smoking. The fumbling in pockets, the stroking of lips, the constant hand movements, the ceaseless chatter—all dictated by nerves on edge.

Hyesun knew the feeling—a compulsion to ramble on, followed by a sensation of utter emptiness. In her experience, unspoken words and all that they signified would ossify in this emptiness, making her realize all too miserably how much her own thoughts, her own world, was governed by words. She imagined her mouth forever widened in a desire to speak, her ears perking up at a breath of air, her eyes constantly flashing with suspicion. That is, it wasn't the words themselves that were hardening in the gray matter of her brain, but rather all the things they symbolized, all the dreams, all the ardent desires.

The bus driver kept glancing at the street and grimacing. The bus had sat idling more than ten minutes, but none of the passengers complained. Hyesun rose.

"Where are you going?" the driver grunted. "We're leaving."

"I need some fresh air—I'll be right back."

The driver shut up. For all he knew, his passenger needed to use the toilet.

Outside, the late-autumn sun wasn't as warm as it had looked through the bus window. Its rays shimmered with a delicate light like a shard of transparent glass, and Hyesun could feel them come to rest on her eyelids. That the bright sunshine left her feeling chilled but clear-headed, as if it bore columns of frost, was it a lingering result of the fog that had risen from every depression along the serpentine mountain road and made all shapes— mountains, road, trees—suddenly vanish?

The tower stood alone, no sign to identify it as mid-Koryŏ or as a provincial cultural asset. Behind it was an undeveloped lot with the kind of posts you might see for hitching stock at a cattle market. The shops that lined the road on both sides of the tower fronted decrepit old houses in the traditional style. The front and side walls, unable to bear the weight of their roofs—or was it the weight of time?—had been torn out and replaced with large sliding doors. The shop signs—CONVENIENCE STORE, GROCERY—were the only modern feature. Otherwise, the shops looked just as outmoded as the marketplace Hyesun remembered from her family's refugee days during the war. The sundries shop, the purveyor of Chinese medicine, the modest inn, the Chinese restaurant, and the dingy granite tower merged agreeably with this tableau from Hyesun's memory and its associated images of rain, wind, sunlight, and time as inert as sodden ash.

There had been a period when Hyesun would walk out into the morning, rubbing her sleepy eyes—the newly dawning morning that had repeated itself unchanging since the day of her birth—to find a world of sound and light. *I want to scream, let me scream!* her blood harangued her as it surged through her arteries and veins, and she felt a scream actually would burst forth from her the way it did from her children. Venturing outside like this was surely the way to the world of the future. But this was before she had arrived at the numerous tomorrows she'd awaited. And now she hesitated to equate the new morning she welcomed, the world outside her door, with the future. Before going to sleep she would grit her teeth, hoping for a night devoid of dreams, fake solace, and false compassion, and the next morning her temples ached miserably from the effort.

The first task Hyesun had set for herself upon returning from her four years in America late the previous spring was to take her picture in an instant-photo booth at a subway station in Seoul. Not that she needed the photo. To her eyes, the embarrassment on the faces of those who lifted the curtain and emerged from the booth bespoke unemployment, poverty, the demands of a pressing life, vagrancy. This prejudice of hers felt odd. It was like when she saw someone glued to a pay telephone, feeding coin after coin into the slot and making call after call. Hapless they were, people trying to anchor themselves, awaiting a message, a person, a job; buying a newspaper and scouring the help-wanted ads; attaching the yield of the fast-photo booth to the resumé ever present in an inner pocket; anxiously awaiting the postman for a reply, finally to receive the plain yellow business envelope containing a courteous rejection letter.

Hyesun had been aware of the glances of passersby as she entered the booth. She felt an awkward twinge, like when she had to resort to a public toilet. She drew the plastic curtain, shielding the upper part of her body, and turned to face the dark surface of the mirror. Following the instructions, she rotated the seat, sat down squarely, and adjusted herself so that the top of her head was exactly at the level of the red line above the mirror. She fed 2,500 *wŏn* in coins into the slot and after setting her expression, fixed her gaze on the lips visible in the mirror. There would be two flashes in the space of four seconds. And finally a suggestion that seemed helpful: the subject should pose differently for each shot. So, why not look impish for the second photo? No one was watching. She felt silly making these adjustments, only to wait expectantly for the smile in the mirror to be developed into a photograph, but she went ahead and pressed the button. For the first photo she produced a meek smile; for the second she bared her teeth and glared fiercely. And afterward she waited patiently for the required three minutes and fifty seconds until the photographs slipped out of the machine. She let them dry. Her face looked swollen and its outlines were blurry. She had followed the instructions to the letter, but her hesitation was visible in the photos and it was obvious she was forcing the expressions.

Was it really necessary, this proof of her return? Into her billfold went two photos she wouldn't be needing anytime soon, and off she went to ride buses and subways around the city, like a good farmer surveying the land he would till. And then, like a solid citizen, she bought a newspaper, and, for luck, an Olympics lottery ticket. More variations on the theme of convincing herself she was drifting no longer. And yet she felt suspended in ambiguity, not yet recovered from jet lag. Was she postponing the inevitable, like a diver terrified of falling?

The girl from the ticket booth skittered up breathless to the bus. In her hand was a small white bag.

"You little twit!" shouted the driver. "It's going to be dark soon—what did you do, make that stuff yourself?"

"It's Sunday—what do you expect? I had to go to the other end of town to find a place that was open," she huffed, handing him the medicine and a paper cup.

"It left ten minutes ago," said the woman in the ticket booth at the Yanggu bus terminal.

When was the next bus? Hyesun and Kim asked in unison, showing their frustration.

The woman gestured with her chin toward the schedule posted on the wall.

There were two departures a day for Wŏlmyŏng-ni, one in the morning and one in the afternoon. The afternoon departure, at 3 p.m., was the bus company's token effort to cater to hill dwellers wishing to come to town, see to their business, and return home without having to spend all day there.

On this short autumn day Hyesun and Kim didn't want to wait for the afternoon bus. They also had to consider the return trip. The creation of Lake P'aro, resulting from the construction of the dam at Hwach'ŏn, had left the old highway underwater, so that Sangmuryong-ni, site of the ruins Kim and Hyesun wished to visit, remained inaccessible by road. The local people had been using the lake to reach most destinations, but boat travel was no longer possible now that Lake P'aro had been drained. Instead, Kim said, you could take the bus to Wŏlmyŏng-ni, where you left the main road and walked a couple of hours across the lakebed.

Over an early lunch of beef-broth soup, they decided to take a taxi. They began negotiating with an elderly cab driver, who grumbled that he'd have to wash his vehicle after a trip to that out-of-the-way place and it would probably be his luck to get stuck in the mud. Hyesun and Kim had to agree to a round-trip fare plus the cost of a car wash before the man would oblige.

Outside the town, habitations became infrequent, replaced by quonset huts bordered by cement walls and barbed wire. When an occasional convoy appeared, headlights shining, bearing banners that read EXERCISE or DRIVER TRAINING, the driver pulled off to the side of the road until the vehicles had passed.

"I didn't realize the area was so undeveloped," said Hyesun. "All you see are soldiers. . . ."

"Well, it's tense here," Kim sighed. "The area was recovered from the North during the war, and it's a border area. . . . It'd be different if we were unified. . . . Back in the old days, the paddies here produced such good rice it was served to the king. Now most of them are underwater."

They turned onto a narrow dirt road hidden from the highway by tall clumps of withering grass. The end of the drained lake came faintly into view below them.

"Look over there."

Hyesun's gaze followed Kim's hand. A line of trucks was moving through the valley at the far end of the lake, where it was fed by a shallow stream.

"Those trucks, you mean?"

"They're hauling gravel to the Peace Dam construction site. . . . No, what I meant are those rocks." Meaning an irregular line of huge stones jutting out of a pool of standing water as if they'd burst forth from a thick stratum of earth like a mythical serpent or a Paleozoic creature.

"Ah, the dolmens," Hyesun said, thinking of the universal longing for eternity that she considered the essence of religion.

"Given an area this size and the scale of those dolmens, there must have been a kingdom with a couple thousand people here."

"There were a lot of those rocks when I was a kid," the driver said, looking at Kim and Hyesun in the rearview mirror. "The grownups used to sit on 'em and take in the breeze after supper. We kids climbed on 'em year round. Now we got this hullabaloo about fantastic remains—tombs of prehistoric people, altars, and whatnot. All they were to me back then were humongous rocks. The elders used to tell us Granny Mago's son put 'em there to show everybody how strong he was. That was before the war. I'm trying to remember when they got buried—maybe when they put in this road. . . . What brings you folks to Sangmuryong-ni anyway, some kind of scientific research? Can't be fishing, seeing as how the water's pretty much gone. Must be something worth seeing if an outsider makes a point of coming here."

"We're looking for rocks."

"Rocks? You came here to study rocks?"

Kim merely chuckled.

The taxi crept down the slope. The occasional gaudy slate roof had vanished, and all they saw were the scattered mountains that ringed the broad expanse of the lakebed, looking like they would collapse under the weight of their scarlet foliage. The lake's high-water mark was a ragged line across their midsections, leaving the nether regions disfigured and the bases resembling layered rice cakes. At the bottom of the slope a paved road materialized, traversing the lakeside mountains. Before there was Lake P'aro, the driver explained, this road connected Yanggu with Hwach'ŏn. It was used by charcoal trucks and horse carriages during the Japanese period. Flanking the road and spaced at regular intervals were tree trunks that looked like ash-colored bones. "They chopped down those poplars before the area was flooded over. . . . See where it's built up over there? Those were dikes for the Hamch'un rice paddies—productive as hell, they were. . . . We had no objection to putting in the power plant, but then they had to go and cover up all this good land with water. . . . Now see those foundation stones? That was the grade school—and over that way was the police box."

It turned out the driver was born and raised in the Yanggu area and had never left except for ten years during his youth. Sifting through his memories of the time before the lake, he explained at length every detail that caught his eye. His native village had been submerged; in fact, it didn't even show up on the map anymore. Fields, villages, roads—the sediment of forty-odd years beneath the water. Lost villages, an absence of human life.

Hyesun knew Kim's objective—to find polished stones in an old streambed newly exposed to the light of day. But what was *she* looking for? What ardent longing, what thirst had drawn her to this dried-up lake?

The corn growing head-high on both sides of the road formed a grove of dried stalks, the fronds swaying desolately and grazing one another with a rainlike patter.

After crossing a succession of valleys and ridges, they were well into the drained area when a village appeared.

"Here we are," Hyesun exclaimed as she peered at the surroundings. "Sangmuryong-ni, the end of Lake P'aro."

They couldn't have gone farther anyway, since the village lay at the foot of a mountain. Promising to return at five, the driver swung the taxi around and departed.

Hyesun and Kim set out toward the village, wanting to talk with the locals and find out where the excavation was taking place. But the first to greet them were a pair of yellow dogs. Alert to the approach of strangers, they darted into view but then slunk about, tails between their legs, barking intermittently.

Perched on the mountainside across the lake was a white one-story building with a banner reading LOVE YOUR COUNTRY hanging from a window. A flagpole bore the national flag and that of the New Village Movement. It was the annex school, and Hyesun searched her memory for the time and place she associated with it. But matching the rough sketch in her memory with the scene she now beheld was like trying to piece together a scattering of fragments. The gap between her memories and the reality shocked her. Was it a matter of time at work? Or the changes that come with time? Without the water that had contained and mirrored the mountain, the lakeside dwellings and hill paths that clung to its midsection looked oddly out of place. There was the plank where Pyŏng'ŏn used to sit when he fished, and next to it, likewise incongruously high on the hillside, the dugout boat that reminded her of an upside-down old-fashioned rubber shoe. Was it the second house in, or the third, where she and Pyŏng'ŏn had put up?

Seven years ago, Hyesun had taken sick leave from school and come here for a week with Pyŏng'ŏn. They had traveled up the lake by boat. Situated beneath the annex school were some twenty houses that followed the contours of the mountain—a "natural village." The residents made a living by fishing the lake and farming the slopes above the waterline, and accommodating tourists who had come to fish. Every other day a boat motored up from the dam to purchase mainly carp, trout, and mandarin fish. Hyesun wondered if the elderly man who sounded like he was coughing his life away had passed on.

She remembered awakening at dawn to the sound of water lapping against the shore and finding Pyŏng'ŏn gone from her side. Looking out the small window of their room, she would see him in the light of a carbide lamp, hunched up on the plank, bundled in a parka, fishing rod drooping toward the water. And she heard the tin lid of the lacquered lunchbox rattle as he filled it with *soju* to ward off the chill before the sun rose. Leaving the window open, she watched the onset of dawn, the lake's blurry surface seeming gradually to rise, the plants at the lake's edge straightening as if revived by the water, the outline of the mountains growing indistinct.

It was so calm at dawn beside the water. The reflections of the mountains floated on the surface while the mist blooming from the lake grew thick in the valleys. Clams emerging for nocturnal peregrinations had fallen victim to a flock of white birds before they could regain the safety of the water, and all that was left of them were empty shells.

Before the fog had lifted, a leaf-light dugout would appear with children from across the lake who rowed here for their classes at the annex school. Hyesun and Pyŏng'ŏn had twice made a similar passage, only their destination was the mountain across the lake. Rowing out into the water, they saw plants swaying long and rootless beneath the surface. Concealed among them like submarines were golden carp swimming in leisurely fashion. To Hyesun, the dugout felt precarious even on delicate ripples, and as Pyŏng'ŏn worked the oars, she wondered if he felt as uneasy as she did. She was pregnant then, jumpy and irritable. It would be their third child, and maternal instinct had left her with feelings of hostility and defensiveness and at the same time an excessive compassion and tenderness—the combination producing a vague, confused state of isolation and loneliness. But despite her uneasiness and apprehension, she felt that the baby inside her womb was a charm for her, a safe anchor for a nervous mother crossing deep water in a flimsy boat.

The morning of their last day here Hyesun, rubbing her sleepy eyes, had gone barefoot to where Pyŏng'ŏn sat. He made room for her on the plank and with bloodshot eyes indicated a spot on the shore maybe fifteen paces away. She saw there the daughter of the family with whom they were staying, a girl who couldn't attend school because she was a deaf-mute. She was stooping and straightening, throwing clams back into the water so they wouldn't be pecked open by the birds. It was a morning ritual, Hyesun realized. After the girl's playmates left for school she would wander about the vicinity of her home, playing by herself.

Because she made no sound she was like a shadow, weightless and insubstantial. A child born of the water, Hyesun thought when she saw the girl at the shore; a child of the woods, when she saw her beneath a tree.

Pyŏng'ŏn, gazing at the girl, had said she reminded him of an old song from his childhood: "So still is the river in autumn that the *ŏryong* falls asleep; oh, you in the pavilion, taking the autumn breeze." His grandfather always used to sing that verse, and now here it was echoing in his head. Pyŏng'ŏn parodied his grandfather singing, his face taking on a sheepish look that he tried in vain to erase. An *ŏryong* was their word for a dragon that enters the water in autumn and falls into a deep sleep, he added.

Hyesun had wondered if on that still morning the far reach of the speechless girl's vision and the moisture rising from the lake like the respiration of a sleeping dragon somehow reminded Pyŏng'ŏn of that old song. Did he harbor illusions about the distant object of the girl's vision, a place he couldn't see? Was he trying through such expectations to overcome the helplessness and frustration that confronted him? If so, thought Hyesun, it was a desperate measure.

Never was he told why he and two other junior teachers at the high school had been fired. For a time afterward he had avoided others. He was afraid, for example, that a friendly conversation might suddenly turn sour, his counterpart changing his expression and tone of voice and slapping him or spitting in his face. On the whole he'd been a respectable social science teacher, inconspicuous in speech and conduct. Strange, then, how the school authorities had dealt with him in such a roundabout way, charging him with incompetence. If not for the fate of the other two teachers, Pyŏng'ŏn might not have survived his humiliation and shame. The other two had confessed in writing to having made radical remarks in class criticizing the establishment. Hyesun's guess was that Pyŏng'ŏn had been a convenient target in the disputes between the school and the foundation, or that he had fallen easy prey to a reduction in force ordered by the school board. Whatever the real reason for his discharge, Pyŏng'ŏn liked to rationalize the matter: he had gotten off lightly. In contrast, one of the other two teachers had, along with his wife, been taken into custody in the middle of the night and detained without cause, their baby left home alone to cry the night away, crawling inside the house and out, a mass of bruises and abrasions. The second teacher had been hauled out of class and taken away; his wife appeared thereafter at the school gate every morning, to wait in vain for news of him. Pyŏng'ŏn considered himself lucky indeed—in his mind he had narrowly escaped terrible misfortune.

The houses Hyesun and Kim passed were empty, the gates barred or propped shut with rocks. The children playing on the teeter-totter called out to them that the grownups were out tending to the crops.

"Let's try down this way," said Kim.

Following him, Hyesun was surprised by the texture of the soil, different from what she had expected from her vantage point above. It felt resistant, defiant almost, an accumulation of fine sediment so firm that their footprints were as faint as bird tracks. This uncultivated land was the domain of sage, fleabane, and reeds—plants that must have sprouted from windblown seeds and now were withering. The ground cover of shepherd's purse and plantain had stabilized the soil. Ants and mole crickets were busy infiltrating the shells of clams and snails.

"Didn't this used to be underwater?" Hyesun asked, sounding more breathless than she felt. In actuality it was an awkward situation, going to an indeterminate destination with a friend of her husband—and Kim's silence as they descended into what used to be the lake did not help matters.

"I'll say—we're a good twenty-five feet below the old waterline."

The land lay between the two forks of the stream that had fed the far end of the lake. The stream looked like it had held stubbornly to its course, not mixing with the lake water even when the lake had been full. In a sunny area sheltered from the breeze, two figures were bent over, a man and a woman, working the soil. Scattered plots of Chinese cabbage were visible, some of the cabbages abandoned and rotting—apparently unsuitable for kimchi. Straightening, the couple—husband and wife?—stared at the visitors.

Kim approached them and asked directions.

The man, short, balding, middle-aged, willingly obliged after lighting a cigarette. He seemed ready for a break.

"Just follow the stream to a wooden bridge. Cross the bridge, go up the hill, and you'll see where they're working. People from ancient times supposedly lived there. . . . They've been hard at it all this fall—hillside's torn up, and they're digging out all those useless old rocks. TV crews been out here, and there was a big article in the paper. Those rocks, you know, to us they're just rocks. Can't be much more than a mile from here. They're working right below the villa where Dr. Syngman Rhee used to live."

As the autumn days grew shorter, night was falling earlier in the mountain valleys. The sky was still bright, but already the mountains were casting shadows and the breeze had stiffened. Propaganda leaflets from the North had given parts of the uncultivated areas a colorful covering almost as thick as the undergrowth. Kim bent to retrieve a couple of the leaflets, scanned them, then crumpled them and threw them aside.

"Why don't the two sides drop flower seeds instead of paper, for heaven's sake. You know what my children told me when they asked for a donation to take to school for the Peace Dam? They said it would pay for a shovelful of cement and a brick for peace. Well, I've never seen so much waste and consumption. And both sides are doing it. It's crazy. . . . So, Pyŏng'ŏn's coming back this winter? Did he get a teaching job? It's political science he's studying, right?"

Hyesun felt her face harden. Those who knew her assumed she wanted to settle in back home before Pyŏng'ŏn arrived. They never doubted he would return once he finished his dissertation. But Pyŏng'ŏn had other ideas. "Stay here another six months— that's all you need," he had said to Hyesun. Six months would be enough time for her to tackle the root cause of her homesickness (others had called it maladaptation) and to realize she'd developed a façade in order to hide it.

Early on, Pyŏng'ŏn had taken to spewing out the opinion of a friend they had met in the States, who had bought a burger shop: "Everyone comes here to study—I did--but back home there are more poli-sci Ph.D.s than you can shake a stick at—who's going to give you the time of day? Cramming your brain just to pick up a degree won't make any difference. But here, if you make a killing in the lottery, your status changes overnight. Korea's not the only place where a son of a bitch with money turns into Sir Son of a Bitch." In their four years in the United States, Pyŏng'ŏn had learned to mimic the man convincingly.

Kim's questions were too bothersome to answer, so Hyesun merely said, "No, it's computer science now—it's supposed to be easier to get a job in that field."

When Pyŏng'ŏn realized he couldn't persuade Hyesun to stay, he dispensed with his standard approach to her and turned serious: Why couldn't she be more flexible? Maybe her rejection of life in the States came from the false front she projected. What did she plan to do back in Korea? On the surface he seemed concerned about how she would get along, but in fact he was reproaching her: *You leave the family, you give up this life we've worked so hard to build, and what do you get in return? Do you think you can make a new life for yourself?* For their part, he declared, he and the children had no intention of returning. "I'd like to write if I can," Hyesun had said. "Write?" he replied in consternation, a peculiar smile forming on his face. Wishing she could wipe that smile off his face, Hyesun had stubbornly repeated, "Yes. I know it won't be easy, but I want to try again." It surprised her that she had expressed this vague thought so readily, unconvincing though it felt.

She thought of her life in America only in terms of suffering, remembering the anxiety and the animal instincts she had felt while raising her children and surviving in an unfamiliar land. For ten years before that she had taught language and literature at a middle school, introducing her pupils to poetry and prose that was beautiful, conventional, and safe. So occupied was she with school and home that she had no time for desultory thoughts. And there was the matter of Pyŏng'ŏn's unemployment. Where was there room for the false entity called fiction? And what was so special about her that she could offer to the world? Writing was a different sort of enterprise from the business of everyday life; it demanded a special talent. Long ago she had entered a literary contest, submitting a story framed in textbook sentences. She had failed to capture the prize, which would have conferred upon her the coveted status of Writer. This and subsequent abortive experiences with fiction writing had left Hyesun with scars she did her best to hide. The more intensely she wanted success, the deeper the scars. She came to realize, albeit vaguely at first, that the world and life could never be depicted in a few sentences, however beautiful and refined, and that she lacked the strength (or was it the courage?) to shatter that world, that life. From that point on she lost confidence in her ability to write. She had been complacent about literature, considering it a thing of beauty, something to savor. Was it any wonder that her creative impulses withered as a consequence?

But in the United States, those impulses had been revived. Why? To Hyesun it was a combination of two impulses a deaf-mute might feel—an urge to shout and a growing anxiety over a hardening tongue. What had caused her to declare to her husband and children that she wanted to write again and would return home by herself? Was it the desire for revenge on the power of expression she felt she was losing? Or was it the love she felt for that power?

Pyŏng'ŏn didn't trust those who professed to reveal and express their inner selves, and he scorned Hyesun for declaring her intentions: "It really gets me how people fancy their life is so special. And how they're always grousing about some nonsense or crap. And some of them actually end up writing! So what are *you* going to write about? How sad you are about poverty in America? About the loneliness here? The racial discrimination? Or maybe your own alienation?"

Hyesun couldn't deny it: when Pyŏng'ŏn had decided to go to America, she had felt an urge to see the world and experience a new life. Oh, the illusions that come into play at such a time: "It was spiritual poverty that made me leave; it was material poverty; it was loneliness; it was fickle despair." How vain! And what better way to deceive yourself when you come up against a dead end? The grass is always greener; what you see is not what you get. Maybe that's why a land unknown and never visited is "the land of the future." And why the dragon sleeps deep down in the water where you can't see it.

After making the passage to America, Hyesun had learned to say "Go to hell" in English before she could memorize the name of the city where they lived. Pyŏng'ŏn had found a job at Yamaguchi's Fish Market, and on nights when he had class he would shower, change, and for good measure apply aftershave to kill the fish smell before he left. He got back around two in the morning after finishing his night classes and studying in the library. Hyesun, when the children were asleep in bed, would sit in front of the television with her glass of water while she waited for him. *Tales from the Crypt* came on at midnight. Dedicated to the bizarre and the prurient, the program featured grotesque murders, sex, incest, and deviltry, inviting viewers to open the lid to their unconscious and reveal all manner of desires hidden in its deepest and darkest recesses. The episodes were superficial and second-rate, they lacked the logic of inevitability, and they ended with a psychoanalyst or a pseudo-psychic talking about the "chaos," the "codes," and the "dark, boundless mysteries" that lurk beneath the thick layer of human consciousness. These experts always sounded like they were reporting the results of a clinical test. It was while she watched this program that the telephone rang one night and a deep, suggestive voice had asked, "Are you alone?" When Hyesun answered, the caller knew from her thick accent and awkward pronunciation that she was a foreigner and he became more persistent: "Are you lonely? Do you need a man tonight? I'm ready for love." "Go to hell, *kaesaekki*," she had replied. No language other than her native Korean could express so graphically the contempt conveyed by the last part of this curse, to which the English equivalent, *son of a bitch*, could not hope to do justice. Hyesun imagined a sex fiend at the other end of the line, an unmarried man clutching his penis and panting as he gaped at a hard-core film. She watched the rest of the program, then went to the bathroom to wash her hands, which felt sticky. Pyŏng'ŏn still hadn't returned. Hyesun opened the door to the children's room and lingered to look at their sleeping forms, feeling that all of them—she, the children, and her husband—were tiny islands, all alone in the world.

Surrounding the apartment building were dense woods where hunting was prohibited and you could sometimes hear the drawn-out, plaintive calls of animals in heat. A lonely road ran nearby, and occasionally the headlights of a car fanning out in the darkness would find a dirty gray cat slinking out of the woods, a stray searching the vague warp of memory for a long-lost master, its domestic instincts stimulated by light and all that it suggested.

Kim and Hyesun found themselves approaching a knot of men who were peering down toward the ground. Among them was an elderly man in a black traditional topcoat and a fedora. Flanking him were a younger man in a windbreaker and two youths; the three of them bore a family resemblance to one another. The focus of attention was a scattering of large, flat stones no different from those Hyesun had seen elsewhere along the way. She and Kim were about to move on when the older man's voice, muffled and sunken, brought them to a stop.

"You can see the family room here, and this was the kitchen. The shed was over there, and that was the vegetable garden."

Where the old man was pointing they could see the faint outline of a foundation—two wings of a house joined at a ninety-degree angle. Green moss carpeted the ground where the man had indicated the kitchen garden.

"From the front yard you could see the top of Samyŏng Mountain—look, there it is, doesn't it feel like you could reach out and touch it? Out back was a well. . . . I'll bet you could sink a hole right now and get water."

The elderly man and the youths, who looked like his sons, nodded in amazement.

"Do you happen to know what kind of tree this is?" Kim asked, indicating a light gray tree sawed off at the middle. It had a forked trunk that resembled a pair of extended arms or upside-down legs.

"It's a persimmon. And this one's a Chinese date. . . . Trees can last centuries underwater."

"Did you used to live here?"

"Yes, I did. This very spot! Born, raised, married, and had children here. Forty-three, forty-four years ago it was, they bought us out. So we took their money and left. And then we heard they let the water out of Hwach'ŏn Dam and the old hometown is high and dry again. So I brought the boys over for a look—spent half a day getting here."

"This must be a very special occasion for you," said Kim.

"Let's see now, that was Showa—you know, during the Japanese occupation—but Showa year what, it's not coming back. Anyway, I was thirty-three. We had to move the ancestral graves, then pack up and leave. Back then I never dreamed this day would come. But then, you never know." The old man spoke as if reading from an epitaph, punctuating his words with sighs that could have been lamentations or exclamations. "There was a road down there, and places where you could get a drink. The village was pretty good-sized, actually. And look here—a cotton plant, see?" The man took a withered plant that was poking out from his coat pocket and held it up. It was about a foot long, its soil-encrusted roots secured with plastic wrap. "This was good land, and the Japs made us plant it with cotton. In autumn that's all you saw, cotton fields. And this is what I found. Forty years the seeds were buried in ground that was underwater, and here they sprouted after all that time—what a mystery."

Hyesun studied the cotton plant, marveling at the old man's ability to have recognized it instantly by its thin purple stalk and the few leaves. If, as he said, the plant could remain hidden in the earth for forty years, waiting for the water to drain before sprouting, then it was indeed unfathomable.

With great care the old man tucked the plant back into his pocket. Then he squatted and like a carefree child playing in the dirt, scratched at the ground with his liver-spotted hands until he accumulated a handful of soil.

"Grandfather, why don't we take one of these home as a keepsake? Wouldn't it look good in the garden?" asked one of the youths as he struggled to heft one of the foundation stones.

The old man shook his head and waved him off. "Ought to leave it here where it belongs. This way, even if it was underwater till the end of time, we'd know where our house was."

Wind began to roar through the empty basin, sounding like the bellowing of a wounded beast. Hyesun turned and noticed the desiccated vegetation, stalks indomitably rubbing up against each other and swaying, seed pods opening and launching their contents.

Kim and Hyesun resumed their journey and before long their steps had brought them far into the lakebed, which followed the former streambed into the distance. Kim occasionally paused to turn up a stone. The faraway echo of explosions began to ride in on the wind. Hyesun looked around, trying to determine the origin.

"Dynamite," Kim said with a bitter expression. "We say it's the Northerners building Kŭmgang Mountain Dam, they say it's us making the Peace Dam."

And now the wind was whirling and clawing like an unappeased spirit at the vast, light gray basin with the dry lakebed at its bottom, and at the mountains looking so forlorn with their lower parts despoiled. It was an odd scene, made all the more strange by Hyesun's feeling that there was also something familiar about it, in spite of the sheer impossibility of imagining what might lie beneath the surface if the lake were full. She'd sometimes experienced a similar sensation going into a house for the first time and yet feeling there was nothing unfamiliar about it. As they walked into the lakebed, Hyesun felt that something indistinct and blurry was coming into focus, as if she were adjusting the lens of a camera. Surely she was capable of writing about such devastation and dreariness. But once again she realized just how long it had been since she'd lost the ability to write. Her words had hardened like a cirrhotic liver. Fossilized words, lexical trilobites and archaeopteryxes, unborn words, words lost in darkness—such was her vocabulary.

During the past month Hyesun had copied out on manuscript paper an author's lengthy novel, complete to the last punctuation mark. It was sheer madness, but she had justified the effort by telling herself that painters practiced by copying the best works of other painters. What was even more dubious, after finishing with this task she had experienced an inexplicable sense of fulfillment and achievement, as if she had painstakingly put together an entire two-thousand-page creation and all that remained was to edit it. But then came the horrible thought that every age has its authors who upon completing their last project give themselves up to empty bravado, claiming to have written such a massive work that their writing hand will function no longer; as well as authors who sink into carnal and alcoholic excess in their life and redundancy in their work while parroting to the end of their days the excuse that writing can have no meaning in an era of political repression. What could have devastated her confidence to such an extent? Was writing fiction the surest means of vengeance toward the words that had deserted her?

Their apartment became the weekend hangout for Koreans. On weekends Yamaguchi's Fish Market was closed and Hyesun had a respite from cleaning Marion's house. Guests came and went, invited or not—it was quite the cozy destination. Most of them were younger students who had finished exams or had no plans for the weekend. Some of the old regulars might stop coming, but newcomers would nonchalantly replace them, with the result that Hyesun always saw a variety of faces to which she couldn't attach a name. Some callers marched in just as Hyesun was finishing the dishes, and she'd have to cook all over again, Pyŏng'ŏn having issued a blanket invitation to any and all who craved a meal of rice, kimchi, and bean-paste stew.

Although Pyŏng'ŏn was hard-pressed to combine daytime work with graduate school at night, he was not treated with due respect. "Studying doesn't guarantee you anything," the cheeky ones would tell him. "Why don't you just do some sightseeing and enjoy yourself? That's what living abroad is all about." Ridicule was implicit in these words: What was Pyŏng'ŏn going to accomplish with a decrepit, hardened brain? On the other hand, the weekend crowd were the only ones to address him politely as "Sir." To non-Koreans he was simply Moon, his family name.

Every weekend Hyesun grilled beef, cooked bean-paste stew, and stir-fried potato noodles along with sliced vegetables and meat. At first she worried about the strong odors of the soybean paste and kimchi, but after preparing several such meals she became insensitive to the smell. Other concerns took precedence. "We don't have enough to live on," she complained. "We spend much more on Saturday dinner than we do on all the other meals of the week combined." But Pyŏng'ŏn would cut her off, saying, "Don't forget, our guests are someone's precious children, each and every one of them. It's hard being away from Korea, so what's wrong with offering some home atmosphere once in a while?" Hyesun wanted to tell him, but couldn't, that he was indulging in a flimsy rationalization, that she had heard their visitors also liked to feast at a Korean restaurant on weekends. "And now they're putting out sushi," she had overheard one of them say. Rather than outrage and shame, it was pain she felt. "Very tasty," others would say. "The same thing would cost over a hundred dollars at a Japanese restaurant. And you wouldn't believe how stingy those restaurants are—they give you half a dozen pieces no bigger than rat turds and call it a serving." Molding steamed rice into compact oblong shapes and adding a slice of raw seafood on top, Pyŏng'ŏn allowed their praise of his sushi-making skill to go to his head. Next time, he declared, it would be fresh sea bream and lobster. "You've become Americanized quicker than we thought, Sir," the guests would tell Pyŏng'ŏn, absorbed in his cooking, looking clumsy in an apron, Hyesun looking on with a mixture of pity and exasperation.

At the fish market Pyŏng'ŏn wore rubber boots and a plastic apron as he went about his duties of scaling, shelling, and deboning. The fish heads, innards, and bones, which would normally have been discarded, made excellent ingredients for a spicy stew.

The visitors behaved well when they drank, making sure to observe proper etiquette for invited guests. They ate their fill, then rose to leave. "You're welcome to spend the night," Pyŏng'ŏn would tell them. "We can stay up all night and have fun shooting the breeze, just like in Korea." This repeated offer was met with the reply that they didn't want to trouble Pyŏng'ŏn or they had to work on their dissertation. The only difference between these guests and customers at a restaurant was that the guests didn't pay.

The only one who got inebriated at these gatherings, the only one who got sad and sentimental and rambled on about 'most anything, was Pyŏng'ŏn. The one surefire topic of conversation was the situation in Korea. Memoirs and autobiographies packed with lies, books bearing such brazen titles as *Witness to the Truth*, passed from hand to hand. Also circulating among the group were sensational exposés of influential politicians and financiers, the titles including such phrases as *Fact and Fiction*, *The Inside Story*, or *Stand Accused*. An author's use of anonymity or an alias to avoid liability signaled to the group just how much they were being deceived by surface appearances of the situation back home. The tactic was all the more infuriating because of the possibility that the author too might be deceiving them.

It didn't take long for Pyŏng'ŏn's guests, once they learned of his firing by the school, to begin treating him as something of an antiestablishment figure. But as far as Hyesun was concerned, he was merely a timid malcontent. She had already concluded that his inexplicable dismissal, his two years of unemployment, and the prospect of living the rest of his life feeling he'd been victimized were the practical reasons for his decision to go to America. Out of a sense of helplessness, he revived a wispy dream of studying abroad that he'd entertained in his youth and in a frenzy sent out applications to universities throughout the United States. Finally he was admitted by a graduate school in New York State. He had worried that it might be difficult to leave the country, but it didn't take long to obtain his passport. The day he had his visa interview he lamented, sounding already like an exile, "They figure they can get rid of all the damned troublemakers this way." Arriving in America, he was asked by other Korean students about the situation back home. His reply became predictable: "The whole country's a mess, a total police state. That's the kind of regime we live under. They barge into a classroom, haul away a teacher, and you don't see him again. . . . It's the cancer ward on a huge scale." He liked to say that no one had come to take *him* away, and he always sounded amazed that he'd been spared. Impressed, the students would say, "You mean you've never been jailed and tortured?" Pyŏng'ŏn shook his head, gritting his teeth in indignation. It pained Hyesun to see Pyŏng'ŏn, a man who had aspired to be a reputable, trustworthy teacher, being cast as a contentious anti-establishment type.

Hyesun and Pyŏng'ŏn had once accompanied one of their more frequent guests, a student named Pak Chingyu, to a meeting of a human rights association.Her realization that in America it was possible to have comparatively free and uncensored discussion of both domestic and foreign issues led Hyesun in turn to the understanding that freedom in America meant more than just being able to watch a Soviet film, see the uncut version of *Emmanuelle*, or sunbathe nude. It would be a sad situation if all you could see of America was what American movies showed you.

The human rights association was a group of radical Quakers, and the meeting that night was devoted to Korea. The program consisted of videos and reports. In the small meeting room, dark curtains were drawn and the video was shown. The images danced about the screen and the outlines of people and vehicles were difficult to distinguish, but Hyesun instantly recognized the setting—the southern city of Kwangju. Though she'd never been there, the opening scenes—the shapes of the mountains and the color of the sky—were instinctively familiar. The dizzying scenes that followed—a torchlight procession, buildings on fire, corpses with mutilated faces, the eyes hardened in glares—were accompanied by staccato rallying cries, the sound of rifle fire, and a chorus of hoarse voices singing "Our Wish Is for Freedom." Rifle-bearing youths stood in utter isolation before the capitol building on the final day. Later, the speaker explained, all of them were found dead. A row of prisoners strung together like fish on a line were loaded onto a truck beneath a banner announcing a May Festival celebration at a university. A young man lying prostrate on the ground, hands tied behind his back, jerked his head up toward the sky. Bushy hair, limpid eyes overflowing with sorrow, not a hint of rage in his expression, no sign of imminent outcry, no urge to shoot. After glimpsing the sky, he buried his face in the ground. Women keened endlessly beside coffins shrouded in white. Hoses washed away bloodstains as if in the aftermath of an evil plague.

The poor quality of the video prompted the group to rerun the particularly atrocious scenes, but those had instantly been inscribed in Hyesun's mind. That sky, that earth, those faces were not in the least unfamiliar. Here was the reality of the rumors that had stubbornly persisted for years. Here were the roots of the grief and rage with which people asked, "Is there poetry after Auschwitz?" Only this time they asked, "Is there poetry after Kwangju?"

In the discussion that followed, someone asked how many people were killed and how many injured. Wasn't there any response, any support from neighboring cities? someone else asked. Kim Yŏngju, one of the coordinators of the program, responded that the general public in Korea weren't aware of the facts because news reports were under the strictest government control and transportation and communication to the outside had been cut off. People had gone about their business but had sensed something was wrong. "How could that be? Korea's a small country— from Seoul to Kwangju isn't like New York to Los Angeles," said a young blond-haired woman, cocking her head.

Next on the program was a video shown by Kim Yŏngju. She was the daughter of a retired general and had immigrated ten years earlier at age sixteen. The title of the video was *Korean Society and the Present State of Human Rights*, and it showed people living near the Seoul city dump on Nanji Island; a community of blind people in To-dong, a neighborhood of cheap inns and boarding houses located behind the headquarters of the Dae Woo Corporation; Moon Village in the upper reaches of Shillim-dong; the Five-Eight-Eight red-light district; the demolishing of squatters' homes; camp towns near the American military bases. Each year forty thousand Amerasian children were born in these camp towns, explained the speaker in an agitated tone. "That can't be right," responded a voice in Korean from the dark recesses of the room. "There are forty thousand American soldiers in Korea—are you telling us that every year they each produce a child?" "Well, that's what a survey said," the woman responded without skipping a beat. "There's nothing in the GI service contract that says they have to produce children," came the same thick, low-pitched voice. His next utterance was loud enough for every Korean present to hear: "Stupid, socialist bitch!" And he left the room. In the darkness Hyesun, sitting toward the front of the gathering, couldn't identify the man. She turned and asked Pak why he and the others were involved in this sort of group. Well, there was of course some danger, and they were concerned about their future, but it was something they did for the sake of the country, he replied in a confident tone.

Hyesun subsequently learned that Pak and Kim had each received a threatening phone call that night: "There's something you don't seem to understand: keep up this shit and you'll never see Korea again. And even if your father's not involved, don't assume his business won't be affected." It was widely rumored that there was a rat among the Korean students and that a KCIA agent had arrived from back home.And then something happened during one of the Saturday night gatherings that imprinted itself in Hyesun's memory, an incident that gave her a glimpse of the deep rift among the students. At first all had seemed harmonious enough, due to the closed nature of their lives abroad and a pervasive individualism in which the rules of conduct were tacitly understood. But in reality there was jealousy, hostility, and profound class hatred among them. Normally these problems were invisible—there was an unwritten rule that they saw of each other's private life only what the other would show. Even so, two rumors were flying everywhere. First, there was an exclusive society composed of the "royal family." Second, a former dignitary's son, watchdog of a family fortune stashed away overseas, lived in a posh condo, drove around in a hundred-thousand-dollar car, and kept a mistress. The mistress, who was indiscreet, was heard to whine, "I pity him. He has a Cadillac but he's afraid to show it off, so he goes around in a beat-up old Chevy."

On that particular Saturday, trouble broke out between Yi Ingŏl and Yŏm Chungi. Yi was the son of a former general. Yŏm was a frail-looking embassy official enrolled in the university's Department of Communications. Hyesun had never met either of them until that evening. She was in the kitchen refilling serving dishes when she heard from the living room an outburst of shouting and the sound of dishes breaking. She found Yŏm, eyes blazing but his face otherwise drained of color, screaming at Yi: "You pro-Japanese son of a bitch! Do you and your goddamn family have anything good to say about your country and your people? Look at your grandpa—look at your daddy! Your grandpa was in the House of Peers—had himself made a noble by the Japs! And your daddy's a chameleon, changing color every time someone new's in power. Doesn't he have any sense of shame, the old skunk! My father was a school custodian for fifteen years! I'd like to know where you assholes got all your money! Sons of bitches!"

The dinner table had been overturned, dishes sent flying. The neighbors on the floor below rapped on the ceiling with a broom handle in protest. Peacemakers were leading Yŏm away, their arms encircling his waist—"Now calm down, Yŏm *hyŏng*—you've had too much to drink"—but it seemed they were enjoying the quarrel, and it was obvious they were waiting to see what happened next. This clash between the descendant of an independence patriot and the offspring of a renegade, a pro-Japanese traitor, was erupting not in a movie or a work of fiction but right before Hye-sun's eyes.

"While your grandpa was decked out in all his medals and sell-ing out the country to the Japanese, my grandfather was active in the independence movement! Thanks to your parents, you grew up in a greenhouse—don't know shit about the world—assholes, all of you—bourgeois assholes—sons of bitches with a little bit of money—and you think an embassy official is nothing but a ward-office clerk!" Yŏm continued to screech even as he fell vomiting to the floor and was dragged outside. "Come out here, you bas-tard son of a Jap-loving traitor. All of you yapping about politics, society, the masses. . . . If you're so concerned, if your little hearts are so pained by it all, then why did you come over here? You're a bunch of half-assed Yankee sons of bitches, shooting off your yaps about freedom, conscience, democracy in America! You shit on your country as soon as you're away from it, you cozy up to the Yankees and squeal to them! . . . If you're so heartbroken and patriotic, then why don't you go back home and do something about it! You're babies playing the exile game—don't pretend you're patriots! I know the likes of you and your scheming little games—I know how good you are at covering your asses! All you cunning little princes! Don't you tell me we're the same blood!" Yŏm was still shouting as they loaded him into a car: "Don't you tell me we're the same blood!" His words, chill and startling and spear-point sharp, touched Hyesun.

It was an ugly, confused spectacle. No, that was too simple. It was a shameful, deep-seated, festering sore that couldn't be treated.

Yi tried to appear nonchalant as he tended to his food-splattered clothing, but his face was already hardening in displea-sure and humiliation. As the others brushed off their own clothes, they set about reassuring Yi: Sometimes mad dogs bite; Yŏm must have had an ax to grind and was taking it out on him. "Who is that guy, anyway?" "Got me. I've seen him in the dorm—oh yeah, and a couple of times in my poli-sci seminar." "Always flying off the handle. What can you do—the guy's bent out of shape." "If he's the rat, then he better learn how to keep his cover." "What a sad sack. Poor, fucked-up young guy. Already a Korean-style bureaucrat—totally brainwashed."

Finally everyone was gone. Where to begin with the chaos left behind—the white walls spattered with soybean-paste stew and kimchi juice, the carpet scattered with food, porcelain fragments, and beer bottles? Suddenly Hyesun was shrieking at Pyŏng'ŏn: "Please, please, please, don't ask anyone over anymore. What do you get out of it? Do you realize that before I can spend a dollar I've got to go over it in my mind a million times? Look at us—a part-time housecleaner and a man who works at a fish market. It's too much for me—why are we living like this? What did we come here for? The others, they're young, but we'll be forty soon. If we don't make it this time, we won't get another chance. That's what I worry about, that's why I'm all wound up. We're getting more and more like beggars. And it's not just about money—I feel wretched. What happened to my pride, my self-respect, my soul? I feel like I'm going nowhere. Are you going to spend the rest of your life making sushi? How long are you going to read those stupid books and articles and argue with your friends about the situation back home? Why do you play those intellectual games anyway—is it love of country? So what if you're sincere— where do you get off criticizing if you don't love your country? When I go to Marion's, I don't take my handbag, just like house-keepers back home—they don't want the owner thinking they're stealing.

"You say you're not going back. Well, I am—I really am. I'm going to start writing again. And don't tell me Conrad produced masterpieces after learning English when he was past twenty. Don't tell me experience is important. Don't tell me a vocalist can sing anywhere, that painters' eyes don't open till they go abroad.

And don't you tell me birds will sing anywhere, that flowers will bloom anywhere, in any soil.

"I know a painter who's been here more than twenty years. He says he still can't do *portraits*! He always does snow scenes, and once in a while birds and flowers show up in them. A lot of people would call them barbershop art—standard run-of-the-mill stuff—but what I get from those pictures is honesty. You think I got honesty from that exhibition where each canvas was a Hahoe dance mask—with a title like *Portrait of a Korean* or *Smile of a Korean*? Now there's an artist whose imagination has dried up. I could tell he was impatient for the fame he'd get from that show—all ten minutes of it. It annoys me to see a painter that hard up. I think it's the same with writing. And as far as the kids are concerned. . . ."

The children had shut themselves up in their room. They couldn't possibly have fallen asleep during the commotion, but no peep could be heard from them. They were sensitive to unrest and were learning through silence and withdrawal—a child's way of protesting, of expressing a wish to disappear without a sound, leaving no trace—to deal with their father's sudden outbursts of anger and rough tone of voice and their mother's frequent irritability. Hyesun found it pathetic, her children trying to grow up before their time. Children may represent false hopes to their parents, but there's nothing false about the children themselves. They are the living message sent by parents to a future the parents can't see—this was one of Hyesun's favorite quotes. Even so, she kept a nervous eye on her children as they grew, and on the changes accompanying their growth, as if those changes were time bombs that would detonate inside them. Her nervousness frequently erupted in violence—she slapped the children over nothing, and once when they didn't come in from playing until dinner was over she stripped them to their underwear and sent them back outside. She often wailed or broke dishes on purpose in front of them.

"There's something wrong with me," she would mutter to herself. But the frightening thing was not so much the illness itself as the cruel pleasure she took from seeing herself grow ill. For the first time, she had become the object of her own revenge.

Another frequent visitor was the stray cat that emerged from the woods in the wee hours of the morning to yowl at the stairway that split the four-plex across from Hyesun's apartment building—that being the place where Mrs. Thompson, who lived downstairs from Hyesun, left food out for it. "It belonged to Chris, the man who used to live in your apartment," she once explained while setting out the food. "He was a retiree, lived by himself here, and then he moved into a nursing home. It's a tomcat, and Chris let it stay out at night and apparently it found a mate. When a tomcat finds a mate, it leaves its master. That's why they're usually neutered, but I don't think Chris had that cat fixed. Anyway, when it's really cold or hungry it tries to find its old home."

Less frequently, and early in the evening, the cat prowled the apartment complex. When it encountered Hyesun pacing restlessly about the neighborhood after dinner, it would hesitate a moment and then flee. To Hyesun it resembled a dirty rag, and the time came when she could no longer abide the filthy cat, its mournful wailing outside the apartment building, its abject slinking. Like embers heating toward a flash point, all of her animosity, cruelty, and rage focused on the ash-colored cat; Hyesun herself couldn't understand it.

She lured the cat with chunks of ham and fish. Close up, the animal looked old and sickly. It was too heavy and moved lethargically, its long, sleek waist swollen into a fat ball. The cat devoured the fish, then licked the bones, moving as if it were used to Hyesun's presence. For a few days Hyesun fed it fish and watched it eat. The animal relaxed its guard and old habits reappeared: it would approach Hyesun and rub up against her leg, purring in satisfaction and licking the back of her hand with its sandy tongue. Finally Hyesun grabbed it. Holding it by the scruff of the neck, she stuffed it into the knapsack the children used for picnics and pulled the drawstring tight. Into the surrounding woods she went, farther than she had ever been, until the sound of traffic on the bordering road had faded into the distance. The old cat made sporadic attempts to wiggle out of the knapsack, yowling louder than Hyesun believed possible; it seemed finally to have sensed it was in mortal danger. Nonchalantly packing the knapsack like a girl out picking wildflowers and berries, Hyesun continued into the woods until the path ended and no other human traces were visible.

On this spring day the fields were a yellow carpet of dandelions in riotous bloom. But here in the woods Hyesun was surrounded by dank, gloomy clusters of pine, alder, and white oak. Untouched by the sun, the snow having melted only recently, the ground was soggy and crisscrossed with trees uprooted and collapsed beneath the weight of a winter's snow, doomed by their unrestrained growth and shallow roots.

As a girl Hyesun had heard if you abandon a cat, no matter how far off, you can be sure it will return to do you no good. So you first have to blindfold it or else put it in a sack, and then secure it somewhere. When she was far enough into the woods and had made sure there was no recent sign of other people, she hung the knapsack from a pine branch, tying it tightly so it wouldn't fall and the branch wouldn't break. Then she perched herself on a fallen trunk. As she wiped her sweaty forehead and hands, her gaze was drawn to some gnarled roots nearby. No, not roots, but the long, spreading antlers of a dead deer. The head and antlers still bore a thin layer of velvet, but the hollow eye sockets were a busy haven for ants and other insects. Had it been hit by a car and staggered into the woods to die? Or was it an old beast that had died a natural death? Either way, from the looks of the carcass it had been dead for a while. As Hyesun was trying to imagine how the empty sockets might once have looked, the cat struggled and yowled, fell suddenly silent, then struggled so convulsively that the branch seemed about to break. Hyesun broke into tears and sat there and sobbed.

She returned the next day. The soggy earth was carpeted with last year's autumn leaves and she couldn't see her footsteps from the day before, but instinct led her straight there. The knapsack still hung from the branch, a dirty stain now showing at the bottom. She thought she noticed faint movements inside, then wondered if her eyes were playing tricks on her. She thought she heard feeble meowing, but when she strained to listen she detected nothing. The woods sounded ever more still, and then she thought she heard a whistling as of the wind, and something inside her collapsed.

She continued to return to the woods on the days when she wasn't housecleaning. The contents of the knapsack seemed to diminish even as the knapsack itself stretched out and grew tattered and its slate color faded. The reeking, rotting thing inside, no longer turning colors, no longer fat or long but a shapeless mess, was not the cat but rather herself, degenerating into depravity.

Off in the distance where the two forks of the stream met, human forms in colored parkas were visible on a south-facing slope. Hyesun and Kim crossed the wooden bridge that spanned the flow and climbed the sunny slope. There was no path, and as they forged through the ground cover of Spanish needle plants, the dark, spiky needles stuck to their sneakers, pants, and sleeve ends.

The activity beside the rocky streamside slope was their first indication of the prehistoric archaeological site. The work sites were about twenty-five feet across, and within their plastic-tape borders university students were clearing soil with shovels, prods, and hoes. To Hyesun, it was as if they were spooning away the earth's surface.

"Must be from the TV station."

Stopping above Hyesun, Kim indicated a man with his back to them and another man, bent at the waist, a large camera on his shoulder, who was stepping backward as he filmed. Both wore yellow windbreakers with a network logo. A grizzled, middle-aged man in knee-high boots who appeared to be supervising the dig was describing to the reporter an array of stones laid out on the ground.

"The part that touches your palm is naturally round, but you'll notice that every one of them has been shaped so it fits nice and comfortable between your thumb and index finger. Now this one here may have been used for tough meat—see, it has a chiseled edge, kind of like a saw. The inhabitants of this particular site used percussion-flaking tools . . ."

The camera panned the archaeologist, the back of the reporter's head, the dry lake, the mountains, and the display of stones, then returned to the archaeologist. Hyesun eased herself outside the camera's range.

". . . and these tools, made from Paektu Mountain obsidian, seem to have been especially valuable—we're pretty sure prehistoric man took them along when he migrated. And judging from the places these tools have turned up, we can speculate that he migrated from Unggi in Hamgyŏng Province down the east coast to Yanggu on the upper branch of the North Han River, then along the Han to the upper branch of the Kŭm River, at Sŏkchang-ni near present-day Kongju. . . ."

Whether it was the length of the interview or the archaeologist's awareness that he was being filmed, some of his answers sounded forced, his voice shaky.

"I'm wondering, do your thoughts and feelings about present-day life ever change when you discover these sites and excavate the artifacts—could you comment on that, sir?"

The archaeologist grinned and asked his students digging a short distance away to stop. He pointed to a palm-sized stone half buried in the ground.

"Would you pick that up?"

The reporter did as he was asked, an awkward expression on his face.

"That stone could be fifty thousand years old—no, make it a hundred thousand years. What you have just picked up, Mr. Song, is a tool used by someone in Paleolithic times, a hundred thousand years ago. How does it feel? Can you feel the touch of the man who held it back then?"

The reporter stared intently at the stone, the reddish earth still fresh on it. As if to indicate that the interview was over, the archaeologist removed his glasses and rubbed his weary eyes. The camera scanned the piles of stones on the slope, then lingered for an instant on the bare incline Hyesun had climbed and the faint outlines of distant mountains that were everywhere being obliterated by wind-driven dust.

As he was climbing farther up the slope, inspecting stones along the way, Kim was brought to a halt by a student. "Can I help you with something?"

"Just looking at the rocks."

Kim adjusted his porkpie hat and produced a strained smile.

How many times had they heard that question on this trip? Hyesun wondered with a smirk.

"This dig is sponsored by the province and strictly speaking, it's off limits to anyone not directly involved."

The student's tone hardened as he sent a suspicious look toward Kim's stout canvas knapsack. Below, the archaeologist, arms crossed and haughtily erect, looked up toward them—the student must have been acting under his orders.

"Really? I wasn't aware of that. Well, I guess I'll head down to that streambed then." Kim forced another smile. "Huh—never thought I'd see the day when I'd be called a rock thief." And down the slope he went.

Across from where he and Hyesun had climbed the slope was a brook, and beside it two young women cleaning a bucketful of stones. After they had washed the dirt off and dried the stones with a towel, they wrapped each one in white rice paper as if attending to human remains.

Hyesun squatted beside them. "Is it fun?"

The two women grinned, their faces bronzed from nearly a month of working in the sun.

"Not so much fun as . . . well, it's kind of like being shut up in a great big time capsule. They date back so far—fifty or a hundred thousand years. And the only thing you ever hear is the wind."

"It's not just the wind," said Kim. "Can't you hear all those wandering souls crying? The Paleolithic people from way back when, and the tens of thousands of Commie Chinese soldiers who drowned here?"

The two women pretended to be scared, then broke into a giggle.

Recalling the farming couple they'd encountered, Hyesun looked uphill from the ruins, wondering where the Syngman Rhee villa might be. The man had definitely said the ruins were below the villa. When she had come here with Pyŏng'ŏn, their host in the village had explained that during the war a division of Chinese troops had drowned in the lake, then known as Hwach'ŏn Lake, and in the flush of victory President Rhee had renamed it P'aro, which literally meant "smash the barbarians." Hyesun and Pyŏng'ŏn had intended to visit the villa until their host informed them they'd have to cross a rugged ridge to reach it, whereupon Pyŏng'ŏn held back out of concern for his pregnant wife. And then back home, Hyesun had aborted the three-month-old fetus. She had considered the baby her hope for the future, but her situation then felt too gloomy and uncertain.

Again she told herself it wasn't prehistoric relics or water-polished stones that had drawn her here, but instead the bleak, empty lake appearing in the fuzzy black-and-white newspaper photo. In fact, hadn't she expected to see, there where the water once was, a clue to what lay inside her?

"Mr. Kim, this doesn't look like much of a stone-gathering place—nothing much except dirt here. So I thought I'd head up toward the old villa—what's the best way?"

"You'll probably just get depressed. Roof's gone, only things still standing are a few walls. You can follow that path through the pines. You'll see signs for the guard house and the gym, but that's about all."

Squatting beside the stream and absentmindedly dipping a hand in the current, he indicated a pine grove above the ruins.

From down below Hyesun couldn't make out the path. The grove looked dark and dense, and she had trouble visualizing a building there. She would have to re-climb the slope where the excavation was under way. Up she went, following the path she and Kim had just come down.

"Next year they'll begin filling it up. Then all of this will be underwater forever. We'll have to find a way. . . ."

Hyesun was surprised to see the television reporter lingering on the slope. Snatches of the archaeologist's imposing voice rode past her on the wind. The sun was sinking and the wind felt all the more fierce.

"Look, sir, look at this!" cried a young woman in a navy-blue parka from one of the pits. She rushed to the archaeologist. "It's weird."

The archaeologist's face lit up as he examined the palm-sized oval of white quartz that the student had handed him.

"This is really something. It's a person's face. This is quite a find."

Other students quickly gathered around.

"What is it? Did we hit the jackpot?"

Before she knew it, Hyesun was approaching the group. As the archaeologist cleaned the stone with the palm of his hand and picked dirt from its cavities, a vivid expression came to life. It was indeed a human likeness, and a woman's at that. Three holes had been chiseled in the unpretentious white stone, producing a becoming expression that was startlingly rich and profound. The students regarded the stone, some saying it was smiling, others that it was weeping, and still others saying it looked sad. But Hyesun couldn't find words to describe the face. A profound grief, an extreme longing, an earnestness—if she were to admit to seeing these emotions in the face of this woman of antiquity, they would have been what she herself wanted to see there.

One day ages ago, a young man had left the communal work area in search of a stone suitable for fashioning into a hunting tool. He had come across an attractive piece of white quartz, and on it he had carved the face of a young woman who occupied his heart. Had he kept the stone? Had he given it to her? Or had he simply made it for a lark and discarded it just as casually?

Hyesun made her way among the gathered students and brazenly stuck out her hand.

"Could I see it for a second?"

With a look of dubious surprise, the archaeologist silently handed her the stone.

Hyesun rested it in her palm and tried to fathom the cryptic expression. Through the eyes of that woman who had risen from the dirt after tens of thousands of years, she tried to see a lake with no water and a swirling wind that murmured like an endless conversation.

THE RELEASE

The day was bright and clear. The wind was up, and the sharp chill of early spring sliced through my clothes. I always felt rootless and disowned when I visited the cemetery. The cold was my only anchor.

What a stark difference from two years ago, or even a year ago. The cemetery then was a bleak, denuded, sectioned hill. Now it held so many burial mounds in its grassy expanse that scarcely an empty plot remained.

I had come to feel that the boundary between human life and death was vague and insignificant, but I guess I wasn't the only one—Mother, hastening to keep up with me, more than once came to a sudden halt and gazed at the ridge and the valleys bristling with mounds.

Before my husband's grave on the upper reaches of the hill I arranged the *soju*, dried fish, and fruit I'd prepared for our simple observance. After lighting the incense and pouring the ritual cup of spirits, I bowed, then bowed again, prostrating myself each time. Not until I was done did Mother look my way. Where she sat, she had virtually turned her back on me to gaze down at the river below.

The sight of me, a twenty-nine-year-old widow facing years upon lonely years, must have been more than she could bear, for she too had been left husbandless when young.

Today was the anniversary of my husband's death. Two years ago he'd accompanied a friend to his father's grave and their car had tumbled over a cliff. This terrible event, which I would never forget, was like a death sentence to me, the beginning of desolate, frightening days. But in his absence I lived on as before, and the seasons returned without fail. By now the sparse sod on his grave had sunk deep roots and sprouted new growth. But the burial mounds, so alive with green, ignored our state of mind.

Mother sat listlessly, having bundled up the offertory items and dishes in a large cloth. Then suddenly, "Look at all the mugwort." Half waddling, half squatting, she began to pick.

"What are you going to do with that stuff?" I asked her. "Don't you have anything better to worry about—like dead husbands, for example?"

She produced a bitter smirk. "Crazy girl."

I scowled at her back as her hands darted, picked, placed the herbs in a plastic bag. She would gather every last one, and then what? Use them for soup? Flavor rice cakes with them? As long as the dead were dead, the living must live—so she must have been thinking. Pick mugwort at the grave of a son-in-law who had met an unnatural death at an innocent age? Well, why not?

She'd been like that even when Father passed away leaving four children behind, close in age and close in size, with me, a fourth grader, the oldest. The three days of mourning at the hillside grave had passed, and on the following day, a Sunday, Mother went through the wardrobe and laid out all of Father's clothing on the veranda, every last thread, and called the taffyman to take it away. And not just his clothing, but his glasses, his leather belt, his books, his razor, everything he had possessed or used. All of it she unloaded on taffyman in return for a sack of popcorn and more white taffy than we had ever seen. And then she sat us down, fed us the popcorn, and handed us the long strips of taffy, helping herself to these edibles in the process. I was a bit precocious and had accepted Father's death, and the meaning of death in general, as a matter of deep sorrow and grief, and the rage and anger Mother's behavior produced in me remain vivid in my memory. All that was left of Father's life and the time we had spent with him was a new toothbrush and several pictures in a photo album.

For over a year, until all the bristles fell out, that toothbrush was used to scrub our sneakers. Why had Mother, having disposed of every trace of Father, saved just that toothbrush, a trivial item ultimately tossed in the wastebasket? Father's family shook their heads—what a hateful, heartless woman. Afterward she never mentioned Father, shed no tears for him that others could see, let no sigh escape her lips. Had this husband and wife never held affection for each other? Was Mother simply callous by nature? There was only one other possibility: Mother might have been so busy getting on with her life that she'd shunted aside all compassion for her departed husband. All right, life *is* harsh after a fashion. I had felt like worthlessness itself when my husband died. Even before his burial I'd been reduced to mealtime hunger, nighttime drowsiness, and perpetual worry about how to plug along in life.

Her plastic bag full of mugwort, Mother was finally ready to go back. It took a good half hour to walk the path down to the river, where we had to cross a bridge to reach the bus stop. At places along the riverbank fishermen had dropped their lines.

We crossed the span of concrete and Mother came to a stop at the far end, where a woman squatted in front of a large plastic basin. The basin was full of water, and in the water were three huge carp, golden scales gleaming. They were motionless save for an occasional wave of their fins; I wondered if fish felt claustrophobic. I could feel myself frown. How long could they hold out?

"Put a spring chicken inside one of these and boil the whole thing nice and slow," said the woman, "and you'll have yourself the best tonic a woman could want. Try it, ma'am."

Staring into the basin, Mother asked how much. Five thousand *wŏn* apiece. Too expensive. But before I could utter a word of protest, Mother had bargained the price down to ten thousand for all three. She paid the woman, who filled three clear plastic bags with water and added a fish to each. All I could do was look on, stewing with displeasure.

"You take one."

Mother handed me a bag, and from the bridge we turned onto a path along the riverbank. I pointed to the cloud of dust approaching from a distance—if we missed that bus we'd have to wait two hours for the next one. Mother glanced back at me but continued toward the river. When we had passed all the fishermen and no one else was around, she squatted beside the water. I simply couldn't understand it and chafed in irritation as the bus went its merry way before my eyes, thanks to Mother's ridiculous behavior. Mother placed one of the bags in the water and ever so gently and carefully, almost tenderly, she opened it.

The carp's hefty bulk drifted free. And then she opened the second bag.

"Now don't be stupid and take the fisherman's bait—just swim far, far away," she murmured, as if she were speaking to a human being. And then to me she murmured, almost as if I wasn't there,

"How could women like us ever understand life and death? It's so basic, and yet we'll never get to the bottom of it. I couldn't bear to think of your dead father—it made me so upset, and to comfort myself I'd save a doomed life, just like I'm doing now. I know, I'm only trying to ease my pain, but the fact is, he's dead and I'm still alive. What else can I do for him?"

THE OLD WELL

On the morning of my forty-fifth birthday, I opened my eyes like on any other day to the clock striking six. The sun in its winter-ending passage greeted me with beams that stretched ever higher into the attenuating dawn, awakening me to familiar objects and the routine of my life. As I navigated among the electric rice cooker, the gas stove, the frying pans, the obsolete refrigerator with its stubborn clamor—each certain to be found in the place I had seen fit to position it—it briefly occurred to me that I could never have imagined looking the way I did today, forty-five years after my birth. And that was the only peculiarity about my birthday. On an early spring day that was probably not so different from this one, I'd left the womb of a thirty-three-year-old woman who had given birth every other year since the age of twenty-three, a woman who probably wished mine would be her last childbirth. And so I had entered the matrix of time.

For almost a decade more she continued to produce. Her last delivery was a boy, born when I was eight, after which her uterus shriveled up like a prune.

There's nothing in particular I can associate with the day I was born. Was it windy that spring day? Rainy? Clear? Cloudy? It's pointless now to ask my mother, so aged and senile she can't remember how to climb the stairs. She was of the last farming generation of her family and was blessed with many births. To her way of thinking, bearing children was as natural as chestnuts falling to the ground and ripe balsam seeds scattering on the wind.

I can remember when my youngest brother was born. Grandmother filled a clean gourd with rice, added a dried frond of seaweed, and after placing the gourd on a shelf in the inner quarters, consecrated it to the Three Spirits. Next she procured a handful of clean straw. This made me wonder if children, like animals, were born on a bed of hay. My glances toward the inner quarters, silent inquiries because I had no one to ask, grew progressively covert and dubious.

Grandmother proceeded to stack the fuel hole of the firebox with split wood, then boiled water in the cast-iron pot. All through the evening the bubbling water steamed up the dark, roomy kitchen. No one offered the children the particulars, but we were given to understand from the bustle and the guarded whispers of the grownups that Mother was preparing to give birth.

Grandmother instructed my fifteen-year-old sister to draw water from the Old Well and fill the water jug. "Don't let your hair fall in it," she warned. "And no chattering—it's vile if your spit gets in it." My sister found this task humiliating, and I was sure she would pout, but to my surprise she located the tin water pail without protest, and I followed her out with the bucket. All during our journey beyond the big shade tree to the distant well my sister kept to herself. After we had returned with the water, Grandmother inspected it for any mote of dust, blade of grass, or shred of leaf, then filled a white soup bowl and removed it to the terrace where the condiment crocks were stored. Next she filled the ceremonial bowl that we kept near the cooking area to propitiate the kitchen god. Father kept out of sight. "Go see one of your friends," Grandmother had said, ushering him out. "Childbirth is women's business." Men, she seemed to be suggesting, were useful only when it came to *making* babies.

We children were gathered in the chill of the outer room, the one farthest from the firebox, pretending to be engrossed in our games, when actually we had ears only for the groans escaping from Mother in the inner quarters. We found no amusement in our games of cat's-cradle and pick-up stones. Nor did we engage in our inevitable squabbling. "It's showing . . . her water's broken . . . she hasn't opened up yet . . . she has a ways to go." Every time my fifteen-year-old sister heard these observations from Grandmother, interspersed with Mother's cries of "*Aigo!*" she shuddered and her small face hardened. "I'm not getting married. I'm not going to have babies." I was sobbing because Second Elder Brother had knuckled my head after I reported that Chŏngok's mom, the Undertaker's wife, had died in childbirth along with her baby. The inner quarters remained lighted well into the night. We strained anxiously for the buzz of voices and the moans of delivery, ultimately falling asleep in our clothes, sprawled out every which way, to awaken on our own early the next morning. It would scarcely have been daybreak, but the white paper panes of the door were as bright as if reflecting an overnight snowfall. All was still, as after the passing of a great event. And when we saw a meal tray loaded with white steamed rice and seaweed soup, its oily surface glistening, we realized that Mother had given birth while we slept. We ventured to the inner quarters, and there on the coolest area of the heated floor lay a heap of straw and a crumpled, bloodstained cloth that looked most peculiar to our eyes. The newborn was dressed in baby clothes that each of us in turn had worn, imbuing them with a bit of our own life before casting them off or outgrowing them. He had fallen asleep breathing a thick blend of blood, perspiration, and mother's milk, all of it suffused with the night's suffering.

Grandmother went out back and burned the bloody straw and the umbilical cord and afterbirth. Up in smoke went the world from which we had emerged, black soot coming to rest on the clean well water in the white bowl that Grandmother had placed on the condiment-crock terrace. In this way we bid farewell to a world that had forever been cryptic and secret.

Father had braided straw into a length of rope, festooned it with charcoal sticks and red peppers, then trailed it between the posts of the front gate to ward off evil. The yard had been swept, and as we departed for school our feet left small prints on the bare ground, otherwise untrammeled but showing the sharp outlines of the bush-clover broom. We hush-hushed the news to every group of children we met along the way: "Mom had a baby—it's a boy."

I have an image of a baby being born, an image tinged with brightness, coziness, and a kind of sorrow. We are, every one of us, born a bloody mass from the crotch of a pitiable woman, and our deliberate passage into a lifetime of existence is like a walk down a familiar path. If we try to imagine what it is to live, in the majority of cases either we find it too perplexing or we're quite content with it. When we visit a burial ground, we experience the contradictory feeling that peoples' lives are both more than and no more than the dates inscribed on the stone. And yet, compared with that simple chronicle of birth and death, the epitaph recording their life and works can reveal the most flimsy excuses, or else that which is superfluous.

What is forty-five years of a person's life? Time enough to grow wealthy or penniless, to become a president or a charlatan, sufficient time to be dead and scattered by wind, fire, water, or dust and come to rest at the foot of a hill. Time enough for me to have traced the course of evolution since the dawn of time, to have journeyed across the water 600 miles below the Equator to the Galapagos Islands, to have gone to Africa and spread the love of medical healing. I could have been Robinson Crusoe on his desert island, or a prophet in the wilderness. I could have written a splendid book singing of Divine Providence at work among blooming flowers and withering leaves. I could have been a dancer dancing barefoot in the grass. I could have written a volume about the law of the constancy of mass, about the existence of the soul, about reincarnation and the transmigration of the soul. I could have been an alchemist, working lead and iron into gold; I might have learned, observing the stars in the nocturnal heavens, the path I must take.

But instead I'm living the life of a middle-aged housewife in a small provincial city, a life aggravated by migraine headaches and by the hemorrhoids I still have from my last pregnancy. I read the latest poetry and essays, I watch the evening news, and I subscribe to two dailies, one held to be conservative and the other progressive, and all of these I consider my window upon the world. I attend the monthly PTA meeting at my son's school; twice weekly I go to market; once a week I visit an herbal sauna, traversing the same streets and alleys; and every Thursday I volunteer at a rehab center, helping the disabled with their physical therapy. On the rare occasions when a celebrated ensemble or performer comes to town, my husband and I will dress up and have a night out.

What had brought the Galapagos to mind a couple of days ago was an afterimage skimming across the surface of my consciousness in the wake of a television special on endangered species, a hot topic for over a week now. The original impetus was likely the word *dodo*, which appeared on stickers my son had attached to his belongings. When I asked him what a dodo was, he said it was a bird that had lost the ability to fly and had gone extinct four centuries ago. Which made me wonder if any of us can help regarding our youthful self as something extinct that exists only in legend. And isn't this in turn a manifestation of the fear and resistance we feel when we find ourselves compelled to enter the world of custom and order?

So weak are our powers of imagination that it is foolish for us to rely on them in our conventional lives. That I'm able with clear conscience to briefly consider the possibility that life has selected *me* must mean that I've stumbled up against the latest of the growth rings of my life. By now, though, I know to wear the very same clothing to different functions, weddings or funerals, but perform the role appropriate to the occasion, and I take pride in the structure I bring to the things I do. I know the flavor I'll get when I mix garlic and ginger; I love the predictability of the washcloth and the dishrag; but I also know that there is a kind of method in an occasional escape into chaos.

My husband and son quickly finished breakfast and left for work and school. I was about to launch into cleaning the bathroom when I caught myself smirking. My neat and tidy husband often forgets, uncharacteristically, to flush the toilet. Never have I pointed this out to him. He's a modestly successful white-collar man who's beginning to lose his hair and gain the bulge of middle age, who over long years has grown accustomed to workplace, drinking party, and bed, who retains virtually nothing that calls to mind his childhood—just as no trace remains of the extreme hunger I felt as a child, or of my kleptomania, or of the worm medicine that brought a yellowish foam to my mouth. But when I see him curled up asleep on his side with his hands in his groin, when I notice his waterlogged stool there for all the world to see in the toilet he forgets to flush, I see also a vestige of the poverty of his childhood: a smaller, unchanging, deeply rooted version of his larger, aging present self, a boy who gazes raptly with eyes of wonder at the strange sight of the stool he has just excreted.

Among my husband's acquaintances from the university was a man somewhat older than he who worked an orchard in the Kyŏngsang countryside. We once visited this man and his wife and came upon them composting manure and grass. His wife, concerned, I guess, about the odor, had said to me, "Manure turns such pretty colors when it's composting." To which I had replied that once people begin avoiding the sight of their own excrement, maybe they've grown oblivious to their own essence. These two had gone to Germany for doctoral programs—one in German literature and the other in education—in the years before that nation was reunited, but shortly before finishing they became involved in some litigation or other and were deported. Upon his return to Korea the husband was jailed for a year, and after his release he developed a peculiar illness—a distance phobia. If he moved beyond a one-mile radius of his usual location, his heart began to pound and he grew jittery. When he returned to his ancestral home in the countryside he covered his eyes with a black handkerchief, learning to feel the radius within which he would have to live from then on. And so it was his wife who would drive us back to the bus terminal. He who was once honored as a proud young farmer said good-bye to us amid the profusion of apple blossoms in his orchard. "Ironic, isn't it—I always wanted to be a wanderer," he chuckled.

I finished cleaning up, in the process making the house seem all the more quiet and desolate. I lit the teakettle, then took the receiver from the phone mounted on the kitchen wall. I pressed the area code and, more quickly and forcefully than necessary, punched in the number. The ring was indistinct. Ten times it rang, fifteen, twenty. I replaced the receiver and slowly stirred the hot water in my teacup.

The city is divided north and south by a river. To the north are farms and to the south businesses, and near one end of the bridge between these two areas stands a farmers' market. I've been going there ever since I began preparing fresh vegetable juice for my husband and son. The prices are comparatively cheap, and most important, the produce is direct from the farm.

If you show up at the market early in the morning, the dew on the green leaves and the tubers gives the illusion that they're still planted in rows in the ground. The sight of this produce gives me the satisfaction I've felt standing among green plants at sunrise, my ankles damp with dew. At such times I find myself thinking it would be nice if I had a small plot to tend. I've learned that most of the produce we buy is grown not in natural conditions of sunshine, wind, and rain but instead in hothouses where temperature, humidity, and light are regulated, and that there's a way of taking withered greens and showering them with water to give them the vibrant appearance of freshly picked vegetables.

As I left the market, lugging in each hand a large plastic bag of kale and other vegetables, I wondered if I ought to apply for my driver's license before summer. Neighbors and friends had told me that being able to drive made a difference in their lifestyle and sensibilities—they felt so much more functional and independent. But when I reached the end of the bridge and saw a line of cars, motionless, all notions of driving were cast from my mind. Three streets emerged from the city to converge like the ribs of a fan there at the end of the bridge. Granted, under normal conditions the congestion was enough to form a bottleneck, but it was rare to see a tangle of vehicles at a standstill.

In the middle of the street stood a frizzy-haired woman in a heavy winter coat with her mouth full of cigarettes. She was directing traffic. Passersby smirked and horns blared hysterically. Among the row of vehicles I spotted a familiar navy-blue car—my husband's—with passengers front and rear. It was a good guess that he was on his way back to the bank after lunch at the sashimi restaurant across the bridge. One of his important duties as a department head was to take meals with customers. His hands rested on the wheel; his face, unseen by his passengers, was filled with fatigue and tedium. The men in the back seat had stuck out their heads out the window to laugh at the woman.

I managed to keep out of his sight, though it wasn't a conscious decision. His gaze was fixed straight ahead and he didn't seem to have noticed me. He was dressed the same as in the morning, but he looked somehow alien. I was puzzled by this quirk—I was close enough that had I watched him a minute longer or called out in anything above a whisper, he would have recognized me.

The madwoman directed traffic as if she had been born to the task, and when a policeman clamped a hand on her shoulder and led her away she followed obediently, with enough presence of mind to wave at the occupants of the dark, beetle-like throng of cars. The vehicles finally began to move, the navy-blue car blended into the traffic, and the next I knew it had left my immediate field of vision. I followed it with my eyes till it was no longer visible, then shuffled to the bus stop.

Buses came and went, but I remained rooted to the spot where I stood. The bus fare clutched in my hand felt clammy. *Sure you want to lug all that stuff on the bus?* I asked myself. *It's only three o'clock, nothing waiting at home, dinnertime's a long way off.* The light at the nearby intersection turned green, but still I stood, no thoughts of crossing, gazing across the way toward a building, before I managed to mutter to myself, *A hot cup of coffee would be nice.* Taxis proved elusive. An empty one might come along, only to disappear before I could hail it. More frequent were the ones heading in the direction opposite where I had to go. Better to catch one of them, even though it meant the driver would have to turn around, so I crossed the street. I located a taxi stand, ventured toward it, and was brought up short in front of a coffee house from my past.

"Brought up short" isn't exactly right. I can't deny that the distant route from home to this place was a detour, and one I hadn't taken in years. I pressed my forehead to the window. On a table next to the window, which faced out onto the river, lay a still life composed of a pack of cigarettes, a coffee cup half full, and a ring of keys. Smoke drifted from a cigarette in the ashtray. The chairs were vacant. Above the table my reflection flickered ghostlike in the window. I gasped, my eyes gaping—perhaps out of fear of what was empty, of that which had disappeared. This place was a world apart, where an apple might fall without a thunk.*

A world where from time to time I listened to the ringing at the other end of a telephone line before it was sucked into the heart of darkness, there to fade and die. A world of impersonal references that could be spoken of only in the past tense. But a world in which I could muster the energy to utter the word "him."

The coffee house was a place where lovers lingered till dark, looking out at the river. The heavy wooden door creaked open as if to say, *The first time in years.* At mid-afternoon there were virtually no customers and the place was still. Everything was just as I remembered it, an evocative stage set. The only difference was that the owner in his ivory-colored dress shirt and neat cuffs had grown a beard—and that the interior was more antiquated and subdued. I took a seat in the innermost area, a place where the table with the half-finished coffee was directly in sight. The occupant of that table must have been the man in the phone booth next to the counter. His back was toward me. I could see him dialing, but the glass enclosure of the booth rendered his voice inaudible.

"Looks like spring is here to stay," said the owner as he handed me the leather-covered menu. In an incongruous raspy undertone, the me of years ago ordered Blue Mountain coffee. If I had been with *him,* the owner would have said, as he had then, *Isn't the color of the water nice?* And if *he* said, *Indeed it is,* the owner would have added, *There's no real spring or autumn around here. Just when you think it's spring it's summer, and as soon as autumn arrives it starts to snow.* The owner knew that *he* had moved here

*Author's note: From a poem by Pak Mogwŏl.

from a crowded metropolis. The people in this area don't usually say things like *Isn't the color of the water nice?* That's more the casual utterance of a wanderer, one who is forever departing elsewhere after a momentary stop; a wanderer who lingers in my eyes only for the time it takes to smoke a cigarette, drink a cup of coffee, finish a glass of beer.

Bluish smoke no longer rose from the cigarette in the ashtray. The white ash listed precariously, then crumbled.

I gazed at what *he* had once viewed over my shoulder: the river and the small island choked with reeds.

The man in the phone booth returned to his table and slumped into the chair. His hair was speckled with gray. He lit a fresh cigarette. The owner arrived with my coffee. The bold aroma set the subdued interior atremble as it wafted through the air. The man might have noticed—he turned in my direction and his gaze briefly met mine. There was something dreary and unsettling in his eyes. My eyes remained fixed on his as I slowly stirred in sugar and cream. I knew the owner was famous for the taste of his coffee, and I knew he was gay. In this small city nothing could be hidden. He was not an elderly man and his beard, so lush it seemed artificial, was a façade.

The plaster death mask of Beethoven still sat high on the wall. I had probably told *him*, sitting across from me, that we used to make plaster masks in art class. I had probably told *him*, in a desperate effort to catch the hazy gaze that was directed over my shoulder, that when they stopped up my nostrils, covered my eyes, and applied the thick plaster to my face I had thought that the cold, dark, blank-monitor sensation must be what death felt like.

The man at the other table finished his cigarette and returned to the phone booth. I turned my gaze to the river. It was altogether the color of spring. The distant hills were a fuzzy brown without their spring growth, and the willows lining the river were a baby green haze. Halfway across the bridge, a woman had bent far over to look down at the water. There were frequent suicides at this bridge. These were reported in short notices tucked away in the local newspaper with small headlines such as CHRONIC ILLNESS, HARD LIFE, LOST LOVE. The current, swifter than you would think, swept past the pillars beneath the middle of the bridge and would suck a drowned body deep, only much later delivering it to the surface downriver.

When I was young, I knew death as a white envelope. There had been times when I returned home from school or left the house in the morning and saw such an envelope wedged halfway between the gatepost and gate. None of the family knew who had left it there or when. The grownups never told us it contained a death notice, but we learned somehow that it was ominous, something that would bring bad luck if we willfully touched or opened it. It was a strange, terrifying secret, death in its blank white envelope slipping into our gate when no one was aware.

Even in summer with its bright, swelling greenery, Father on his deathbed said he could hear over and over the snapping of branches. His ears, open to the afterlife, were hearing sounds from another world, one that existed only in images of cellophane clarity invisible to others. Knowing it was the auditory hallucination of one facing death, the gathered family paid scant attention, responding instead by pretending frequently to look outside in the course of their vigil, and in doing so they put Father at peace. We did not know that what he heard were the sounds of death, and death was something we were too young to recognize. "It was truly a lovely, peaceful passing." But as proud Mother said this, Father, not yet encoffined, had started to decompose. In life his body had shaken with laughter; in death it reeked. Mother didn't realize that what she had said was taboo. The people of old were right, in spite of their long-standing superstition. They knew how to show dignity in the face of death. It was forbidden to speak of the person who had died. When at the midnight hour the shaman had gone up on the roof to wave a white traditional jacket of the deceased in order to usher the first outcry of his soul toward the inky heavens, my little son said he saw a huge white bird, wings outstretched, flying into the dark of the sky.

The ringing in my ears that had tormented me for some time after *his* death finally went away. When I had reported this ailment to the youthful ear, nose, and throat specialist—a feeling that my ears were swelling without letup, a seething medley of indecipherable murmurs that gave me wracking headaches—he had ventured a guess that something was wrong with my inner ear. And now there is no trace of *him* left in my mundane everyday life. I eat, I sleep, and the sex act is for me brief and mechanical, like the meaningless sighs that escape from me when I'm alone. But *he* lives on in my trivial gestures and rituals, just as all of the dead, even after memories of them are eradicated, seem to be nestled in the genes of those who survive them. From the time I read in the newspaper of his passing, I fell into the habit of summoning his telephone number from where it drifted in my mind, and punching it in. Over and over I sent the ringing of a telephone toward the depths of darkness; again and again the sequence of digits he could no longer use issued out into a dark void. How could he have died? And why? But such questions were no longer meaningful.

For a time after *he* died everyone looked like a corpse to me. Corpses that ate, drank, gave hearty laughter, walked about, enjoyed pleasure, suffered pain. Perhaps my childhood friend Chŏngok's father was right. Chŏngok told me her soused father, the man who shrouded corpses, slept in a coffin every night.

The man re-emerged from the phone booth and his eyes drew mine as they looked out over the bridge. It was the gaze not of a man looking at a woman but of one who had fallen into confusion. As the years go by, I've come to feel that a stranger's gaze is not simply a matter of a man looking at a woman, me. The cast of the eyes, now inscrutable and fleeting like the reflection of a glass bead, now boring into my innards, is most likely signaling to me that I'm a woman who's seen better days.

I looked squarely back at the man. He smoothed hair that was already neatly combed, rubbed his face, and his bewildered eyes became flustered. The owner didn't seem comfortable with the resolute, almost palpable silence encased in this room and put on a record. Needle scratched on vinyl and Ravel's *Bolero* commenced.

With difficulty the man removed himself from my gaze and spread open his newspaper. But I could sense him observing me as before, his eyes above the newspaper page that shielded his face; I could hear gasps that sounded ever more strained. He was obviously disoriented. He wouldn't have been so embarrassed had I been a beautiful young thing. *Who is she and why is she staring at me?* I imagined him breaking into a cold sweat as he ransacked the jumbled storehouse of his memories, the faces of women he had known, embraced, and discarded coming faintly to mind. The gradually accelerating rhythm of the castanets sounded closer and closer and I imagined the collected threads of his memory scattering, setting him adrift more deeply in the labyrinth of his mind.

Finally he came to a decision: placing the newspaper on the table, he lurched to his feet. In doing so he bumped against the table, knocking his coffee cup to the floor. With a sharp crack it shattered, and the last of the man's composure was lost. As the *Bolero*'s breathless whirl of eighth and sixteenth notes gave way to the finale, the owner inched toward the flustered man and intercepted him as he bent to pick up the pieces. They exchanged a few words, which I couldn't hear over the constant crescendo and ever-quickening tempo of the music. Not the slightest glance did the man send in my direction. His back set firmly toward me, he crumpled and disposed of his empty cigarette pack, gathered his keychain, paid the owner, and left.

I could see him through the broad glass window, unsteady as he traversed a crosswalk. At a tobacco stand he purchased a pack of cigarettes, then produced a handkerchief and mopped his face.

I left the coffee house. Feeling on edge but unable to explain why, I scurried after him, following his footsteps along the crosswalk before arriving at the river.

I found him resting against a willow where parched grass carpeted the broad expanse of the riverbank. He took a series of deep breaths, his left hand massaging his chest. Either he was about to vomit or he was wrestling with an irrepressible force that threatened to burst out of him. His face was terribly pale. I couldn't tell if he had seen me. Brow furrowed, he peered through me at the sun, which had begun to sink.

Anxiously he loosened his necktie. For a moment it struck me that he might want to strangle himself with it, but then he placed the necktie in his suit jacket. Next it was off with his jacket. He lay down on his back, using the folded jacket as a pillow. By now he was gasping for breath. He covered his face with his handkerchief, then uttered an agonized cry as his body began to wrench back and forth. Before long his white dress shirt and his light-colored trousers were soiled with dirt and grass. "What's wrong? Are you sick?" I heard myself ask in a choked voice as I stepped back from him. In no time there was a crowd of street vendors and people who had been in line at the dock. "Shouldn't we call the police or take him to the hospital?" But they ignored my urgent words. Someone suggested the man was epileptic and was taking precautions to avoid striking his head during his spasms—judging from how he'd selected a quiet place, loosened his clothing, and lain down, it probably wasn't the first time and he'd soon be back to normal, so there really wasn't anything to worry about.

Like a frog twitching in its death throes, the man continued to writhe. The outlines of his face became visible through the sweat-soaked handkerchief. The onlookers exchanged anecdotes and conjectures while awaiting the outcome: Was epilepsy hereditary or not? Did you hear about the man who had an attack the first time he met the woman his matchmaker had picked for him? And then there was the man who had a fit on his wedding night and scared his bride away. The scene felt unreal, seemed somehow fabricated. I myself knew of a man who had passed the application test at a promising firm but was seized by a fit during the final interview; I knew of a man who had suffered an attack the very moment he managed with great difficulty to win over the woman he loved. How long would this episode last? Five minutes? Ten? The convulsions gradually subsided, and rather abruptly the man shuddered and heaved a great, whistling sigh. *It's over.* As if on command, the swollen front of the man's trousers suddenly soaked through in a relentless, spreading stain that darkened the fabric.

The man rose to his feet. Ignoring the bystanders, who had fallen mute, he brushed off his clothing and smoothed his hair. He picked up his jacket and at the very instant that he turned to leave, I felt his gaze. I will never forget the emptiness and solitude I saw in those eyes.

Over dinner my husband mentioned what a hot day it was, then asked if his summer suit was ready to go. I responded that it *was*, after all, spring and that spring weather was unpredictable. My husband then said he wanted to spend part of June at a quiet resort in the woods; that way we could avoid the summer vacation madness. He also suggested we could take a trip overseas after our son left for college in the big city. After dinner he read the paper and declared that polluted water and dirty air were taking a terrible toll on us. I agreed with him. The paper carried photos of people protesting contaminated reservoirs and a city water supply in which earthworms made occasional appearances from faucets.

Our discussions of a quiet vacation and clean air and water, of a pension and a country home, make me feel we're aging. My husband has been an indifferent Catholic since his late teens, when he was baptized with the Christian name Peter, but he says he wants to spend a peaceful retirement volunteering through the church for neighborhood and society. This may sound like a passing fancy, but I think it's fair to call it a plan. While it's true that we can't predict people's lives or even what will happen tomorrow, it's likely that my husband and I will enjoy our old age in this fashion unless we somehow become more adventurous. My husband wishes to grow old in dignity, free of ambition, and I want to trust him in this. I happened to learn that he takes part in church-sponsored campaigns and that he's pledged to be an organ donor. That he hasn't informed me of this I regard as a measure of his respect for my freedom of choice. For my part, I find it difficult to accept the notion of being stripped naked while I'm still warm, opened up by some stranger and my internal organs removed, and then deposited in the ground like an empty sack. If my husband should precede me in death, I might very well have him stuffed before burial.

It pleases me to hear my husband and son discussing issues I know nothing about—global warming and unusual weather patterns, foreign wars and nuclear bombs, newly discovered planets more distant than Pluto. Their conversation makes me realize that we live in a new and different world, makes me at once proud and apprehensive.

"I thought everyone had soured on the India craze, and now I see that meditation is all the rage. It says here that when you reach the highest level you're capable of almost anything—you can even have an orgasm while you're sitting still! How's that any different from masturbation?" I asked my husband as I read a newspaper insert advertising a meditation center. "Maybe it's a matter of what's productive," he answered. But is there anything more productive than the life we live from one day to the next? Consider the ingredients of that life. There is the son born of the legalized relationship between my husband and me. We watch over that boy as if he's a tree we've nurtured in health day by day, and at the same time we share hopes and worries, the minute issues of our daily existence, food and sex. To be sure, there's also a measure of betrayal, disillusionment, and rage. There is the peacefulness of water in a bowl and the stubborn mold in a crock of soy sauce that has cured, and there are the customs and order with which we embrace all of these. We rely on the virtue of ingrained habit to ease our tendency toward insomnia and put our feeble, painful memories to sleep. At some point, side by side in bed, we cease talking about the dreams we each dreamed the previous night. *How do you put up with me?* Every now and then I silently pose my husband this question. He probably asks me the very same thing. It's a valid question, but not once have I voiced it. After all, someone who's afraid of the water won't go beneath the surface, for fear of drowning.

But it wouldn't be honest of me to say our relationship is simply one of habit, a relationship tempered by time. To do so in a conscious attempt to ingratiate myself with others would be cowardly and hypocritical, tantamount to self-contempt. There is clearly something between us, but I can't describe it in terms of habit.

My husband and I were born the same year. We grew up in different areas, one of us in the west and the other in the east, but we share the experience of being born during the civil war and coming of age amid its ruins. We know the hunger and the hollow feeling of spring days and long summer afternoons without lunch, and the taste of roots, which we dug from the ground with dull knives or scraps of metal to fill that hollowness. We know the crack of the night watchman's clappers and the inexplicable sorrow it brought, making it difficult to sleep through the long, cold winter nights; the combination of regret and drowsiness felt upon waking from a late-afternoon nap; the horrible sight of a maimed soldier with a hook in place of a hand; and the beatings and curses that came from beaten-down parents. We were children who grew up reciting timetables, dates, oaths, and pledges of revolution.

When I look at my seventeen-year-old son I see the image of my husband at that age—though I did not know him then—and I never fail to be startled at the terrible cloning instinct in human DNA.

My husband mentioned the traffic jam that afternoon. By doing so he implicitly criticized the city officials, whose vision apparently extended no farther than the narrow streets immediately before them. "Shouldn't we sell the little house while it's still moving season?" In response I said I would see a realtor the next day about putting it on the market, and I left it at that.

Not until I finished the dishes did I realize I'd left my market vegetables at the coffee house.

Fronting our high-rise is a hill of mixed woods and acacia thickets. Across that hill is the "little house," as my husband and son are wont to call the unit we own in the Yesŏng Apartments. And on the way to that apartment building is the Lotus House. To get to the Yesŏng Apartments you have to go out onto the street that connects with the entrance drive to our complex and make your way around the wall that encloses it. Normally I take a shortcut across the hill instead, ignoring the PRIVATE PROPERTY, NO TRESPASSING sign and crawling through a dog-sized hole in the barbed wire. Fortunately there remain on the hill some large, stout trees—pines, oaks, huge paulownias—and the sight of them never fails to bring me to a stop. Even when the leaves have fallen and the hardwoods are bare, if I stand beneath them around nightfall I feel somewhat akin to a sage and find myself staring with measured breaths at the advancing dusk.

From where the slope of the hill levels out, a fence used to extend around the Lotus House—except to the north, where the house is backed by the foot of the hill. The fence consisted of closely set wooden posts that were uniformly man-high and thick as the rafters of a fair-sized house, and strung between them was a dense mesh of thick wire. With the onset of spring the fence began to come down, starting from the east. Rumor had it the house was to be demolished and replaced by a sashimi restaurant specializing in carp and trout.

I was passing by the Lotus House on my way to the Yesŏng apartment when suddenly I noticed, wound about the fence, my scarf. Several days earlier Dimwit had cut his leg; I had used the scarf to bind the wound and promptly forgotten about it. It held no great attachment for me, fading and fraying as it was, and I had meant to throw it away, but for some reason that day I'd put it around my neck before heading out. With its garish red pattern, the scarf looked so out of place on the fence it embarrassed me—I kept thinking it belonged around my neck.

Dimwit had been spending his days taking out the fence, but on this particular day he was nowhere to be seen. Others call him Dimwit and so do I. He's past the age where you call a person by name. I never feel awkward calling out to him. My only reaction is that the two syllables of his nickname, like the two syllables of anyone else's given name, are merely a combination of consonants and vowels. He might be in his thirties. Then again, maybe his forties. He's one of those people whose age is easy to reckon but difficult to pinpoint.

A few days earlier I was watching him take out the fence. He was using a small saw to cut the wire. I could have suggested pliers, but I knew it was useless. As always, Dimwit had an audience of neighborhood children too young for school. They gave a running account of his every action: "Dimwit's smoking"; "Dimwit's peeing"; "Dimwit's laughing." Try as he might, he couldn't cut the wire, and then I saw him squat down, arms around his legs. Blood appeared on his dirty sweatpants. It turned out the saw blade had snapped, poking his knee. His face was melodramatically contorted and he was boo-hooing. There was no sign of life inside the Lotus House. The bloodstain spread. I had Dimwit roll up his pants leg, and then I loosened my scarf and wrapped the cut. The wound wasn't that deep, considering the amount of bleeding. His pants leg kept coming down, so I rolled it above his knee. When I touched his firm, sinewy thigh, he began writhing as if I were tickling him. "Dimwit's got hair, just like my father!" the children clamored, pointing at his leg. Dimwit ceased crying and the frown on his face was replaced by a look of pride. Although I didn't think he would understand, I told him to make sure he disinfected the cut and applied ointment. He only grinned. "He's Dimwit—he doesn't know anything," the children answered in his stead.

Perhaps Dimwit wanted to show he was clever by fixing the scarf about the fence as a way of returning it to me. I felt embarrassed leaving the scarf behind as I continued on to the Yesŏng apartment.

I opened the mailbox as I always did—never with a feeling of expectation but only because it bore the number of the apartment I owned—and extracted the water and electricity bills, which always showed the base rate. As I proceeded upstairs I encountered the woman on the third floor who volunteered as building monitor. She hadn't seen me for such a long time, she said, making me suspect she had tried several times to find me and was displeased that I was not a resident owner. From the standpoint of the building monitor, who has to shoulder all building-related errands and the chores others won't do, people like me must be vexing— people whose apartment is empty save for the name on the door, who never take part in cleaning the stairwells, canvassing for signatures, flocking occasionally to City Hall to file a petition, staging rallies, and such. But even if she thinks I'm never there, the fact is that I come and go at irregular times. The woman asked me for the club dues and several other minor payments that I'd neglected, and I promised I would pay her before long. I briefly entertained the thought of cheering her up by asking her to find a suitable buyer for the apartment, but instead I offered a cursory good-bye and brushed past her.

At the end of the corridor on the fifth and topmost floor I opened the forest green metal door to my apartment. As I entered, it occurred briefly to me that it was perhaps because of the strangely solitary and yet comfortable feeling I experienced when I opened the locked door that I had not sold the apartment, even though I had no specific need for it. As an argument for selling, my husband had mentioned the disadvantage of one family having two residences, and while I placed no stock in his remarks, I also said that we stood to profit because the people here had high hopes that the area would be redeveloped. The result was that we put off a decision from one day to the next. To be perfectly candid, though, I think I needed a space of my own.

It was a very small apartment built long ago for humble folk. You could feel the heat radiating through the flues running beneath the floor, but gathered together with the dust and its thin overlay of desolation was the chill you feel in a home where no one lives.

We had purchased it two years earlier, and lived here for three months before our new apartment was available and after we had sold our former home to take advantage of moving season. There wasn't much difference between the low purchase price and the deposit we would have had to pay on a rental. After the three months we moved into the new apartment and rented out this one. Our tenants had moved out the previous winter and the apartment had been vacant ever since.

It was as the renters had left it. I had swept and mopped it once but otherwise hadn't touched it. My cleanup job was made much easier by the fact that the young couple who had lived here were quite levelheaded and responsible and had left nothing behind. Except, that is, for the notepad in the pantry drawer—an item they had most likely forgotten. The pad had a hole at the top with a rubber band threaded through it and a pen hooked to the rubber band, making it resemble the credit book that the owners of a small sundries shop might keep. The contents included what looked like a shopping list—*one block of tofu, three mackerel pike, one bunch of spinach,* all written by the wife in a painstaking hand, along with the date. *One toy car, two pounds of bananas, a box of condoms.* As well as lines that might have been taken from poems or popular songs, I couldn't tell which. And regrets at having spanked their child or thought hatefully of her husband. *It's as I thought—he's a good man but pitiful. I should try to understand him. Poverty dries us up; it makes us forget the words and the gaze of love. Today I'm especially melancholy and full of dislike—I can't stand it. Perhaps it's the rain. All I want is to go somewhere....* The lives of the young couple jotted down in clumsy handwriting made me smile. I couldn't bring myself to throw the notepad in the wastebasket, and I held out the possibility that I could return it should I happen to meet the owner, so I kept it in the topmost compartment of the pantry.

The previous winter I had come here almost every day on the pretext of fueling the coal-briquette water heater so the pipes wouldn't freeze and burst. Nothing is in the apartment save broom, dustpan, and the forgotten notepad. You can see, though, where framed pictures and the wardrobe used to be: squares and rectangles on the wall where the color is less faded. It seems that their existence is revealed only after the object itself has disappeared. I take naps here and look out the window; there's no work for me to do. I'm alert to the recording of "Für Elise" that comes from the laundry truck, the shouts of peddlers hawking from their trucks over loudspeakers, and—a sound I'd forgotten—a baby bawling. When I look out the west-facing window around sunset I can almost visualize among the fleeting golden rays the short period in which we lived here, and it fills me with sadness.

If I open the window I can look right down at the Lotus House. It's a large, tile-roof structure that's lasted some two hundred years. The local people call it the Chinsa House or Dimwit's House as well as the Lotus House. The "Lotus" part of the name presumably comes from the pond in the front yard with its marvelous summertime display of pond lilies. I'd heard several accounts from the owner of the sundries shop near the entrance to our building: born in the Lotus House were at least five high government officials but also nine idiots; their descendants— teachers, officials, and peddlers—had scattered to all parts; and Dimwit, unable to take a wife, had remained at home with his elderly mother, looking after the house and hiring out for various chores. The sundries shop owner had been born in the area and had lived here all his sixty years, and there was nothing he didn't know about the Lotus House. I'd learned from him that the hill between this building and the high-rise where we now lived used to belong to the Lotus House, as had the sites where both apartment buildings now stand, but that the property had been sold off a chunk at a time, that the squabbles over assets when the family gathered for the ancestral rites were a sight to behold, and that the house itself, in such a state of disrepair that it looked haunted, would likely be torn down and replaced with a fancy sashimi restaurant that would inevitably bear the name Something-or-Other Garden. "Times are different now," he added. "Making money's number one—spend a hundred years fussing over your glorious family history, and you won't have a copper to show for it." He was referring to the Lotus House.

Among the imposing roof tiles were desiccated stalks of grass that now and then were startled into motion by the breeze. In the backyard a tangle of forsythias had put forth yellow blossoms; splashes of red marked the azalea buds. Spring growth flowed between earth and heaven. Trees surrounded the house at a distance and the swelling buds of the apricot and pear trees beside the pond resembled fleshy red eyes.

A vegetable plot had appeared, but the lot was vast enough that the front yard and the gardens in back remained ample. The house itself, along with its pond, tower, and pavilion, vestiges of the past, was disintegrating like ash amid the riot of spring growth. Most likely none of the surviving family members was up to maintaining it.

Out from this moribund house came Dimwit. He washed his face at the faucet in the yard, then hefted a shovel and set off toward the east-facing part of the fence, seemingly ready to take out more of it. I assumed he wouldn't touch the saw again after cutting himself with it before. My old scarf was still there beside the wide-open gate, a reddish knot on the fence. He was a powerful man. Dancing back and forth, he dismantled the fence and tossed the posts aside with never a pause. Dimwit was always there, hovering about the house like a yo-yo, part of the wind, part of the scene I saw when I gazed out my window.

In the steam-filled sauna, naked women with pained expressions sit silently on the narrow benches, their mouths covered with towels. Thus do I imagine the pain of those who died at Auschwitz. But the pores of these women are wide open and their peachy skin resembles flowers in full bloom. Clumps of mugwort hang from the walls, as if to reassure us that this is, true to its name, a "mugwort sauna." Covering my mouth with a towel soaked in cold water, I try to count to a hundred. At first I had trouble counting to twenty, but now a hundred is not so difficult.

After the sauna I rinse my sweaty body with tepid water. Among the public baths in our neighborhood this one has reasonably good facilities and the water is clean, so it always draws a lot of customers. There's a whole range of women here, industriously scrubbing their skin clean, soaping their bodies, and getting a massage—young women; pudgy, waxy, middle-aged women; women in the last stages of pregnancy; and elderly women with stretch marks that attest to their former fecundity. Last autumn my husband brought me a *matryoshka* doll from Russia. It's made of thin wood and on it is painted a young woman with rosy cheeks and wearing traditional clothing. It's simple in shape and appearance, like a self-righting doll, but inside it are a series of replicas, each one smaller than the previous one. It strikes me that these nesting dolls could represent life's iterations. How many women do you suppose there are within an elderly woman whose skin is drooping like a huge, ragged layer of outerwear on a gaunt frame? A woman less elderly, a woman who has begun to age, a young woman, a pubescent girl, a little girl whose existence is like the tiny secret of a fruit—a seed waiting to be opened?

Beside me a young woman whose belly was swollen with child was washing her daughter. The girl—I guessed her to be four or five—was absorbed in washing a plastic doll. Was the maternal instinct already at work? I myself had settled into the maternal role shortly after marrying, with no more doubt than if I'd crossed the veranda from one room to another. This very morning I had hurried out the door to see off my son, when a chill swept my heart. I called his name, but when he turned back to me I merely smiled and waved as if nothing was wrong. What had struck me so suddenly and powerfully was a feeling of compassion for the purity that was sprouting inside him like a radish shoot. At this realization I had turned away and closed the door.

Since my son was born I haven't had the dreams that were so frequent before, the dreams of flying or of nose-diving to the ground. Or the dream that I was tiny and was looking for a place to hide.

"Ow—that's hot, you bitch!" A half-lathered girl bounced up screaming. Her mother had just poured a tub of rinse water over her. At the clarity and suddenness of the obscenity, the other women ceased their silent washing and giggled at the mother and child. Startled, the mother ceased her ministrations and looked about in confusion. The girl burst into sobs. "I'm sorry, Mommy, I thought it was someone else." Her hoarse crying echoed against the cavernous ceiling.

I stood under the shower, hot water pouring over me, and shuddered. I couldn't see myself in the mirror. I knew it was because the mirror was steamed up, but still I found it frightening that what should have been there was not.

I turned off the shower and looked into the mirror. The steam gradually cleared from its surface to reveal the outline of my face coming slowly to life, as if approaching from the far distance. My face, asymmetric like a patch of reject fabric—this was the slight change that appeared in me after *his* death.

When I saw *his* name in the obituaries, where I'd glanced as I folded the laundry, and after I read the details and knew it was in fact *him*, my first reaction was to look in the mirror. I can't describe my mental state, but whatever it was, it led me to the mirror like an automaton. The face that greeted me was cracked and broken. It wasn't that I'd suddenly discovered wrinkles, or that the mirror itself was cracked. Rather, the face I saw there had in a single instant shattered all of my ingrained customs and habits. Before a scream could escape me, the broken face disappeared and the face I knew came into view. My own face, true, but one I wouldn't have known if not through the medium of a mirror or a photograph. I removed myself from the mirror, rushed through the remaining laundry, then took the Chinese cabbage I was soaking in salt water and added the necessary ingredients for making kimchi. What else could I do but continue my routine? I prepared fixings for my son's lunchbox, shared a joke with my husband as we watched television, and let out a moth that had worked its way through the shabby moth netting and was whirling and flitting about the light.

Thus was *his* death made known to me, in an anonymous and very ordinary manner.

The impact of my realization that *he* had disappeared forever from this world, that he no longer existed, drifted by, as did the calm and ordinary hours of evening, no different from any other day.

He died and something within me died. What that something was, I don't know. And perhaps I don't wish to know. I fell into

204 THE OLD WELL

the habit of stopping short and gaping at my reflection whenever I saw it—in a display window, in a grocery store mirror, in water. Rinsing the evening rice, I would find myself looking out at the darkening woods and the twilight to see, melting gently into habit, like a drop of blood dissolving in water, the reality of his existence and nonexistence. He exists at the farthest reach of a gradually receding scene in a painting that's a model of perspective, at an indistinct vanishing point that's disappeared from my range of vision. As in bygone days, the me of the present moment is on occasion happy and on occasion unhappy. And that's how I'll grow old, keeping in mind a mutually acknowledged image of old age, an image no different from that held by others.

I returned home from the bathhouse, settled into my easy chair, and fell into a deep slumber. I dreamed I was a little girl standing beside the Old Well. I was crying because I'd accidentally let my bucket fall in. I tiptoed to the wall around the opening and peered down, but nothing could be seen in the well's obscure depths—not the bucket and not the golden carp that glided to the surface at night when no one was there. The desolation I felt in that dream remained after I awakened. These days I sometimes dream about that well. The dream is more or less the same: I'm crying because the bucket's fallen in; or I'm with Chŏngok, my childhood playmate who died, and we're looking down into the calm, settled water and its perfect roundness; or some sort of ritual is going on.

It was my great-grandmother who told me about the well and the golden carp.

In the neighborhood where we lived when I was a child, there was a large well. Because it was so large it was sometimes called the Big Well, but ever since the old days people had customarily called it the Old Well. "Old" meaning that the well had been there for as long as anyone could remember. The water was deep and it had a clean, sweet taste. That's what Great-grandmother told me. And in the Old Well there lived a golden carp. After a thousand years it changed into a serpent, and after another thousand years, on a night of thunder and lightning, it became a dragon and rose to heaven. When Great-grandmother was in her nineties, black hair appeared on her head and her hollow mouth produced a tooth as spotless and white as a silkworm egg. Mother took this as an ill omen. The old woman was growing senile, she said. Mother didn't respond to anything Great-grandmother said, didn't make eye contact with her, and fed her only small amounts. There was a saying that the senile live long lives, and this prospect bothered her. But Great-grandmother was not like Kwangja's grandmother, who was supposed to have been possessed by the spirit of a cat and who went around at night yowling and trying to catch mice. Nor was she like Odol's grandfather, who ate his own feces.

When we looked into the well on a moonlit night we almost expected to hear the golden carp gliding through the water. The girls had half-day classes, and after they returned home they had until sunset to draw water. If they let their bucket fall in, they caught a beating or went without supper, but still there was always some child who would lose her bucket and remain in helpless despair at the well until dusk, scared to death and crying. Carelessness was an unforgivable vice. Chŏngok, the Undertaker's daughter, who came to draw water with her stepmother's baby riding on her back, was someone whose bucket often fell in.

EAST SEA FUNERAL HOME, a respectable enough sign, hung from Chŏngok's house, but the neighbors called her father the Undertaker. Word had it that he slept inside a coffin. Maybe it was true, who knows? People didn't die that often, and the Undertaker, when he had nothing to occupy him, spent most of his time drunk. With her stepmother away selling rice cakes at the market, Chŏngok did the cooking and the laundry, and her hands seemed perpetually swollen and too large. She always carried a baby on her back, but she was spirited and full of zest and nothing seemed to faze her. If we wanted to find her we didn't need to go to her house, which we suspected produced a strange and terrible odor. For in spite of her stepmother's reminders to stay home and watch the baby while she went out, you could count on finding Chŏngok half a dozen steps behind the woman, the baby on her back and a smile on her face. She played jump rope, baby and all, and if the effort caused her accidentally to bite her tongue, she suspended the baby in its quilt wrapper from a utility pole and played tag and more jump rope. Sometimes she played hide-and-seek and forgot about the baby, leaving it to hang, sleeping, like a cloth bundle till dusk. If her bucket fell into the well, she was given a pail and sent back out. Which meant, more often than not, that she would stand crying at the well till sunset. Older girls in the neighborhood or women who had come to draw water scolded Chŏngok for her carelessness, then lent her their own bucket with a warning: "If you let this one fall in, you're going in after it."

When you marshaled all your energy to draw the water-laden bucket from the well, you'd feel a burst of panic, as if some superhuman force was about to pull it back into the water, and either the rope would slip from your tense grip or the knot around the handle would come apart, leaving you with nothing on the other end. And even when you managed to complete the task successfully, your heart would pound if the rope were to suddenly slip partway through your fingers.

The other children didn't believe me when I told them a golden carp lived in the well. They called me a liar and a bigmouth. But Chŏngok believed me. She said the carp would make our dreams come true.

During the summer a ceremony was held at the well after the monsoons had come and gone. It was the grownups' belief that national disasters on the order of droughts or flooding made well water and condiments turn bad. And the monsoons that year were something to behold. The school became a shelter for flood victims, classes were canceled, and the children flocked to the river. The grownups, for their part, set out from home with long poles and nets. Soaring out of the water, a roost for large birds, were the branches of the poplars on the island. The river itself swelled into a broad plain of muddy water. The adults were up all night for fear the water would breach the riverbanks. But still they set out for the river in the morning with their poles.

At the riverside the children sang:

The rains bring out the turds,
Watch them float along,
Hear them sing their own name,
Durdurdurdurd, turdturdturdturd.

For the final refrain we all joined together and screeched, our faces and lips pale in the wind and rain. And in fact the river held everything imaginable. Pumpkins, wardrobes, nickel-silver pots, chickens and pigs still in their pens: all were carried off by the strong flow. Inja's father, trying to retrieve a squealing pig as it floated by, was swept away and very nearly drowned.

The ceremony at the well was held when the monsoons ended. While we all waited for the silt to settle out of the well water a date was set; rice cakes, a pig's head, and fruit were prepared; and an offertory rite for the spirits was held. Afterward the men emptied the well dry. Then Sunok's uncle, recently discharged from the service, removed his shoes and socks and was lowered in stout netting, like the man in the folktale, into the well. The children looked on uneasily as he descended into the depths. It was as though he were being swallowed by a dark, infinitely deep circle. Tiny frogs hopped among the crevices between the mossy stones, their calls amplified by the hollow profundity of the well. We heard scraping against the ground at the bottom, and when Sunok's uncle asked for the net to be brought up, his voice reverberating against the walls, the men above began to haul in the line. The net held a seemingly endless variety of items—a container of dirt from the bottom, rusty buckets, a metal bucket claw, a pair of flabby rubber shoes, a rotted chunk of wood, porcelain chips. From above, Sunok's uncle, bent over in the gloomy depths of the well, looked like a dwarf. Each time the net was brought to the surface, everyone avidly inspected the contents. Perhaps we expected these unknown objects from the depths of the well to be something fantastic. When the last haul yielded only sandy dirt, the work was stopped. And finally Sunok's uncle was brought up. I remember thinking that he could have been five hundred years old. He looked about uncertainly while his eyes readjusted to the light, then produced an incongruous burst of laughter. After he and the other men who had performed the offering went off to drink, the children lingered at the edge of the well, gazing silently into its empty depths.

The golden carp was no longer there. Still, when I saw clear water pooling at the bottom I continued to believe the fish was alive. Chŏngok was convinced that it wanted to hide from the gaze of humans and had hidden itself in a spring deep within the well, to emerge only when clear water had filled it again.

Late that autumn Chŏngok fell into the well and drowned. A villager who had gone to fetch water before daybreak discovered an empty pail beside the well and Chŏngok's body floating within. No one was supposed to draw water after sunset but it was certain—notwithstanding her stepmother's declaration that she had never sent the girl for water at night—that Chŏngok had done precisely that. *The little thing was taken by the ghosts,* the grownups whispered among themselves. Others said the girl's prematurely deceased mother had called her, or that something had polluted the offertory rite at the well.

The Old Well was filled in. After a day of shaman rituals, the demon in the well was buried once and for all under thudding heaps of dirt. Not even in the broad light of day did the children resume hovering near the well, and at night they wet their beds—because on nights when the wind moaned, the dark, angular shadows of tree branches on the paper panels of sliding doors took on the semblance of Chŏngok, her stepmother's baby riding on her back and her huge, water-swollen hands waving to them as over and over she called out their names. I wondered if she had gone to the well that night because she wanted to see the golden carp.

The old folks yearned for the cold, sweet-tasting well water, but the growing children quickly forgot their dead friend and their fear of the closed-up well. Water pumps were being sunk in every yard and no longer did the children have to go afield to draw water; the days ended when they would be thrashed for letting their bucket fall in.

It was only when my husband took up fishing that I learned that carp live in dirty, turbid water surrounded by moss and decaying plants. It was my job to prepare the fish he caught, and it was with a feeling of debasement and at the same time apprehension at the prospect of opening that which has always been sealed that I sliced open the still-living fish. A faint puff escaped, and there before my eyes were its innards. Like ours, they had been created, closed up, and never seen by others. Imagine darkness in a closed space, followed by the instant of first light. Suddenly exposed, the reddish blue entrails convulsed, these dark, clammy smaller entities sensing the destruction of the only world they knew and writhing in agony like Jonah in the belly of the whale.

Back when we still lived in a house, I used to bury the head and guts in the flower garden after I'd filleted the fish. They made good fertilizer—or so I thought, until I realized that all through the night the garden was swarming with rats. The holes they dug in the ground became larger and more numerous, easily catching my feet. I sometimes put out a mousetrap, only to hear for the rest of the night a big fat rat whirling the contraption around and squeaking. It may be that recollection is like a stone out of water. Pick from the water a beautiful, multicolored object and you discover a stone with an ordinary pattern and texture drying into something as desolate as the bleached bones inside a burial mound. What invests the stone with its brilliant pattern is the flow of water and time—this I realize. Even so, I continue these days to dream frequently of the Old Well and the golden carp.

The spring drought continued. The thermometer read upwards of 85 degrees. Overnight the magnolias at the Lotus House burst into bloom; the removal of the fence, which had started to the east of the house, had proceeded almost to the front gate. With only the fence to the west remaining, the house appeared half-naked. My scarf, still tied beside the gate, was at the height of the branches of the old apricot tree near the lotus pond. Was this Dimwit's idea of a joke? I smirked. Or maybe he'd forgotten who it belonged to and remembered only that he must return it to its owner.

Dimwit was watering the vegetable plot with a hose; the plot looked bone dry. Suddenly he seemed to notice the road, which was now in clear view with the fence gone, and he cocked his head anxiously. The fence posts, which he had neatly stacked off to the side, were being loaded onto a truck. The house, normally silent and devoid of human presence, was bursting with life. There was a constant stream of men in work clothes, reservist garb, or blue jeans, as well as a middle-aged man in a suit. His attire and the way he seemed to visit whenever he pleased made me wonder if he was the family patriarch. He parked his midsize silver car in the yard. The bags of cement and sand stacked there seemed to bear out the rumor that a sashimi restaurant would be built on the site.

The majority of my time at the Yesŏng apartment I spent looking out the window at the Lotus House. The previous day I'd gone down to the sundries shop to buy toilet paper and had innocently asked if it was true that the Lotus House was to be torn down. This was the answer I received: There was a lot of fine old lumber in that house, and a lot of greedy people eyeing it, and some rich fellow had decided to use those timbers in their original state to build himself a nice Korean-style villa in the hills, so a while back he had bought the crossbeam, rafters, and doors, and none of it came cheap. "Building a house is a bitch, tearing it down is a snap," the sundries shop man added.

I myself couldn't understand my persistent interest in the Lotus House, but I told myself it was because I had nothing else to occupy me here, it was the only sight that presented itself when I opened the window, and it seemed a waste that a beautiful old house was destined to vanish.

Dimwit put down his hose and squatted. He stared vacantly at the soil. Water continued to spurt rhythmically from the hose, wetting his feet and forming rivulets, but his gaze remained fixed on the ground. From time to time he dug intently through the soil with his fingers, looking for something.

The day grew hot, and the flower blossoms rioted against the spring light. The trees surrounding the Lotus House put forth leaves seemingly by the minute, and Dimwit grew busier. The guest wing disappeared, and the next night a small tile-roof structure that appeared to be a shed was dismantled as well, leaving a space occupied only by pieces of roof tile and piles of dirt. Day by day the Lotus House was erased, both its location and its appearance.

Workers began to put up a brick wall where the fence had stood. In the yard they mixed cement. By the time the sun reached its zenith a steady cloud of cement powder and gritty dust was rising from the men's truncated shadows. The vegetable plot lay in disorder, the Chinese cabbages—evenly spaced, bluish-green, a hand-span high—smothered in dirt.

Dimwit had a new task—felling trees to the rear of the house. With an ax he hacked away like a lumberjack at the trunks of the old trees. He was a strong man and worked straight through the day without rest. He must have been working under someone's orders and been eager to carry them out. Even so, he seemed to be in a great fluster. As if he had just remembered something, he would stop hacking at the pines, scurry about, then take a shrub by the base and strain to pull it from the ground. When mopping the sweat from his brow or setting down his ax to massage the small of his back, he would take a look around and shake his head in a most peculiar way. The transformation and disappearance of this world in which he had been born and lived, the only world he had ever known, must have unsettled him.

If so, then his anxiety had infected me as well. Back home, as I attempted such undemanding tasks as dicing scallions and slicing bean curd, I ended up with nicks in my hand and I broke a glass. I explained it away as the result of the heat or my headache, but my headaches were nothing new, though they *were* more intense in the spring. My husband asked if I'd listed the Yesŏng apartment with a realtor and repeated his belief that we should sell before summer. I nodded equivocally, but I was doing nothing to prepare for a sale. Instead I had lately been visiting the apartment even more frequently. At times I had stolen off at night when my husband and son were asleep. For some strange reason my head felt clear when I stood among the trees, which by now were quite leafy. My husband criticized me when I spent a lot of time there, saying that when he was away and had to get in touch he couldn't chat with me the entire day. It never occurred to him that I could spend the day in that vacant place doing nothing.

A motorcycle sputtered into the yard of the Lotus House. The rider toted a metal container, most likely a meal ordered from one of the Chinese restaurants. The workers abandoned their labor and gathered around the faucet. One of them shouted toward Dimwit, who was still wrestling with the trunk of a stout tree, but the man's voice was swallowed by the clanking of a yellow bulldozer as it pulled up on the road in front.

A crimson radiance filled the room. Had I been sleeping? I jerked myself upright. Through the open window it looked as if the heavens were on fire. I must have gone to sleep on the floor without a pillow. From where I sat I gazed up blankly at the thick glow in the sky.

At sunset and daybreak we remember them—the epitaph of the unknown soldiers in the First World War. In this way do people justify the fact that they themselves are alive.

I sometimes ask myself why it is that the sublime sight of twilight occasions a feeling of defeat in me.

When I was young I used to bawl my eyes out when twilight dyed the sky. They were inexplicable, my sorrowful choking sobs that continued even when my parents spanked me and called me a bad-luck girl for making such a scene. Perhaps my response was caused by willful fate, by this feeling of defeat and dread in the knowledge that humans are all too cowardly and weak.

When *he* called me that summer I was nursing my son. Sensing his mom's flustered state, the boy clung desperately to the nipple. And then, with a shudder, he bit down on me. His teeth had started to come in and he bit with alarming force. I cried out in spite of myself and slapped his face. The boy wailed as if he had touched fire. The nipple began to bleed as soon as he released it. It hurt as if it had been bitten off. The boy's mouth was bloody as well. I put some gauze packing inside my bra to stanch the blood flow, asked the neighbors to look after the boy, who was crying with an anxious urgency, and hurried to *him*. Together we crossed the river and found our way to an old temple set deep in a mountain valley.

The temple showed the effects of its thousand years of existence. Azaleas were in full bloom in the temple yard under the midday summer sun. "That red could reach down to hell," he said, dazzled by the color of the flowers. I think my response to him was silent: "I'll go as far as hell; I'll go to the farthest reaches of light, sound, and darkness."

From the temple to the boat dock below, the valley seethed with tourists. Arrayed along the river were merchants beneath awnings, selling spirits and soft drinks.

The day was waning but the sun remained hot. He and I ducked under one of the awnings, a place with a few low tables to sit at and a plastic mat covering the ground, and found it occupied by two families. Judging from the children asleep there and the flower cards spread over a folded army blanket, they had decided to relax here rather than venture into the crowded valley. The proprietor was serving *soju* and acorn jelly. She asked *him* in an obliging tone if he'd like to try some badger liver; it was supposed to be very good for men. A man at the next table seconded her opinion, a reddish chunk dangling from his chopsticks. "Yes, this is a rare delicacy." With an awkward smile *he* shook his head. The woman and her customers talked about the marvelous efficaciousness of spirits produced by soaking a badger in alcohol.

The evening sun gradually declined, and until it set and the twilit sky was revealed on the surface of the river, *he* silently emptied a bottle of *soju*. Up close, you could see the river water was filthy. From the gentle flow of the river a steady stream of garbage was channeled to the edge, beneath our feet.

I asked the woman when the last boat left. She told me not to worry, that boats ran late this time of year and that above the river we could find bungalows or else clean rooms in private homes. Leaving behind two sleeping children, those next to us ducked out beneath the awning, saying they were going to buy themselves a badger. "What a nice man and wife you are," the vendor woman said to us, but it was flattery and I knew she thought otherwise. We were questionable in her view, him with his bloodshot eyes and me sitting casually across from him, arms around my upraised knees—*one of* those *couples*. Couples too clumsy to hide their desire to go to a place with no other people and conjoin. I think our nonchalant expressions, as if we actually were married, were the result of the discomfort we felt with each other, a feeling that commenced with the woman's empty words. Was that discomfort simply a reaction to our flouting of system and order? No, it was more than that. I believe it also involved my disgust with all relationships in which discomfort could be covered up with a nonchalant expression.

In a filthy toilet I urinated, then looked inside my bra. Beneath the blood- and milk-clotted gauze was the sharp outline of two teeth. I suddenly felt queasy and retched.

The children woke and began a piteous wail. Their parents had yet to return from their badger-buying journey. The older child, a girl, tried to coax her brother into silence. She placed his feet inside his shoes and did likewise herself, and they went outside and proceeded along the river hand in hand, leaving behind this place with its liquor and badger-blood stains. Soon they were out of sight, the dusk underlying the evening glow enveloping their ever more distant forms.

If the river hadn't been so dirty, if the twilight hadn't been so deep, if it weren't for those two children, we wouldn't have looked with a penetrating, all-encompassing gaze at the essence and the fallacy of the desire that we were trying so hard to conceal. And perhaps I wouldn't have noticed that the happiness I'd go as far as hell for now wore a different face.

There is no doubt that our thoughts coincided then. I thought of my home and baby, and of his family, which I had never seen, and of the supper and the lighted house that awaited him. He must have thought likewise. He checked his watch. There was time until the last boat, and despite my hopes and efforts (whose desperation he was unaware of) to extend our time together, I was reassured by the approach of the boat that would deliver each of us to the place we had left behind.

The Lotus House was no longer there beneath my window. During my dreamless sleep, while the midday sun descended the heavens, two hundred years of time had crumbled like ash. The sublime glow of sunset faded to violet and dusk filled the sky, but strangely enough, the site of the house, suddenly level, loomed more prominently. It seemed the construction work continued at night. A string of light bulbs, already lit, extended across the yard. Dimwit was alternately rummaging through the remains of the house and making agitated circuits around the area. He seemed to be looking for something. And then, with a grunt of annoyance, he fastened his arms around the trunk of a tree that had escaped cutting and began to wrestle it back and forth. Why was he doing this? Why? What was he looking for? His very movements constituted a colossal question. Most likely Dimwit didn't know what it was he sought. The disappearance of something familiar, the unfamiliarity that succeeded it—these he would not understand. I think for a brief moment I must have wept.

As I locked the door and descended the steps, I must have thought I would soon put the apartment on the market. I came out on the road that went past where the Lotus House fence had been, then turned back toward the apartment building and went to the phone booth near the front entrance. I deposited a coin and punched in the numbers. Before the second ring a woman's voice answered. When I remained silent the voice said, "Must be a wrong number." I didn't know what to say and carefully replaced the receiver. Again I deposited a coin and this time took care to dial the number correctly. The same voice answered, again before the second ring. I produced a faltering apology and the woman replied in a considerate tone that she'd just been issued the number. I slowly turned to go. I felt peculiar knowing that this series of numbers *he* had possessed for so long was now being used by someone else. Did those numbers remember him? Did they remember the endlessly complicated emotions that lay hidden beneath his tone, his manner of speaking, his words? A familiar voice from the dim past had startled them—would they someday search their memory for that voice? *I'll be there. It's raining here; what's it like there? I just felt like calling. That's it for now. So long....*

When dusk settles over the woods, I feel like a sage. I like to stop and place my ear against the body of a tree, but I'm too old to understand what the tree is saying. So with this tree, I held my arms wide and embraced it instead. I thought I could feel something warm. I removed my shoes and began to climb. The sap flowing deep within the rough bark produced a fine scent. The tree was so straight I tensed, feeling I could slip or fall at any moment. I twined my legs about the thick trunk. My body grew warm with desire. I clutched at the tree, squeezed my legs about it with all my might, and writhed. A scream escaped me. I felt a momentary rapture, then dissolved into a white mass and sank into languor. I believe I shed a few tears.

The violet flowers of the paulownias bloomed and swayed in the darkness. *He* had died on a night glorious with stars and flowers. And for generations to come, when I no longer existed, this tree where I stood would flower and leaf, would provide nesting for birds.

I surveyed the hills, the trees, the stars. All would outlive me. And finally I recalled, just as she had first spoken them to me, my great-grandmother's words: *Once upon a time a maiden lost her gold hairpin in a well. She died of a broken heart, and the hairpin turned into a golden carp. . . .*

AFTERWORD

With the passing of Pak Kyŏngni in 2008 and Pak Wansŏ in 2011, O Chŏnghŭi has become the elder stateswoman of contemporary Korean fiction, a writer who enjoys critical, if not widespread, popular success and who is proving increasingly influential among younger Korean writers. She was one of the first Korean writers to receive training in creative writing at the university level, at Sŏrabŏl College of Arts. Like Pak Wansŏ, Hwang Sunwŏn, Kim Tongni, and Ch'oe Yun—four of modern Korea's most accomplished authors—she emerged more or less fully formed as a writer. She began writing "The Toy Shop Woman" (Wangujŏm yŏin), which was honored with the 1968 New Writers Award, sponsored by the *Chungang ilbo*, a Seoul daily, while still in high school. She then published approximately a story a year until her first collection, *River of Fire* (Pul ŭi kang), appeared in 1977. If by that time there were any doubts about her commitment to her craft, she dispelled them by remarking in a brief afterword that while writing a story she is constantly plagued by doubts as to whether she has given her all to that particular work.[1] *River of Fire* is remarkable for the tension created by the juxtaposition in each of the twelve stories of a first-person narrative and a nameless narrator, an unsettling combination of intimacy and distance. In these stories, O became arguably the first Korean writer to carry out Virginia Woolf's dictum that killing off the gentle, egoless, self-sacrificing "angel in the house" is part of a woman writer's job.

The decade that followed was O's most productive period. Her second and third story collections, *The Garden of My Childhood* (Yunyŏn ŭi ttŭl) and *Spirit on the Wind* (Param ŭi nŏk), appeared in 1981 and 1986, respectively. Receiving the Tongin Literature Prize in 1982 for "The Bronze Mirror" (Tonggyŏng), she became one of the first writers to capture both of the major Korean prizes for short fiction and novellas, "Evening Game" (Chŏnyŏk ŭi keim) having been honored with the 1979 Yi Sang Literature Prize. The stories in these two volumes are more diverse in character, theme, and technique. "Chinatown" (Chunguggin kŏri, 1979) is one of the most accomplished coming-of-age stories in contemporary Korea. "Words of Farewell" (Pyŏlsa, 1981) utilizes stream-of-consciousness technique in depicting parallel spiritual journeys by a husband and wife, the former having left home to avoid surveillance by the authorities. The title story of *Spirit on the Wind* is a dual narrative that examines trauma from the point of view of the victim and her uncomprehending husband. At the same time, the stories in both collections, like those in *River of*

Fire, continue to portray families broken by desertion, infidelity, sterility, madness, and death. These holes in the family fabric parallel the breakdown of a traditional agrarian society built around the extended family, which was accelerated by the industrialization of South Korea under a succession of military dictatorships from the 1960s to the 1980s.

By the mid-1980s O's writing had become more discursive as she responded to criticism of her works as lacking in historical consciousness and awareness of contemporary realities—two catchphrases applied indiscriminately by the conservative and patriarchal literary establishment of South Korea to writers who did not focus overtly on social, political, or historical problems in their fiction. Always an intertextual writer—in one of her earliest stories, "Weaver Woman" (Chingnyŏ, 1970), she adopts the herder boy and the weaving girl of one of Korea's best-known folktales, who are separated forever for neglecting their duties, and recasts them as a barren wife and her wandering husband, who are estranged by her inability to produce the all-important male offspring—O began to incorporate more historical elements into her works. "The Monument Intersection" (Pulmangbi, 1983), for example, is inspired by her own family's migration, after liberation from Japanese colonial rule in 1945, from Hwanghae Province in present-day North Korea to what would become South Korea.

O's literary fiction in the 1990s was sporadic; a highlight being the publication in book form of *The Bird* (Sae) in 1996. Curiously, the cover of the first printing of this book identifies it simply as *sosŏl* (fiction). Not until the new millennium and a subsequent printing did this work receive the cachet of *changp'yŏn sosŏl* (novel). In the early 1990s, in an effort to broaden her readership, O published two volumes of *comte*, a genre that in Korea consists primarily of family-centered miniatures and occupies an ambiguous space somewhere between literary fiction and popular fiction. "The Release" (Pangsaeng, 1990) in the present volume is from one of those collections, *The Drunkard's Wife* (Sulkkun ŭi anae, 1993). She has since published children's and young adult fiction and two volumes of essays.

The present volume contains one story from the 1960s, three from the 1970s, three from the 1980s, and two from the 1990s. The first four stories, all originally published in her 1977 *River of Fire* volume, exhibit the clarity and concentration characteristic of her early work, but are not without their humor, which is shown to good effect especially in "One Spring Day" (Pomnal, 1973). The three stories from the 1980s feature a broader cast of characters and, in contrast with the *River of Fire* stories, limited third-person narratives. "Lake P'aro" (P'aroho, 1989) is revealing for its glimpses of the lifestyle of Korean international students and its metatextual element. In this story O draws on two years of life with her family near Albany, New York, while her husband, a professor, was on sabbatical. The final story, "The Old Well" (Yet umul, 1994), has a retrospective quality.

O Chŏnghŭi will be remembered as the writer who pioneered gender parity in contemporary Korean fiction and who raised the bar of accomplishment to a new level. She is one of the few writers of modern Korean fiction to acknowledge in her stories the individual's capacity for evil, and apart from Ch'oe Yun in "There a Petal Silently Falls" (Chŏgi sori ŏpshi han chŏm kkonnip i chigo, 1988),[2] no one has written more insightfully about trauma. It is difficult to overemphasize O's influence on contemporary Korean writers. P'yŏn Hyeyŏng, one of the most prominent of the current generation, wrote her master's thesis on O. According to the dust jacket of O's 2006 essay collection, *The Patterns of My Heart* (Nae maŭm ŭi munŭi), among the authors most influenced by her are Shin Kyŏngsuk (author of the U.S. best-selling *Please Look After Mom* [Ŏmma rŭl put'akhae, 2008]), Chŏn Kyŏngnin, Cho Kyŏngnan, Ha Sŏngnan, and Yun Sŏnghŭi. And the obligatory interpretive essay in a 1994 volume of self-selected stories was written by none other than Kim Hyesun, contemporary Korea's most imaginative poet and a mentor to a generation of creative writers.[3] These accomplishments are all the more noteworthy when we consider that O's "official" oeuvre of literary fiction (the works contained in the five volumes of her fiction published by Munhak kwa chisŏng sa) consists of a mere three dozen pieces— thirty-four stories, a novella, and a novel. That she has accomplished so much on the basis of such a comparatively slender output bears witness to her desire to make every work count.

NOTES

1. O Chŏnghŭi, afterword to *Pul ŭi kang* (Seoul: Munhak kwa chisŏng sa, 1977), 281.

2. Ch'oe Yun, "There a Petal Silently Falls," in *There a Petal Silently Falls: Three Stories by Ch'oe Yun*, 1–78 (New York: Columbia University Press, 2008).

3. Kim Hyesun, "Yŏsŏngjŏk chŏngch'esŏng hyanghayŏ" (Toward a female identity), in *Yet umul*, 375–98 (Seoul: Ch'ŏng'a ch'ulp'ansa, 1994).

SUGGESTIONS FOR FURTHER READING

Fulton, Bruce. "O Chŏnghŭi." In *The Columbia Companion to Modern East Asian Literature*, ed. Joshua Mostow, 701–3. New York: Columbia University Press, 2003.

O Chŏnghŭi. *The Bird*. Trans. Jenny Wang Medina. London: Telegram Books, 2007.

——. "The Bronze Mirror." Trans. Bruce and Ju-Chan Fulton. In *Land of Exile: Contemporary Korean Fiction*, rev. and exp. ed., ed. Marshall R. Pihl and Bruce and Ju-Chan Fulton, 215–32. Armonk, N.Y.: M.E. Sharpe, 2007.

——. "Chinatown." In *Words of Farewell: Stories by Korean Women Writers*, trans. Bruce and Ju-Chan Fulton, 202–30. Seattle: Seal Press, 1989.

——. "Evening Game." In *Words of Farewell: Stories by Korean Women Writers*, trans. Bruce and Ju-Chan Fulton, 181–201.

——. "The Face." In *A Moment's Grace: Stories from Korea in Transition*, trans. with commentary by John Holstein, 215–29. Ithaca, N.Y.: Cornell University East Asia Program, 2009.

——. "Garden of My Childhood." Trans. Ha-yun Jung. *Words Without Borders* (online), November 2005. http://wordswithoutborders.org/article/garden-of-my-childhood/

——. "The Monument Intersection." In *The Golden Phoenix: Seven Contemporary Korean Short Stories*, trans. Suh Ji-moon, 199–248. Boulder, Colo.: Lynne Rienner, 1998.

——. "The Party." Trans. Sŏl Sun-bong. *Korea Journal* 23, no. 10 (October 1983): 49–64.

——. "Spirit on the Wind." In *The Red Room: Stories of Trauma in Contemporary Korea*, trans. Bruce and Ju-Chan Fulton, 25–121. Honolulu: University of Hawai'i Press, 2009.

——. "Wayfarer." Trans. Bruce and Ju-Chan Fulton. In *Modern Korean Fiction: An Anthology*, ed. Bruce Fulton and Youngmin Kwon, 329–44. New York: Columbia University Press, 2005.

——. "Weaver Woman." Trans. Miseli Jeon. In *Waxen Wings: The* Acta Koreana *Anthology of Short Fiction from Korea*, ed. Bruce Fulton, 35–49. St. Paul: Koryo Press, 2011.

——. "Words of Farewell." In *Words of Farewell: Stories by Korean Women Writers*, trans. Bruce and Ju-Chan Fulton, 231–74.

Yi, Hyangsoon. "The Journey as Meditation: A Buddhist Reading of O Chŏnghŭi's 'Words of Farewell.'" *Religion and Literature* 34, no. 3 (2002): 57–73.